I0684767

From Indigo Sea Press
By Donna Small

Just Between Friends

Ripple in the Water

Through Rose Colored Glasses

indigoseapress.com

Just Between Friends

By

Donna Small

Perseverance Books
Published by Indigo Sea Press
Winston-Salem

Perseverance Books
Indigo Sea Press, LLC
302 Ricks Drive
Winston-Salem, NC 27103

First Perseverance Books edition published
December, 2015
Perseverance Books, Moon Sailor and all production design are trademarks of Indigo Sea Press, used under license.

For information regarding bulk purchases of this book, digital purchase and special discounts, please contact the publisher at indigoseapress.com

Cover design by Tracy Beltran

Manufactured in the United States of America
ISBN 978-1-63066-260-8

To my delightful, devoted readers.

—Donna Small

Chapter 1

What the hell have I gotten myself into?

Layne Matthews stood in front of the mirror turning from side to side in order to inspect her appearance from every possible angle. Finally she nodded, satisfied with what she saw in her reflection. Satisfied, perhaps, that what she felt inside wasn't something that was able to be seen in the mirror. To the casual observer, everything was perfectly, immaculately, in its place. It was only if you knew Layne, really knew her, that you got a sense that something was just a bit off. Only then would the small furrow in her brow, the tiny trace of tension in her shoulders, or the fact that her bottom lip jutted out ever so slightly, cause you to look at her with concern in your own eyes.

If you were only a casual acquaintance, you saw what Layne wanted you to see; the strapless Vera Wang wedding gown with a bodice that was altered to fit her torso perfectly, the thick, auburn hair pulled into an elegant chignon, the veil with tiny combs that complemented the dress perfectly, and the matching necklace and earrings that accented the tiny beads covering the gown.

Tiny tendrils of hair had been strategically left out of her bun and were now curled delicately around her neck, providing a look that was both soft and graceful. Her skin, fresh from a series of facials over the past several weeks, was flawless. Her makeup, applied earlier by a professional hand, ensured the photographs from today would be stunning.

She was the picture-perfect bride. This was the image she had had chosen to project, so therefore, she did.

The dress, purchased by her mother, was the "something new" required if one followed wedding legend protocol – and she did. She wore her grandmother's long, white gloves, which fulfilled both the "borrowed" and the "old" requirements of her attire. Underneath her dress, a blue garter sat on her right thigh, waiting to be removed by her soon-to-be husband.

It was overwhelming the amount of effort had gone into planning for this one day. Not to mention the amount of money that had been spent; that would be spent. It was silly really, she thought. Her parents, however, had insisted on the large wedding, wanting to invite all of their friends. Right now, in fact there were well over two hundred people waiting for her to walk down the aisle.

So why today, on what was supposed to be the happiest day of her life, was she filled with terror?

There it was again; that feeling deep inside that told her something just wasn't right. As she watched in the mirror, her brows came together slightly making a small crease between them. Knowing that her best friend, Emma, sat behind her and could read her emotions better than anyone, she smoothed her brow with her gloved fingers, trying to erase any visible sign of whatever it was that had her feeling unsettled.

It had to be nerves. Of course! She was nervous, that's all. What bride wasn't nervous on their wedding day? Layne felt certain that nerves came with the event itself as opposed to the hesitation one might have with spending the rest of your life with one person. For her, that one person was Andrew Harper.

Andy. Her future husband. As she thought of him, a slow smile worked its way onto her lips. They'd been dating for almost a year when he'd proposed and she had been thrilled to accept. When they'd rushed home to tell her parents, they were just as excited as she was. Everyone fell in love with Andy almost the moment they met him. He was the type of man that few women were lucky to meet, let alone fall in love with and marry. And she loved him.

She just wasn't *in love* with him.

It wasn't that he wasn't everything she wanted because he was. On paper, he had all the requirements she'd look for in a husband. Of course he was handsome, but he was also polite and charming and had the ability to put anyone at ease. But it was more than that. He had charisma. When in conversation with someone, he would listen much more than he spoke (a very admirable quality to Layne, who loved hearing the sound of her own voice) which made one feel as though what they were saying was of great importance.

Andy had a great sense of humor that allowed him to see the positive in any situation. Because of this, Layne and Andy had rarely, if ever, fought. She thought about that for a moment and wondered if perhaps that might be what was worrying her.

Sure, they'd *discuss* things, occasionally disagree, but more often than not, Andy would simply give in, unwilling to be ruffled by anything Layne might throw at him. That was Andy, unflappable, always-willing-to-please Andrew Harper. Mr. Compromise. Layne had often thought that Andy lacked the passion to become enflamed about anything. She even occasionally wondered if he was passionate about her. She knew, without any sort of hesitation, that Andy loved her; she'd never questioned that. But there were times when she wondered what it would be like to be *wanted*. She wondered if Andy had the ability to desire something so much that he would actually become enflamed with passion. But that just wasn't who he was.

She loved him but still wasn't sure of the precise moment when she realized it. The feelings she had for him had slowly grown from friendship and companionship into comfort and love, which she supposed was the best way for love to happen. She enjoyed spending time with him; it didn't matter what they were doing. Marrying him was the next natural step, wasn't it?

Things always seemed to flow so easily between them that when he proposed, she didn't even hesitate before accepting. Logically - which was how Layne thought about everything - it was the right thing to do. And of course, it made her happy to accept his proposal (and the 1.5 carat emerald cut diamond), which was why she couldn't understand why she felt the nagging feeling in the pit of her belly.

Layne looked in the mirror one last time and nodded, positive that what she was feeling was completely and absolutely normal.

* * *

Emma Stewart sat on the couch filing her nails. She'd long since given up trying to tear Layne away from the mirror knowing that they weren't going anywhere near the aisle until Layne was satisfied that every bead and inch of material was in its proper place.

She heard the rustle of Layne's dress and looked up to find her turning around to face her. For probably the hundredth time that day, Emma's eyes welled up as she looked at her best friend in her wedding dress. Somehow, it all seemed surreal. The two of them had been planning for this day since they first met nearly twenty years ago. They'd imagined how they'd each be each other's maid of honor, what style of dress they'd wear, what they'd serve and even what color they'd choose for their bridesmaids' dresses. The only unknown was the name of the groom. Of course, they'd both had their share of boyfriends and had written their own name next to any number of differing last names, but none of them had stuck. Until now, that is.

Emma had always known that Layne would be the first to walk down the aisle. When they were teenagers, it was Layne who would use her allowance money to purchase Bride magazine, the one who would drag Emma to every bridal show within driving distance, and the one who had enough confidence to step into jewelry stores and try on ring after ring so she could be certain which shape and size looked best on her hand. While Emma certainly looked forward to her wedding day, Layne had been the one planning every detail since she was old enough to know what a wedding was. And now that the day had finally arrived, Emma was thrilled for her. So thrilled, in fact, that she could barely manage to keep herself from crying, but she gave herself a little leeway; she had more than one reason to be emotional today.

"Layne, you look so beautiful! Oh, god! I think I'm going to cry!" Emma said, as she gently dabbed at the corner of her eyes with a tissue.

Layne giggled. "Again? Emma, you've been crying all day!"

Emma was careful not to smudge her makeup, which had also been carefully applied earlier by the same professional hand. "I know, I know. I'm just so emotional."

"Well, that's what I love about you." Then worry crept into her features. "Are you sure I look all right?"

Emma rolled her eyes. Layne had never looked anything other than beautiful a day in her life. She got up and walked over to her friend, turning the both of them to face the mirror.

"Look at you! How can you even ask that?" Emma looked at the two of them side by side and couldn't help notice how different they were. Layne was tall and slender, with thick auburn hair and olive skin that turned golden brown after any time in the sun. Her own skin, in direct contract to Layne's was pale and almost translucent since Emma rarely, if ever, spent any time in the sun.

Even without exposure to the sun, her cheeks displayed a smattering of freckles which she'd long since given up trying to hide. Earlier today, Emma had tried to convince the makeup artist of just that. However, said make-up artist was not one to shy away from a task such as this, and before Emma could finish her sentence, she pulled out her entire arsenal of concealers, powders, and brushes to prove she was up for the challenge. It was nearly an hour later before she finally gave up, opting instead to enhance the freckles rather than hide them.

Emma was several inches shorter with straight blond hair that fell to just below her shoulders. Today her hair had been piled into curls on the top of her head in a style similar to Layne's. Rather than make her appear more glamorous, Emma felt she looked somewhat like a little girl playing dress up. She noticed that even the layer upon layer of eye shadow, eye liner, and mascara weren't enough to make her look close to her twenty-eight years. She thought she could mostly blame her youthful features on her freckles, which she noticed were clearly visible given the natural light that was pouring in from the floor to ceiling windows.

She squelched a sigh as she looked from herself to Layne, who was completely in her element all dressed up and oozing with glamour. Layne was what someone that was often described as voluptuous or sensual. Emma lacked even a hint of any of sensuality, or so she thought, but she had a pixie-like quality that made her immediately liked by anyone who met her.

As Emma stood there looking at their reflection, she felt a tiny twinge of jealousy followed almost immediately by a small pang of guilt. Today, it seemed, was going to be much more difficult than she initially thought. *Difficult, but not impossible,* Emma told herself, and quickly focused her attention back to her best friend. Knowing how close they were and how much she loved Layne only made her feel worse. She'd kept her feelings hidden for so long but today, those feeling were nearly choking her. Layne was getting married and Emma wasn't sure how she was going to survive given how she felt about the groom.

Emma had been in love with Andrew Harper from almost the first moment she'd laid eyes on him. It was only because of her stupid bladder and her own insecurities that she didn't have the courage to approach him before he met Layne.

It was nearly two years earlier and Emma was meeting Layne for drinks at a bar after work. Emma had gotten there a few minutes early and needed to use the rest room. As she made her way to the back of the room, she noticed a man seated at the end of the bar. As her gaze took him in, her insides turned to mush and she felt a rush of emotion unlike anything she'd ever experienced. She knew this was something serious.

He was nursing a martini with three olives on a toothpick. It was his hands that she noticed first. They were large, which to her meant capable and strong, and his nails were neatly trimmed. Another plus, she thought. She watched as he scrolled through his blackberry with one hand while the other stirred the olive-filled toothpick around the inside of the glass. She stood there, transfixed, and took in the rest of him. He was wearing a neatly pressed pale yellow dress shirt with the top button undone. The tie had been loosened around his neck and revealed a white undershirt beneath. She felt her pulse quicken and imagined what it would be like to unbutton that shirt and pull it out from his waistband in order to run her hands up and underneath it.

Because she was lost in her own imagination, she had forgotten she was in the middle of the path to the restroom and had been standing there, practically salivating and staring at this stranger. Someone bumped her as they tried to get past and the jolt brought her back to reality. She mumbled an apology and once again attempted to make her way to the bathroom. Safely inside, she splashed a bit of cold water on her now reddened face and tried to compose herself. Forgetting for the moment, the urgency in her bladder, she began to figure out how exactly to meet this man who affected her with emotions that were unlike anything she'd ever experienced. But as she would soon find out, no plan was needed. By the time she had made her way out of the restroom, the man had vacated his spot at the end of the bar and was now seated with Layne at a table. Luckily, there was an empty chair -a sign that she'd not been forgotten by her friend- and she walked over and sat down with the two of them. Already there was a freedom in their behaviors that signaled, at least to Emma, a mutual attraction. In that moment, Emma knew that any chance she had with this man had vanished.

Although Emma felt the loss of possibility deep within her, she didn't begrudge Layne for this turn of events. People couldn't help but be drawn to Layne and Andy was no exception. She was a striking looking woman who also possessed intelligence and a great sense of humor – a bonified tri-fecta of admirable qualities. Emma did what any best friend would do; she put on her best smile and immediately set out to determine whether or not this guy was good enough for her friend.

And he was.

Emma could not find a single thing wrong with him, not even so much as a scorned ex-girlfriend. It seemed as though Andy was the one guy in the world who could actually get away with the "we can still be friends" line.

Layne had never been someone who neglected her friends when she was involved with someone. Quite the opposite was true, in fact. More often than not, Emma was asked to come along with Layne and Andy when they went to the movies, out to dinner or just met for a drink after work. While this was a great characteristic to have in a best friend, the merits of this particular situation were not so effective when you were trying to fall out of love with the man you were constantly being forced to see.

To add insult to injury, any time Emma was not included, she was later given a complete debriefing in which Layne and Emma analyzed and discussed every possible meaning to each statement, facial expression and nuance Andy made. The dates were discussed in great detail until Layne was satisfied that things were progressing as they ought to.

In addition to the basic relay of venue, scenery, and conversations, Emma was given a detailed account every time some relationship milestone occurred. When Layne and Andy shared their first kiss, Emma was told how, when, where, and most importantly, whether or not he was a good kisser (He was). When Andy surprised Layne with a weekend at the beach for their one month anniversary, Emma got all the details (Oceanfront room at a bed and breakfast, long walks on the beach). When they had sex for the first time, Emma again, had to suffer through hearing all the intimate details that one shares only with their very best friend. (On the bed, then the floor, then in the shower, and he was an AMAZING lover!) Through all of this, Emma acted as though she were thrilled for her best friend, and she was; she just wished that Layne's happiness were the result of some other man – any other man.

And then, one day after Layne and Andy had been dating for almost a year, Andy proposed. Of course, Emma was the first person Layne called. Emma listened dutifully, shouted congratulation with gusto, hung up the phone, and then drank herself into a stupor, trying to ease her heartache.

Nothing, however, could dull the throbbing pain of her heart shattering into tiny pieces.

What made this all the more difficult for Emma was the fact that she couldn't discuss this problem with Layne. She had to keep it bottled up inside of her, unable to reveal her pain to anyone, least of all her best friend. Every other problem she'd had, she'd been able to discuss with Layne over and over until either a solution was found or she just felt better after talking about it for hours on end. With this particular problem, she wasn't sure which aspect of it was the hardest; the part where she was in love with her best friend's fiancée or the part where she wasn't able to talk about said problem with her best friend.

Of course, the final nail in this coffin was the fact that she was wracked with guilt every time she thought of Andy and felt those flutters inside her belly, which was pretty much all day, every day. She knew she couldn't help how she felt but Layne was her *best friend,* the person who knew every single thing about her and loved her despite it. And though she tried to convince herself of the fact she couldn't control how she felt, and certainly couldn't make herself fall out of love with Andy, she just couldn't shake the thought that she was betraying her best friend. After all, wasn't that the cardinal rule of friendship? You don't fall in love with your best friend's boyfriend. Period. Emma's feelings were inexcusable despite how completely and utterly right they made her feel.

Of course, Emma had tried to fall out of love with him – God knows she tried - but she spent so much time with Andy and Layne that she was never away from him long enough to even begin to forget about him. It was hopeless. She just went about her days aching for something she knew she would never have and carrying the load of guilt she knew would never lighten.

This was the first time in Emma's life that she had kept something from Layne and it was eating her up inside. But while she knew she was hopelessly, desperately in love with Andy, she knew that Layne loved him and was going to marry him. As difficult as it was to suffer in silence, Emma did it, knowing that Layne was happy.

Today, however, was going to be the toughest challenge yet. Seeing the man she loved marry her best friend might prove to be too much for her (She hoped there was plenty of wine at the reception), but Emma vowed then and there that she was going to get through this day, no matter what. She was going to be there for her best friend, as they'd always done for each other.

Layne looked at Emma's reflection in the mirror. "You're sure I look all right?" Her voice sounded almost foreign to Emma as it lacked any of the confidence she normally carried around with her in abundance.

Emma stood up and placed her hands on her hips. "It kills me that you even have to ask. Andy is going to have trouble remaining standing at the end of the aisle when he sees you!"

Layne giggled. "He'd better be standing when I get up there. I want him to be completely coherent when he takes his vows."

"He will be. I don't think anything could make him miss you walking down the aisle."

Layne released a small sigh and felt her eyes mist up. "I don't know what I'd do without you, Emma."

"Well, you'll never have to find out." Emma replied.

Layne gave her friend a smile that is only shared between the best of friends, then turned and stepped away from the mirror in order to reach for the bouquet that had been resting on the table.

"Okay, then. Let's go." Layne said, as she took a deep breath.

Emma picked up the train of Layne's gown and placed it gently over her forearm, careful not to wrinkle the delicate fabric. She then reached for her bouquet of flowers with her free hand and together, they left the room.

They walked silently to the front of the church, each lost in their own thoughts. Layne found herself thinking about the months and years that were to come, and wondered if every bride felt this way. Emma found herself wishing she were the one getting ready to walk down the aisle and spend the next fifty years or so with Andy.

They arrived at the back of the church and greeted Layne's father, who was there waiting for them. She settled Layne on his arm and then moved behind her to adjust her train, lifting it up to catch the air beneath it and then lay it down gently on the white runner that had been laid out for her to walk on.

Emma stepped in front of her best friend, adjusted her veil one last time and nodded. "Are you ready?"

Layne nodded and forced a stiff smile onto her face.

The music began to play inside the church, signaling the need for Emma to face forward. The wedding planners opened the doors slowly, revealing pews filled with wedding guests all turning to face the bride. Emma didn't notice a single one. Her eyes were focused on the man at the end of the aisle waiting for his bride to come to him. Taking a deep breath, she began to walk slowly down the aisle, just ahead of Layne.

She was, after all, the maid of honor.

Chapter 2

Emma reached for the glass of wine in front of her and lifted it up in front of her in a mock salute before taking a sip. She'd gotten through it without making an ass of herself – although she still wasn't sure how exactly she managed to remain standing while Layne and Andy vowed their undying love to each other.

And now she was swiftly realizing that her earlier assessment of the day was correct: There wasn't enough alcohol in the building to numb her from the pain she was feeling. You'd think she'd be used to this by now but somehow, today, she felt the pinch just a little more sharply. Today it became solidified. He was gone forever and she'd stood right there with the best view in the house while she watched Andy give his love to another.

Of course, she'd done all that was expected of her. She was Layne's best friend and was determined to do everything she could to make certain she had perfect wedding day. And there was no part of perfect wedding day that involved the maid of honor collapsing into a sobbing heap of cornflower blue at the foot of the bride and groom.

Nope. That just wouldn't do.

She walked in front of Layne up to the altar, fixed her train so that it showed all the gorgeous details to everyone in the church. She held Layne's bouquet of orchids so that she could hold Andy's hands while they said their vows. She then watched as they said those vows to each other while she stood there trying to hold back the tears since she didn't have a free hand to wipe her eyes with. Both Layne and Andy spoke with such raw emotion that nearly everyone in the church lifted a tissue to dab at their eyes, so touched were they by the display of love they were witnessing. She watched them slide matching rings onto each other's hands and applauded enthusiastically (as best as one can when they're holding two bouquets of flowers) when they had their first kiss as husband and wife.

Emma had stood beside her best friend while she took the vows that began her new life with the man she loved while simultaneously extinguishing any hope she might have had left. It was over for Emma and she knew that now. Once they were married, there was no chance of an amicable break up, a parting of ways, an "it's not you, it's me," or any other separation Emma had fantasized about in which all parties were still friends and Emma was miraculously able to reach out and take Andy's hand in her own any time she felt the need to touch him.

Perhaps the one thing that may have kept Emma sane was what she told herself over and over... Andy was happy. She had always thought that wanting someone to be happy even if they couldn't be with you was a load of crap. But as it turned out, it happened to be true, and made it even more bittersweet for her. She knew that deep down inside, she wanted him to be happy, which convinced her (as though she needed convincing) that truly, and without a doubt, she loved him more than anything.

Throughout the entire ceremony, Emma told herself over and over that all that mattered was that he was happy. He was actually happier than she'd ever seen him. She thought he looked like the kid who, for his birthday, got a puppy, a pony, and every game for his X-Box in addition to flat screen TV to play it on. He had been grinning foolishly for the entire day except for the few minutes it took for them to exchange their vows. Then, Emma watched his expression change from giddy to solemn, almost as though he were paying close attention to what was being said in order to seal them in his memory and refer to them for every day after today. He took them so seriously, in fact, that his voice broke several times while he was speaking. After the first few times, Emma felt certain he was going to cry. The emotion he felt was so thickly laced in his words that one would have to be obtuse not to realize how much he felt for Layne. And as the maid of honor, she had the best view in the entire church. Since Andy was looking at Layne and she was directly behind her, she was able to see the emotion he felt from less than two feet away. What she saw in his eyes was almost too much for her to bear.

It nearly broke her.

Now that the pain of her heart breaking into a million tiny, little pieces had stopped throbbing, she was able to focus on the next step

– getting through the reception. She did fully plan, however, on making and an effort to dull her pain further by consuming several glasses of wine. (She gave a quick thanks to Layne's parents for their firm belief that no one should have to pay for a drink at a wedding.)

She took another sip from her glass and looked out at a sea of two hundred-plus guests. She thought for just a moment that if it were not for the cornflower blue, floor length bridesmaid dress she was wearing, she could take a bottle from behind the bar and discreetly slink off into a corner somewhere to drink her sorrows away. But since her "uniform" told everyone she was a key player in the day's festivities, she knew that wasn't possible.

First, there would be the toast from the best man, Andy's college room-mate Tyler. Tyler took an interest in Emma almost as soon as he met her and as a result, she'd spent the better part of every pre-wedding event fending off advances from him. The man just didn't know how to accept the possibility that a woman didn't fall immediately in love with him. Surely rejection had this happened at least once in his life?

After Tyler spoke, there would be numerous people who would clink their forks against their wine glasses to encourage the bride and groom to kiss. She'd been to weddings where this happened so frequently that the wedding couple could barely eat. She hoped for her own sanity that the guests would use their forks to eat their dinner rather than encourage this tradition that Emma found particularly antiquated. Did people really think you needed someone to clink some glass as encouragement to kiss the person you only moments before, vowed your undying love to? The whole idea was absurd.

Later on in the evening, there would be the cutting of the wedding cake. The bride and groom would then feed each other while the guests cheered them on and hoped that one or the other would cram a piece of the cake in the other's face, creating a huge mess. Emma couldn't help but roll her eyes as she thought of this ridiculous concept and the havoc it would wreak if allowed to go on. Anyone who knew Layne would know that if even the tiniest crumb of cake were to wind up anywhere other than directly in the middle of Layne's perfectly colored and lined lips, there would be hell to pay. Emma knew that Layne had spent a small fortune on her wedding dress and would probably internally combust if any of the butter cream icing were to come anywhere near it.

This fiasco would be followed by the bride and groom's first dance. Emma had to sigh as she thought about this tradition. The bridal party would join in to the dance after a minute or so and that meant that she'd have to actually allow herself to be in Tyler's arms. She knew that the three or so minutes she spent in his arms would be the longest in her life. All things considered, though, after the emotional turmoil she'd been through today, the feeling of irritation would be a welcome change.

The final highlight of the evening was one that Emma found particularly disturbing. Of course, this was the event where the bride and groom would be put in the center of the dance floor and the groom would attempt to retrieve the garter that was located underneath the bride's dress on her upper thigh. Emma was not looking forward to watching Andy retrieve the garter that had placed there for that sole purpose.

She lifted the glass to her lips and drained it. *It's going to be a long night,* she thought.

All of this might lead one to believe that Emma was unhappy or even angry with Layne but that just was not the case. Emma was ecstatic for her best friend and wished her nothing but happiness. She just wished there was some way that Layne could have all this happiness without the pain it caused to Emma. God...she wished for that so badly. She wanted Layne to be happy but why couldn't she be happy with someone else?

Anyone else...

With a small sigh, she turned back towards the bar and focused her attention on the guests milling around the bar. Layne's mother, Claire, was speaking excitedly to her brother Bill. Her hands were flitting around as she spoke and it made Emma wonder what the subject of the conversation was. She smiled thinking of how thrilled Claire had been when Layne told her of the engagement. From that moment on, she had been consumed with the details of the wedding and would offer to run any and all errands involved with the planning of the most important day in her only child's life.

Layne bore a striking resemblance to her mother. So much so, in fact, that often times people assumed they were sisters instead of mother and daughter. They were nearly the same height with Layne only a mere half inch taller than her mother. Both had the same flawless skin that was free from any blemishes despite the many hours they'd each spent in the sun over the years -a detail that Emma was admittedly envious of, given her abundance of freckles. And of course, they shared the same hair color, right down to the subtle highlights that always seemed to catch the light perfectly. Emma was only one of a few people that were privy to the face that Claire's hair color mirrored her daughter's because of a standing appointment at the local salon - an appointment that had always struck Emma as unnecessary. Claire was a beautiful woman and Emma had long thought that regardless of the color of her hair, she would be striking.

She watched as Layne's father Stephen came up and shook hands with his brother in law. He naturally placed his arm around his wife and pulled her closer to him and gently planted a kiss on her forehead. Emma couldn't tell what he was saying to his wife but must have been something complementary because she beamed at him and leaned in to kiss him on the lips.

Emma sighed softly. It seemed that she was surrounded by happily married people. Weren't there any single guys here that she could at least make an effort to be interested in? Well, a single guy besides Tyler. Maybe Layne had a recently divorced cousin? She wouldn't be picky...having a pulse would do...today anyways.

She surveyed the room once again and allowed her gaze to rest on Andy, who was now dancing with his new wife. She noticed how he held her close; one hand on her lower back and his other held her hand close to his heart. She watched as he lifted her hand to his lips and gently pressed a kiss to one of her knuckles and smiled at her with such emotion that Emma had to look away, almost embarrassed at having witnessed such a moment of intimacy.

Looking down, Emma realized that the bartender had refilled her glass of wine and at the moment, it was not being put to good use. The glass was slowly losing its chill and coming to room temperature rather than helping Emma through her depression. Needing to remedy that situation, she lifted the glass to her lips to take a sip. From out of the corner of her eye, she noticed a cornflower blue dress that matched her own coming towards her. She knew it was Vicki, a woman that worked in Layne's office and was also the only other bridesmaid. Vicki wasn't particularly close to Layne, which was why initially, Emma had been surprised when to find out she was going to be in the wedding. Although Vicki and Layne had worked together for a few years, Emma couldn't recall a time when Vicki had been out with Layne for anything other than a work event. Of course, Layne had always been someone whose work defined her so it was only natural that she would feel particularly close to some of her co-workers.

"Vodka tonic, please." Vicki said, waving her hand as she approached the bar. For a brief moment, Emma thought she was going to snap her fingers to get the bartender to move quicker. Luckily, that didn't happen and Emma breathed a sigh of relief. Vicki had always been somewhat abrasive and lacked the filter that told her when others might be upset at something she'd said. As a result, more than one person had been offended by something that had come out of Vicki's mouth. Emma had learned this firsthand when the two of them had first met. It was only moments after Layne had introduced them that Vicki began offering suggestions to Emma on how to cover them up. She then further put her foot into her mouth when she gave her the name of a "reputable dermatologist" who could "laser those puppies off." When Layne gasped and then tried to shush her, Vicki had only shrugged and responded that she was only "trying to help get rid of the dots on her face." Of course, all of this help had been offered without even so much as a hint from Emma that she had any problems at all with the freckles on her face.

No filter. No filter at all.

Emma knew she'd be needed for several things during the reception and she figured now was just the right time to leave the bar and check on Layne. 'Now' being before Vicki opened her mouth.

But…today was not her day. Before she could even turn away from the bar, Vicki had sidled up to her and way squinting at her as though trying to solve a math problem that was written on Emma's forehead.

"Er…Hi, Vicki," Emma said. "Having a good time?"

"You do realize you're supposed to be making sure Layne has everything she needs, right?"

For some reason unknown to Emma, Vicki had assumed responsibility for making sure that the wedding ran according to plan and of course, this meant that Vicki was constantly checking on Emma's whereabouts and reminding her of her duties as maid of honor. Apparently, only moments after being asked to be a bridesmaid, Vicki had run out and purchased all the books she could find on the subject of wedding etiquette, including books specifically related to maid of honor duties. It quickly became clear that if Vicki wasn't going to be the maid of honor, she was going to make sure that the chosen maid of honor – Emma – didn't mess anything up.

Emma withheld any sarcastic comment – quite the feat considering she'd now consumed two glasses of wine - and managed to hold the smile on her face. "Don't worry. I was just heading over to see if Layne needed anything."

Vicki's chest visibly deflated as though she'd been hoping to find an opportunity to either relieve Emma of her job or reprimand her and now the opportunity had vanished. "Well, all right then."

Emma began to walk toward Layne and waived over her shoulder. From behind her, she heard Vicki continue to give orders. "And Emma? Don't forget, you'll need to help Layne a lot tonight. If I were you, I'd stay close!"

She ended the sentence by raising her voice an octave or so, trying make it sound musical and sing-songy. Emma rolled her eyes thinking that no matter what tone Vicki used, the statement would still be judgmental and critical.

Smiling through gritted teeth, Emma said, "I've got it, Vicki," and added a little musical lilt to her own voice.

She began to weave her way through the crowd, careful not to spill any of her wine on the laminate flooring. She finally made it over to Andy and Layne, who were seated at a table on the far side of the room speaking with Tyler and a few of Andy's college buddies. Tyler was the first to notice her approaching and stood up to greet her, sloshing some of the beer out of his glass as he did so. Emma knew instinctively that he'd had too much to drink and steeled herself for another round of fending off his advances.

"Hey, Em. It's about time you made it over here. I've been sitting here waiting for you to come and entertain me."

Emma raised her eyebrows and looked pointedly at the glass he held. "I hardly think I need to entertain you. From the looks of things, you're doing just fine all by yourself."

"Awwwww..come on." He leaned close to her and whispered in her ear. "You know I need you around."

His breath felt a little too warm on her ear and smelled sour from the beer he'd been consuming. She crinkled her nose and tried to

Donna Small

back away but found that she was unable to since he had wrapped one arm around her lower back in order to keep her close. It seemed that Tyler, being the eternal optimist, had not yet grasped the fact that Emma was not interested. Clearly, she would have to be more direct. However, given the amount of alcohol she assumed he'd had to drink, she wondered if anything would get through to him.

Of course, the last thing Emma wanted to do was make a scene in front of everyone, especially Layne and Andy. There was no way she was going to be the story everyone mentioned when they recalled the wedding. So, as much as she wanted to give Tyler a swift kick to the general vicinity of the family jewels, she contained that urge and instead looked him in the eye and crossed her arms in front of her chest.

"Tyler," she said sternly, "I just came over here to check on Layne. Now, if you don't mind-"

"Oh, I don't mind at all," he slurred. His breath was now hitting her directly in the face and the stench was overpowering. She pushed at his chest with her hand and squirmed out of his grasp, nearly dumping her remaining wine all over him. She smiled, thinking how it was almost too bad that she managed to save the wine since it might have actually shocked some sense into him.

"Well, I do!" She hissed, as she smoothed her dress down. She turned away and walked over to the other side of the table and sat down beside Layne.

"What was that all about?" Layne asked, motioning to Tyler with her eyes.

"Ugh. He will NOT leave me alone!" She reached for the glass of water in front of Layne and took a sip. "How much has he had to drink, anyway?"

Layne glanced at Tyler to assess. "By the looks of things, way too much." She shrugged. "But not to worry, he's riding back to Andy's parents place with them and staying the night."

"Lucky for them," Emma mumbled.

"Now come on. He's not that bad....is he?"

"Let's just say that over the course of your engagement, I've had my share of 'up close and personal' moments with him."

"I don't know why you just don't go out with him. He's kinda cute!" Layne glanced at Tyler again and Emma watched as she looked him up and down. "He's nice and tall, has a good build, and he's got a great sense of humor."

Emma sighed. "I don't know, Layne. He's just not my type."

"Well, what IS your type? Just tell me and I'll find him for you!"

She opened her mouth to speak but just then, Andy came up behind Layne and kissed her on the hollow of her neck. Layne giggled and their conversation was thankfully – at least in Emma's opinion - forgotten.

"How are you Mrs. Harper," Andy whispered into Layne's ear.

She giggled again and then turned to him, trying- and failing- to look annoyed. "Would you stop saying that? Whenever I hear it, I look around for your mother."

"Well, you better get used to the name," he replied, "because you're going have it for the rest of your life." He looked over at Emma. "Am I right?"

She nodded. "He's right. You're already married so it's too late to complain about your new name."

"Well, you're no help," Layne huffed. "Aren't you the maid of honor? That means you're supposed to *help* me." She folded her hands together and tucked them underneath her chin, mimicking a damsel in distress but Emma was having none of it.

"Oh, I will...with the cake, your dress, your bouquet..." She counted out the items on her fingers.

"Yeah, yeah..." Layne grinned.

"Speaking of helping you," Emma said, "Shouldn't we get over to the cake table?"

Layne looked across the room to where the four tiered wedding cake sat. "You're probably right." She turned to Andy. "Come on, *Mister* Harper. Let's get this show on the road."

She stood up, placed her hand in Andy's elbow and motioned for Emma to lead the way. As they weaved their way across the room, Emma overheard Layne giving last minute instructions to Andy and had to chuckle. She knew her best friend so well.

"Now, remember. If you get ANYTHING on this dress, I will have to hurt you. The cake goes *gently* into my mouth..."

Andy chuckled. "I know...I know. Don't worry, Layne. I won't hurt the dress."

As the evening progressed, cake was cut, music was played, dinner was eaten, and bouquets were thrown and subsequently caught. Emma gave a good show of reaching for the tossed bouquet, but there was no way she was getting anywhere even close to it. She knew that Andy was going to practically hand the garter to Tyler. She also knew that the recipients of the bouquet and garter would perform a reversal of what the bride and groom had only recently done. That is, instead of removing the garter, the man who now held it would slide the garter up onto the leg of the woman who had caught the bouquet. Needless to say, Emma was having none of that. The last thing she wanted was for Tyler to have his hands anywhere near her upper thigh.

Emma thought back to the conversation she'd had earlier with Layne. It never ceased to amaze her that Layne could somehow slide matchmaking into any conversation – even one at her own wedding! Emma knew that it was only going to get worse now that she was married. She wanted the same happiness for Emma, which meant that she would continue to fix her up with any single man she came in contact with. That was the only argument the two of them ever had. Layne would continue to set Emma up with anyone and everyone she met while Emma would continue to protest to deaf ears that she wasn't interested. Layne held out hope, though, that she would be the one to find the perfect match for Emma. Of course, Emma knew that she'd already found her perfect match but Layne, without ever knowing Emma's feelings, had taken him for herself.

At the end of the evening, Emma slowly walked to her car and climbed in. She slid off her shoes and rubbed her feet against the carpeting of the floor mat, trying to massage them. She drove home slowly, utterly exhausted from the day's events. She was happy for Layne; ecstatic even. She just wished with every fiber of her being that Layne could have found happiness with anyone else. Ever since they'd been kids, Layne had fallen in and out of love more times than Emma could remember. Why was it that this time, Layne didn't fall *out* of love? Why this time, did it have to be forever?

Emma pulled into her apartment complex, grabbed her shoes and purse, and walked barefoot into her building. She was tired and desperately needed to curl up in her bed.

She let herself into her apartment and locked the door behind her. Without even turning on a light, she walked directly down the hall and into her bedroom. All she wanted at the moment was to curl up in her bed and fall asleep for ten or twelve hours. She took off her bridesmaid's dress and hung it on its hanger, smoothing out the wrinkles with her hands. She picked up the plastic bag that the dress had come in and worked it over the hanger, gently pulling it down to cover the length of the dress.

"There," she said, as a tear slowly made its way down her check.

After putting on her pajamas, she pulled back the covers and crawled in, pulling the comforter up to her chin and holding it tightly. Here, in the safety of her bed, she could release the pain she'd kept inside of her for so long. It was over now. Layne and Andy were married. They'd vowed to love one another forever in front of two hundred of their friends and family. It was ironic that is one fell swoop, Layne's marriage gave her a new beginning....possibility....hope, while for Emma, it meant the end of those same things.

Emma was not, by nature, a jealous person and had never been jealous of Layne for anything. Today, though, jealousy funneled through her and she knew that she would give anything to have what Layne had at this very moment.

"They're happy together." Emma whispered into the darkness. "And that's all that matters."

There in the darkness, she let the tears fall. It was only after she reached the point of complete emptiness she was able to fall asleep.

Chapter 3

Emma drove up the long gravel driveway and rolled her eyes as she noticed the addition of several plastic animals in the front of her parent's house. For whatever reason, her mother thought pink flamingos and plastic deer were a nice addition to the front lawn. Although this was a major embarrassment to Emma while she was growing up, she'd learned to live with it. Besides, nothing could convince her mother to rid the yard of the ornaments.

She pulled in front of the garage on the side of the house and got out, noticing that the lawn was still perfectly manicured. Since she'd moved out nearly five years ago, she'd worried about her parents and figured that if there came a time when they weren't quite able to manage as they always had, one of the first things they'd let go would be the lawn. Because her mother was still adding animals to the décor and the lawn was still a green carpet, she figured she had nothing to worry about. Nothing other than the fact that her mother thought the artificial animals added something special to the front lawn. That, in and of itself, might be more than enough to convince an impartial party that her mother might be losing some of her marbles. Emma chuckled softly as she made her way around the side of the house to the walkway.

She walked up the front steps to the house she had grown up in and noticed that the azalea bushes her mother had planted had grown noticeably larger since the last time she'd been here. She felt a pang of guilt seeing the growth in the azalea bushes and she knew that her visits should be more frequent. She promised herself she'd make an effort to visit the home she had grown up in more often.

Emma's parents, Walter and Marjorie Stewart, had lived in this house since before she was born. They had purchased the home after they'd first gotten married, thinking that children would come along quickly. The pregnancies did, but the children did not. Marjorie had gotten pregnant five times and had lost each child further and further along; the final miscarriage being a little past the halfway point of the pregnancy. They had all but had given up; the miscarriages were not easy on Marjorie and with each loss, her sorrow grew deeper and it took longer for her body to recover. Walter, afraid of losing his wife, convinced her that taking a breather from trying to conceive was best. "We have each other," he told her. "We don't need anything else."

It wasn't until several years later, and purely by accident, that Emma was conceived. As each week passed, Marjorie allowed herself to hope a little bit more. She knew it was a girl, just as she knew that this child would be carried to term. And she was correct on both counts.

On May 16, 1982, Marjorie and Walter Stewart held their baby daughter in their arms for the first time. Marjorie was 46 years old.

Emma didn't mind growing up as an only child. In fact, most of the time, she rather enjoyed not having to share her parents with a sibling. There were times, however, when she wondered what it would have been like to have a sister. To Emma, that relationship possessed the best elements of friendship and family to form a unique bond that was stronger than anything else. Perhaps her desire to have a sister is what allowed her and Layne to become so close. Ever since they had met in the first grade, the two of them had been nearly inseparable and Layne had been the only constant in Emma's life outside of her parents. To Emma, her mother, father, and Layne were her family. Of course, she had other friends, always had, but none were nearly as close to Emma as Layne. Perhaps it was because both of them were only children that they formed such a unique bond. Whatever the reason, each had found something they needed in the other and Emma had often thought that they were just as close as sisters could be.

Emma's parents, because they had waited for so long to have a child, were much older than most of the other parents in the neighborhood. Their age never seemed to bother Emma in the least. As a matter of fact, it was her age that made Marjorie quite popular with the neighborhood children. Being older than the other parents, she possessed a grandmotherly quality that made her seem all the more nurturing and subsequently, made the Stewart home the place where most of the children flocked to afterschool and on weekends. More often than not, Marjorie would have a fresh batch of cookies cooling, which Emma now suspected was all part of the plan to keep Emma safe at home as much as humanly possible. And Emma didn't mind at all. She'd always managed to have a friendly relationship with her parents, except for, of course, her teenage years when she felt it necessary to exert her independence over and over.

When she graduated college and got her first teaching job, she decided it was time to move into her own place. As much as she desired the independence living on her own would provide, she worried about her parents and leaving them alone. It was her mother who sat her down one day and told her exactly what she needed to hear.

"Emma, you need to live your own life now. We understand that. We always knew that God loaned you to us for a short time."

"But mom," Emma had said, "I worry about you and dad."

"Oh, honey. Your father and I were on our own before we had you and we'll be on our own again. We'll be fine. And besides, you're only moving 20 minutes away. You'll visit every Sunday for dinner."

And she had done just that....for awhile anyway. After a few months her weekly visits became every other week, then once a month. Today's visit came after nearly a two month absence and again, the guilt swelled up inside of her.

As she got close to the front door, she heard the heavy, wooden door open. She looked up to see her father smiling at her through the screen. As she got closer, she could feel herself regressing to the child and teenager she was when she lived here. She always thought it strange how she managed to run her own life, take care of her apartment, work full time but the moment she walked through the front door of this tiny, brick home, she felt like a child once again. She smiled as her father opened the screen door to let her in.

"Daddy!"

"Hi, Sweetheart. How's my little girl?" He asked, as he pulled her into a bear hug.

"I'm fine. How are you? " She walked into the house and looked around for her mother. "Where's mom?"

"I'm fine. And your mother just went to the grocery store. She realized she was missing a key ingredient and wanted to make you a proper lunch."

Emma rolled her eyes. "I wish she wouldn't do that."

Her father shrugged his shoulders and chuckled good-naturedly. "I've been trying for nearly forty years to get your mother to do what I tell her. You and I both know that's never going to happen."

Emma and her father shared a knowing look. Marjorie Stewart had always had a mind of her own, especially when it involved cooking.

"So, what's mom cooking for lunch?"

"Oh, you know your mother. She was so excited you were coming that she made a turkey, mashed potatoes, green bean casserole, squash, and stuffing. Of course, when she realized she was out of cornstarch so she had to run to the store. You can't serve mashed potatoes without gravy."

"I know. I know. 'It just isn't done.'" Emma said, giving her best impression of her mother's favorite line.

Emma threw her pocketbook on the kitchen table and looked around. Nothing had changed since she'd moved out nearly five years ago. She would bet that if she walked into her old room, her soccer trophies would still be on the top of her dresser, right where she left them.

"Do you want a soda or something?" Her dad had opened the fridge and was rummaging around inside of it. "I'm sure there's a diet coke in here somewhere..."

"Whatever you have is fine, dad." He took out the soda and placed it on the counter.

Emma heard the crunch of tires on the driveway and looked outside to see her mother's Buick pull in. She watched as her mother drove in to her spot, backed up and then pulled in several times in an attempt to park in just the right spot. She'd never been the most confident driver and Emma smiled remembering numerous occasions when they'd pass by a store rather than go in simply because the only parking spot available required someone to parallel-park – a feat Marjorie had never come close to mastering.

Although Marjorie Stewart did not possess great driving skills, she had other, more endearing qualities that made nearly everyone who met her fall in love with her immediately. She had a way about her that made you feel loved, even if you'd only just met her. She took special care of those she considered her friends, either by providing a shoulder to cry on, an ear for listening, or something as elaborate as dinner for a new mother who was overwhelmed with the amount of effort a baby required.

Emma had a smile on her face as the door opened and she walked over to greet her mother with a hug and kiss. She held on a little longer than usual this time, knowing she'd been away for some time.

"How are you, mom?" Emma quickly glanced at her mother and realized that any worries she had about her parents not being able to manage were swiftly eliminated. Her mother's hair, while completely white, was styled in a very chic bob that came to just below her chin. Her makeup was subtle but expertly applied, the result of years of practice, and showcased the clear blue eyes that were mirror images of her own. Her mother had always had an eye for fashion and what looked best on her and though she now carried a little extra weight around her mid-section, she dressed in a manner that made every attempt to minimize it, yet flatter other areas. Marjorie Stewart was still considered a handsome woman, most especially by her husband.

"Hi, honey. I'm good. It's your father here we need to worry about." Marjorie pulled back and pointed a finger at her husband. "Tell your father that he needs to get his annual physical. He's been avoiding again."

Walter Stewart was notorious for avoiding anyone wearing a white coat. During the course of her life, Emma had witnessed her father suffer through many small conditions; poison ivy, sinus infections, and even the occasion strained ligament, only to end up at the hospital because the condition had gotten significantly worse. It seemed he never learned the fundamental concept of seeking medical attention before it turned into something more serious. He simply used the "wait and see" approach, never realizing that it wouldn't work for something that required an antibiotic or some other sort of medical intervention.

For the first few years of her marriage, Marjorie had let him have his way until a case of appendicitis nearly caused her to lose him. From that moment on, she watched over his health like a mother hen and would use whatever ploy she needed to in order to get him to see a doctor if she deemed it necessary. Once, she even told him that it was Emma who was sick and insisted he meet them at the doctor's office only to find out that it was he who had the appointment. Growing up, there were times that Emma thought her fathered was bothered by this, but as she grew to adulthood, she realized that her father actually liked to be looked after. Now the avoidance of all medical personnel was mainly a charade that the two of them carried out anytime there was a witness, like today, when Emma was there.

She glanced over at her father and saw a sparkle in his eye as he tried to look offended at the accusation. "Marji, I told you I'm fine. I don't need to see any doctor."

Marjorie looked back at Emma. "You see what I have to put up with? I tell you, that man is going to keel over and die one day because he didn't go and get his blood pressure checked."

Walter sighed loudly. "I'm fine, I tell you! No need to visit the doctor when you're not sick...." He walked into the living room still mumbling and Emma had to let out a chuckle.

"I'm glad to see nothing's changed around here."

"Nothing at all, I'm afraid. I'm still married to the most stubborn man in North Carolina."

Emma and her mother walked into the kitchen. She reached for a glass and filled it with ice, then sat down at the table and poured her soda while her mother checked on the turkey.

"Mom, you didn't have to go to all that trouble."

"It's no trouble, dear. Besides, your father and I can have sandwiches...I can make soup....I can bring leftover over to Mrs. Billings...."

Emma sighed, realizing that nothing had changed. Her mother was still caring for all the neighbors, even though most of them were younger. At seventy-four, Marjorie could be considered elderly by anyone's standards but was not going to let something as silly as a number dictate her lifestyle, mobility, or (heaven forbid) her behavior.

If you asked her, she would tell you that she forgot about the white hair and the wrinkles until she saw her reflection in the mirror, which by the way, she avoided at all costs. She was lucky enough to realize at a very early age that beauty was not something you saw in a mirror; it was something that came from within when you were confident in who you were, which she most certainly was.

She was someone who had always found happiness in caring for her family. She loved to be in the kitchen cooking for her family and neighbors and had always loved being the home in the neighborhood that all the children came to after school. And if she were being completely forthcoming, she would say that there was a small part of her that enjoyed, perhaps a little too much, the times when her husband came down with the flu or some other minor ailment. It was really the only time that he allowed her to fuss over him without a single complaint.

Marjorie closed the oven door after placing the turkey on the top of the stove. "Now I've just got to make the gravy and we'll be ready for dinner."

"Mom, let me do that, will you?" Emma stood up and took a step toward her mother. Hearing the scrape of the chair on the kitchen floor, Marjorie turned around and placed her hands on her hips.

"Dear, I love you with all my heart but you know as well as I that you never learned to make my gravy properly. Now, just sit down there and talk to you mother."

Emma flopped back down into her chair, properly chastised. "All right."

"So how's work? I'm sure those children get more adorable every day."

"Well, I don't know about every day, but mostly, yes. They are adorable."

"How is that parent you were telling me about last week? The one that stood outside your classroom and watched every day for an hour or so? Mrs... Connor....Connelly! That's it."

Emma looked up, surprised at her mother's memory. Some of her students' families were close to her and she had heard numerous stories of ailing parents who had fallen victim to Alzheimer's disease. She knew it put a tremendous emotional strain on families and it was one Emma's main worries where her parents were concerned. She felt herself breathe a sigh of relief, knowing that her family was far from that, at least where her mother was concerned. Other than a few colds each year and some aches and pains, both her parents were very nearly in perfect health and based on her mother's memory of details like the names of the parents of her schoolchildren, Emma figured she was free from that particular worry

"Mrs. Connelly is much better. I managed to talk to her one day after she'd been standing outside the class for well over an hour. It seems Zachary is the eldest of three children and she's had them all at home with her since they were born. It wasn't that she didn't trust me or what I was doing; she was just having a little separation anxiety."

Marjorie nodded. "That makes perfect sense. Of course, it would be silly for anyone to have a concern about you being their child's teacher. You're great at what you do. Those parents should be glad to have you. Hmphh.." The frustration she felt caused her to whisk her gravy faster, clanging the utensil against the side of the pan.

Emma smiled, knowing her mother would always be her biggest supporter. "Thanks, mom."

Marjorie finished stirring the gravy and tapped the whisk on the side of the pan before placing it down onto the spoon rest. "Honey, would you go and get your father? Tell him it's time to carve the turkey."

Emma and her mother set the table while her father carved the turkey. When all the food was placed on the table, Emma smiled and shook her head. There was enough food there to feed them for an entire month. Of course, this was the norm for Marjorie Stewart since she found it almost impossible to cook for less than ten people.

After lunch, Marjorie and Emma decided to take a walk outside. Emma needed to at least make an attempt to burn some of the calories she'd consumed and Marjorie wanted to show her daughter the progress the garden had been making as a result of Mother Nature bestowing the perfect mix of rain and sunshine. Emma took her mother's arm and tucked it in the crook of her elbow as they walked along backyard.

"So, what have you planted this year?"

"Much of the same. Over here I've got some squash and tomatoes and then over there are some jalapeno peppers."

"Really? But you don't eat those? Why would you plant them?"

Marjorie smiled. "Your father had a little something to do with that. You know how he loves his spicy foods."

"Yes, I do." Emma chuckled.

As they walked between the rows of vegetables, Marjorie removed her hand from the crook of Emma's elbow and placed it on her shoulder. "How's Layne doing?"

Emma smiled. "Oh, you know Layne. She's great. I'm over at her and Andy's place a lot...you know, so she can fix me up with every guy she meets."

Marjorie chuckled. "That poor girl is wasting her time."

Emma looked at her mother, confused for a moment and thinking, just briefly, that her mother doubted her ability to meet someone. "Wasting her time? What do you mean?"

Marjorie turned to face her daughter and seeing the look on her face, realized how what she had just said sounded to her daughter's ears. "Oh, sweetheart! I don't mean it like you think." She hugged tightly and then released her in order to look her in the eyes once again. "I am absolutely certain that every man Layne tries to fix you up with will fall head over heels in love with you. I just meant that you're not going to fall for any of those men....at least not while you're in love with Andrew Harper."

Emma gasped. "How did you...but I don't...I mean-"

Marjorie silenced Emma with a wave of her hand. "Emma, I'm your mother. I gave birth to you, changed every single one of your diapers-Lord knows your father was useless in that category- and I've kissed every bump, scrape, and scratch you've ever had. How in the world did you think I would not know that you're in love with that man?"

"I, uh, thought I had hidden in pretty well."

"From everyone but your mother, dear." Marjorie gently poked Emma on the tip of her nose. "So, what are you going to do about this?"

"Nothing, mom. Absolutely nothing."

"Well, I hope you only feel that way until he comes to his senses and realizes he married the wrong girl."

Emma threw her hands in the air. "Geez, mom! He didn't marry the wrong girl! Andy loves Layne. How can you even say that?"

"Because he doesn't look at her the way you look at him." She sighed. "Emma, you know I love Layne, almost as though she were my own child. And it is only because I love her that I can say without any guilt that Andy married the wrong girl. Layne is wonderful, but she's not for him. She's a bit....what's the word you use? Oh, right. High maintenance. Andy needs someone a little less demanding. Someone like you."

Emma rubbed her face with her hands. "God, mom. Can you try to be a little less biased?"

"Well, of course I'm biased. But that doesn't mean I'm not also right."

Emma sighed. "Okay, I give up. But Andy IS married to Layne."

"Whatever you say, dear." She said with a smile.

Emma stole a sideways look at her mother and shook her head. Together, they walked back into the house.

Chapter 4

Emma walked into the restaurant and scanned the room in search of Layne. Of course at only five –five, this task proved to be quite difficult since she couldn't see over anyone's head. Finally, after leaning around several people, she located Layne sitting at a table on the far side of the restaurant. She caught Layne's eye, waved to her, and began to weave her way towards her through the tables.

Emma thought it funny how so little had changed over the past several months. She had thought with certainty that their weekly lunches as well as the time they spent together, would begin to dwindle since she assumed Layne would be spending most of her time with her new husband. She also thought (and hoped) that her own feelings for Andy would diminish given the fact that he was now married and permanently unavailable. She had managed to convince herself that her feelings for him held fast up until the moment he was married because he wasn't entirely off the market. Sure, he was dating someone…then engaged to someone, but wasn't married. Although it was a mere technicality, while he was only dating Layne, there was still a chance, however slim that might be, that their relationship would end – in a completely friendly and mutually acceptable method, of course.

Once he was married though, she felt certain that she would be able to let go, even just a little bit, with the realization that Andy was now completely and legally committed to another. That, unfortunately, had not been the case and Emma was still hopelessly and miserably in love with her best friend's husband and wracked with more guilt than she ever thought possible.

The only positive aspect of this impossible situation and the only thing that enabled Emma to function on a daily basis was the fact that both Andy and Layne were so happy. She told herself over and over that if she couldn't be with him, the next best thing was for him to be with someone who loved him and made him happy. A poor alternative, but an alternative, nonetheless.

Since the wedding nearly six months ago, nothing had really changed between Emma and Layne and the amount of time they spent together. They still continued to meet for lunch nearly every week. And now that Emma thought about it, the only time they'd missed having lunch together was when Layne was on her honeymoon. That was, Emma thought, seven days that she didn't want to think about. It pained her to think of Layne and Andy lounging on the beach (Layne in the tiniest of bikini's, of course), only returning to the room for yet another round of mind-blowing honeymoon sex. Of course, after that, they would spend time cuddling, staring adoringly into each other's eyes, and profess their undying love for each other. Because she had these graphic (and inaccurate, she hoped) pictures in her mind, Emma had avoided asking about the honeymoon. Instead, she focused on looking at the pictures of the pristine Aruba beaches and the two of them in front of exotic locations with their arms around each other, fruity drinks in their hands, and huge smiles on their faces.

Emma knew from previous experience that Layne loved to share all the intimate details of her sex life and Emma wasn't about to open that can of worms. She lumped Layne and Andy's sex life into the same category as her parents – the category called "Things I Know Happen But Do Not Want Any Documentation Of."

All things considered, Emma felt she was handling things quite well and more importantly, felt certain that before long her feelings for Andy would pass – at least that's what she hoped would happen.

Emma reached the table and sat down heavily, as though the walk across the room had sapped her energy. A diet coke sat in front of her and she took a long drink from it and looked around the room before speaking.

"Geez, crowded today, huh?"

Layne glanced around and nodded. "Some conference or something. I heard a couple of guys saying something about it at the bar." She looked back at Emma and frowned. "You look frazzled. Rough day with the kiddies?"

The teasing sarcasm in the question was not lost on Emma. Because she was accustomed to Layne's teasing about her job as a Kindergarten teacher, Emma simply chuckled in the way one does when they know they have the upper hand in the joke. "You and I both know that you wouldn't last a minute with my class!"

Layne lifted up her soda in a mock salute. "Agreed. Which is why I chose a liberal arts degree over education." She shivered in jest. "I don't know how you can deal with those screaming kids all day long. That would drive me nuts."

"Layne, they're in kindergarten. They don't "scream all day long." They play, they read, they color...."

Layne waived her hand in the air indicating she wasn't at all interested in what went on in Emma's classroom. "I know, I know. So, did George ever call you?"

Emma rolled her eyes, thinking of this most recent matchmaking attempt by Layne. This past weekend, Emma had been invited to her and Andy's house for dinner. What Layne had failed to mention was that George, a pharmaceutical rep that frequented the doctor's office that Layne managed had also been invited. Obviously, Layne saw the absence of a ring on the left hand, checked for a pulse, and then quickly assumed he'd be a perfect match for Emma. It took all of three minutes for Emma to realize that he was not for her. If it wasn't the "I can't believe we let women vote" comment, then it was surely the "keep 'em in the kitchen" comment that sealed his fate. Emma shot Layne evil looks all night while Layne shot back looks of apologies. Although Emma knew Layne had no idea George was such a Neanderthal, she still enjoyed watching her cringe each and every time he said something so out of date and rude that it was actually funny.

Andy, clearly embarrassed by his wife's failed matchmaking attempt, had sat at one end of the table silently eating his steak and consuming glass after glass of merlot while he looked at Emma sympathetically. Leave it to Layne to find the one single man in Greensboro that actually viewed women as chattel. Emma had smiled politely throughout the evening, counting the minutes until she could leave without appearing rude. She was gracious up until the moment he left when she handed him her phone number...well, a phone number that was close to her own but off by a couple of digits.

Emma giggled. "There is no way George could have gotten in touch with me using the number I gave him."

"Did you give him the dyslexic version of your number?" Seeing Emma nod, Layne continued. "I thought we had cured you of that in college?"

"I thought so too but since George spent the evening in the

1940's, it seemed only fair that I regress as well." Emma chuckled.

"Touché. And I am so sorry about him. I had no idea he was so...so-"

"Cave-man like?"

"Yeah, sorry." Layne looked up at Emma sheepishly. "Forgive me?"

Emma waved her hand in a gesture of nonchalance. "Of course! Besides, where else can I get a dinner and a show like that? I mean, you've got to admit, he was very entertaining."

Layne nodded. "That's certainly one way of looking at it."

The waiter came over and took their order. As soon as Layne handed him the menu, she continued their conversation. "So, what's going on at work? Anything new?"

Emma smiled in the way friends do when they know they have a good story to tell. "You know, you ask that only because you know nothing ever goes on where I work. Today, however, I do have a bit of scoopage...."

Layne's eyes widened. "Really? Do tell." She leaned forward resting her chin in her hands, anticipating a juicy story. She then sat upright. "Wait a minute. You're pulling my leg, right? "

Emma shook her head. "Nope. And you're not going to believe it."

Layne resumed her position – chin in her hands, eyes fixed on Emma, waiting for the details to come forth.

"You know, you don't have to look so happy about this. It's really a pretty horrible story. Maybe I shouldn't talk about it," Emma said in an attempt to torture Layne, who was already ready to hear gossip.

"No, no. You should talk about it. And I'll be the judge of whether or not it's horrible. Now go on." Layne waved with one hand, indicating to Emma she should hurry up and divulge the story.

"Okay. Do you remember how I told you that all the teachers thought that Mr. Pendal was having an affair with the secretary?" She watched as Layne nodded, recalling the story of Emma's principal and his possible infidelities. "Well, it's true. All of it."

"What?! You're kidding!" Layne took a sip of her soda, her eyes never leaving Emma's.

"I wish I were. It's been a nightmare."

"What happened?"

"Well, Jeannette planned a birthday party last week for Neil – Mr. Pendal – and then took him out to lunch. It was just the two of them. So while they're gone, his wife shows up at the school-"

"Ooooh. This is going to be good!" Layne squealed as she rubbed her hands together.

"Oh, wait. This gets better." Emma leaned forward as though revealing a juicy bit of gossip. "She brought their daughter."

"No!" Layne tried to feign shock but the smile still remained on her face. Emma thought that perhaps, it had even grown wider.

"Yes! So we're all standing around, waiting for him to come back. Finally, after we all made small talk for the better part of an hour, they stroll in…through the back door!!"

"You have got to be kidding." Layne rested her head in her hands. "I don't think I like where this is going."

"You got that right. Well they walk in and he has his arm behind her, sort of like he's helping her in. Not a big deal, right?"

Layne shrugged. "I guess."

"Well, not to the ordinary person but if you're having an affair with someone and your wife sees you with your arm around that someone, you feel guilty. So you drop your arm a little too quickly which makes you look as guilty as you feel."

"He did that?"

"Yup. Just as his daughter was running into his arms. You could actually see the moment when he realized his wife was there. His face just froze and he looked terrified! It was awful. We all just sort of stood there looking at each other, waiting for her to lose it."

"So did she?

Emma shook her head. "No. She was a class act. She just stood there and stared at the two of them for a couple of seconds and then walked into his office."

"Wow. She must have nerves of steel."

"You don't know the half of it. He's standing there holding his daughter not really sure what to do. We're ALL still standing there silent, waiting for someone, anyone, to say something. Then, his wife comes back in and takes his cell phone from him. She clicks a couple of buttons and begins to read his text messages out loud! In front of all of us!"

"Text messages? I'm not following."

"She read all the messages he'd sent to her! He wasn't even

smart enough to delete the texts from his phone!" Emma threw her hands up, exasperated.

"Oh my god! And all of you were just standing there!"

Emma nodded and then took a sip of her diet coke. "Then-"

"You mean there's more?"

"Oh, yeah. Apparently, she called Jeannette's husband and told her about the affair. Then, she called the Superintendant!"

"The Superintendant? Are you serious? Isn't he like the...."

Emma nodded. "The head of the entire school system."

Layne's mouth was wide open and for the first time in a very long time, no words came out. Feeling a bit impressed that she'd managed to shock her friend in to silence, Emma continued.

"So, the end result is that he no longer works at the school – he was placed at another school as a teacher or something - and Jeannette spent the entire week sobbing." Layne's annoyance at the turn of events enabled her to get her voice back. When she spoke, it was evident she was irritated at how things had turned out. "So, she's still there but he gets the ax? How did she manage that? Wasn't she a willing participant? And why would she *want* to stay there. I mean, everyone knows what happened, right?"

"Who knows why she wants to stay there. Maybe she really likes her job. I don't know. But I'll tell you something....she's going to have to *work* from now on."

At hearing this cryptic statement, Layne's curiosity got the best of her and she momentarily forgot about her irritation. "What do you mean, 'from now on'?"

"Well, for the past year or so, she's done nothing but walk around like she owns the place. She wouldn't do anything for anybody. It was really hard on all of the teachers because we have so little time out of the classroom. If we needed copies made or something, she would just refuse to do it, so we'd have to do it. I guess when you're sleeping with the boss, you don't have to do any work. Well, that's already changing." Emma chuckled, feeling pleased that Karma had stepped into the situation.

"We've got an interim principal until a new one is hired and she is making Jeannette do everything! I guess that's her penance or something."

"Wow. Who would've thought such a small school would have

so much drama."

"I know, I know. It's weird because we all thought something was going on but to have it laid out there in the open like that? Veeeeery uncomfortable. I still can't believe his wife read those texts out loud. Unbelievable."

The sandwiches they'd ordered arrived and both took a few bites before speaking again.

Emma wiped her mouth with her napkin. "Okay, enough about the sexual escapades of my principal. I feel like I've monopolized the conversation. What's up with you?"

Emma absently tossed one of her potato chips into her mouth and looked at Layne, waiting for her to respond. Layne sat still, more still than was normal, save for her hand, which held a fork and absently moved the pasta salad around on her plate. After a few moments, she looked up at Emma.

"Laynie? What's the matter?" Emma, seeing the frightened look in her friend's eyes, automatically reverted back to her childhood nickname.

Layne's lips were pursed together in what appeared to be an attempt to prevent herself from sobbing. Unable to speak, she simply shook her head. Emma sat still, becoming more and more worried as she watched Layne hold back tears. She placed her fork down onto her plate and reached for Layne's hand.

"Okay, what is it? You're beginning to scare me."

Emma watched as Layne's bottom lip began to quiver and two tears slowly made their way down her cheeks. "I'm sorry. I don't mean to scare you. It's just that -"

Layne took a deep breath, lifted her head, and looked into her friend's eyes. Her voice was barely a whisper when she spoke. "Oh, Emma...," she said, "I think I've made a horrible mistake!"

"A mistake? What are you talking about?!" Emma asked.

"Andy," Layne whispered. "I think I made a mistake when I married him."

Chapter 5

"What?!!??" Emma screeched, causing the patrons seated at the tables nearest them to turn their heads. Not wanting to draw any attention to their table, Emma took a deep breath in order to calm herself. When she spoke again, her voice was much quieter. "What do you mean, 'you made a mistake'?' How can you say that?"

Emma sat across from Layne, patiently waiting for her to respond. Layne stared at Emma with a confused look on her face as though she were struggling to come up with the right words to explain her feelings. After several moments, she gave up searching for the right words to explain her emotions and threw her hands up in the air in a show of defeat. "I don't really know. Everything just feels wrong somehow. Look, I know I'm not making any sense...."

Emma could only stare at Layne, dumbfounded. She sat there silent for a moment and then realized that her mouth was gaping open. She forced herself to close her mouth and then tried to say something coherent. "I...I don't understand. I thought you loved him."

Layne shook her head. "I do love him. It's just...Oh, I don't know how to explain it, Emma. I just feel like something's...missing."

"Missing? What are you talking about?"

"I don't know! I just feel like something's wrong."

Emma, who had always functioned best when a task was in front of her, immediately focused on finding a solution to the problem. "Well, what is it? What's wrong?"

"I don't know! I can't quite put my finger on what it is other than to say that I guess I thought it would be different somehow. And here lately I've been thinking that maybe this was all a mistake...a big mistake. That maybe I shouldn't have married him."

"You can't mean that, Layne."

Layne rubbed her temples with her perfectly manicured hands. "Oh, I don't know what I mean. That's the most frustrating part. It's like I know something's not right but I don't know what it is and I don't know how to fix it. I guess that's the best way I can explain it." She released a sigh of exasperation. "What is wrong with me, Emma?"

Knowing that Layne's self esteem had always been sensitive to the slightest hint at inadequacy, Emma was quick to reassure her. "There's nothing wrong with you. You're just...confused."

Layne raised an eyebrow. "Confused? God, I wish it were that simple!"

Emma cringed inwardly. The words had come out of her mouth before she'd even had time to think them through. While she wanted to reassure Layne that her feelings were normal, she knew they probably weren't. Several of her friends had gotten married over the past couple of years and they were, for the most part, happy. Sure, they all had their problems but they were of the "leaving his socks on the floor" or "what color do we paint the bedroom" sort. She'd never heard any of them mention that they thought they had married the wrong person. Instead, it seemed as though they'd found the one person in the world who made them better; more themselves somehow. Emma had noticed a connection of sorts between her friends and the men that would ultimately become their husbands. She wasn't able to identify exactly what made it so but whatever it was, it had become more pronounced once they had gotten married. Once that commitment had been made, they seemed to emanate a feeling that told everyone around them they were a part of something that was better together than separate. Emma longed for that more than she cared to admit and here she was trying to console her best friend who, at least on the surface, had just that.

She wracked her brain for a reason as to why Layne might be feeling this way. A reason, of course, that differed from what Layne was thinking – that Andy was the wrong guy. The answer came to her after only a few moments and even Emma herself wasn't convinced of its merit. Had Layne been paying attention, she would have noticed the hesitation in Emma's response and the lack of conviction in her tone. Because Layne was solely focused on her own dilemma, didn't notice Emma's struggle to provide an answer, nor did she notice her lack of enthusiasm and for once, Emma was glad only to have half of Layne's attention.

"What if it is that simple?" Emma asked.

Layne looked up slowly, as though afraid of hearing what her best friend was about to suggest. "What do you mean?"

Emma wasn't sure if Layne would buy into what she had to say but she had to come up with something to reassure her that her feelings were normal. Years of friendship had taught her when Layne wanted to hear the truth -even if it hurt – and when she simply needed reassurance that everything was going to be okay. Today, Layne was looking for the latter and Emma knew it was her job to provide it. If, at a later date, Layne decided she wanted to hear the truth, well, Emma would tackle that bridge when she came to it. For now, she was in reassurance mode.

"I mean, what if your feelings are just confusion. You've spent the past six months trying to figure out how to merge your live with Andy's. Before that, you spent the better part of a year planning this huge wedding with two hundred guests. I would imagine that after all the showers, the wedding, and the honeymoon, there's going to be a period of time where reality sinks in. I don't know, sort of a coming down period?"

Emma knew she didn't sound even the slightest bit convincing but she knew that given Layne distraction, she'd never notice.

"You know, you may be right." Emma watched as Layne looked down at her plate and moved the pasta salad around with her fork. "I'm not sure what I thought marriage would be like but I guess I just thought it would have a little more excitement, you know? There's so much *comfort* between us that there's no surprises anymore." Layne said comfort as though the word itself had a bitter aftertaste.

"But Layne, comfort is a good thing. It's what marriage is all about."

She shrugged. "I guess. But it is a little boring. I mean, there's nothing new…ever!"

"Don't think of it as boring. Think of it as familiarity." Emma said, grinning slightly.

Layne snorted. "Familiarity, huh? I guess that's one way of looking at it. I don't know, Emma. I just feel like I'm missing out on something. I mean there's got to be more to life than grocery shopping on Saturday mornings and dinner with the in-laws on Sunday afternoons."

"Well, you could always shop on Sunday and have dinner with

the in-laws on Saturday." Emma smiled at her friend, trying to coax a smile out of her.

"You *know* what I mean," Layne huffed.

She placed her hand on top of Layne's. "Of course, I do. I'm just trying to get a smile out of you. But seriously, I thought you wanted to get married. I thought this was what you wanted."

"It is what I wanted. It's just...sometimes? I think I want something more. I don't know what, exactly. Just more."

"Oh, Laynie. Don't you realize that you've found what everyone wants? Someone who loves you, no matter what. Sure, there'll be some times when you need your space or whatever but overall it's good, right?

Layne nodded.

"And you don't feel this way all the time, right?"

She shrugged. "I hadn't really thought about it."

"Maybe you're just feeling like you need to shake things up a bit; add in a little bit of excitement or something to your daily routine." At this point, Emma had no idea what she was saying; she was really just talking to keep Layne from realizing how stupid her idea was in the first place. But something stupid was better than the alternative which was acknowledging that Layne's feeling might actually have some merit.

"I don't know. Truthfully, the thought of doing *anything* with Andy doesn't appeal to me at all. That's what makes me think it's not so much what we're doing; it's the fact that I'm with him. I mean, I pretty much know his response to any given situation, I know that after dinner he's going to watch Seinfeld reruns and read for a bit. I know on Fridays he's going to wear his Levi's with a polo shirt. On Saturdays, he'll read the paper and then call his parents. Ugh. It's all so familiar that it's starting to irritate me."

Emma squelched a sigh. What Layne was finding so unappealing was exactly what was so attractive to Emma. It was ironic that Layne had exactly the life that Emma had only dared to dream of and felt claustrophobic while in the midst of it.

"Why don't you try something that you find interesting?" Emma moved the food around on her plate absentmindedly. "I don't know. Find something that you'd like to try and then have Andy come along. Maybe if you're doing something new, you won't be irritated with what you think he's going to do because it's a new situation. "

Layne raised one of her eyebrows and tilted her head to the side, which told Emma she thought the idea was ludicrous.

"What?" Emma asked. "You don't think that would help?"

"I have no idea. It's just that...."

"Just what?"

"It's just that I'm not sure if I'm even willing to try. I mean, if Andy's the wrong guy for me, then what difference will it make?"

"Well, how will you know unless you try? You've got to at least try, Layne. You made a commitment to him in front of two hundred people, for God's sakes. You're not really just going to give up, are you? "

Layne stared off into the distance and for a few moments, Emma was afraid she was actually considering what she'd said as though it were a *suggestion*. Before the panic fully set in, Emma spoke. "Er...Layne?"

She looked at back at Emma, momentarily startled. "Huh? What? What did you say?"

"You're not going to give up, right?" Emma said, more sternly than she intended.

"I really can't, can I? I've got to make an effort here. Really make an effort."

Emma nodded.

Layne sighed. "It's just that I don't know how to try to fix this. I don't even know where to begin. I mean, how do you try to get back something you never had?"

"I'm not sure I'm following."

"Emma, whatever is missing between me and Andy isn't something that we had and then lost. What's missing is something I don't think we ever had. That's what scares me."

Emma was beginning to become frustrated. She wasn't sure what Layne was trying to tell her but she wished she'd just let it out rather than leak out tiny bits of her feelings like she was doing. Emma wanted to help but she couldn't do that unless she knew what was really going on. "What are you talking about?"

"That 'connection' or whatever you want to call it. We never had it. We've always had comfort and friendship but that's it. I'm afraid I married Andy because it was the next logical step in the relationship and not because I wanted *him*. It's like everyone expected that marriage would be the next step and I'm not sure if I did this because I wanted to or because it was expected of me. I guess I never really thought about spending the rest of my life with Andy."

Layne placed her head in her hands as though the simple act of speaking were exhausting her. Emma would have smiled at the theatrics involved in the sentence had the implications of what she was saying about her marriage not been so concerning. She needed to review what she had just been told to make sure she heard it correctly. Layne wasn't sure if she wanted *Andy?* Wasn't sure if she wanted to marry *him?* She shook her head. The possibility of that was unreal to her. Layne seemed to be so happy since she'd gotten married – at least that's what it looked like from where Emma was sitting. She'd hate to think it had all been just for show.

Emma watched as Layne sat with her head in her hands and her eyes closed as though unwilling to even ponder the possibility of a lifetime with one man. After a few moments, she opened her eyes and slowly dropped her hands back into her lap. She inhaled deeply and then released a long, slow sigh, which Emma knew meant she had more to say. She sat and waited for her to continue.

"This…thing that's missing between us? I want it. Emma, there are times that I want it….so badly." Layne looked down at her hands in her lap. "Am I a horrible person?"

Emma shook her head. "No. You're not. You're just confused and worried about your marriage. The simple fact that you *are* worrying about it makes you a good person. Hey, maybe you're just having a mid-life crisis."

"Emma, I'm twenty-eight years old."

"Okay. No mid-life crisis. Maybe you just need time to adjust to being married and realizing what it's all about? I mean, think about it. You spend a year planning for this party where you get to where this gorgeous white gown, Andy gets dressed up in a tux, and for an entire day, you're treated like royalty! Everything about the day is so over the top that you're bound to have some let down or whatever after that!"

Emma had no idea where this particular theory came from. It seemed today she was just full of ideas, stupid as they were, that were jumping out of her, wanting to be heard. Layne, however, seemed to listen to Emma's suggestion keenly, nodding the entire time, as though buying into it. By the time Emma had finished,

Layne was nodding enthusiastically.

"You know, I think you may be right. That's exactly what it is. Some sort of post wedding funk. It makes complete sense when you explain it that way. There was a ton of buildup before the wedding. Then we had the trip to Aruba. How can I not be a bit down in the dumps when faced with going back to work and the day to day boring stuff I have to deal with? Yeah....that's got to be what it is..."

As her voice trailed off, Emma noticed that she began to sound more like she was trying to convince herself of the theory rather than like she agreed with it. In spite of that, however, she picked up her chicken Caesar wrap and took a large bite out of it, grinning while she chewed. Emma realized that Layne had just summarily ended the discussion so she picked up her turkey club and began to eat as well.

It wasn't until much later, when Emma was walking back to her car that she allowed herself to think just how ironic the situation was. She'd just spent the better part of an hour trying to convince her best friend to be happy in her marriage – a marriage that Emma would give anything to be in. If that wasn't irony, she wasn't sure what was.

Chapter 6

Guilt was a powerful tool and it was one that had always worked particularly well on Emma. Since her last visit to her parent's house, she carried around with her a good dose of it, which prompted a return visit much sooner than she had anticipated. She missed them, of course, but it seemed that she was never able to find the time to squeeze in a visit.

Granted, it didn't help the situation that her most recent visit had reinforced how well her mother knew her and if anything now was when she needed to spend time with someone who knew her so well. She had carried her feelings for Andy around with her for the better part of three years and now that he was married, her feelings – much to her dismay – didn't seem to be waning. The fact that her mother had figured out how she felt was almost a relief. Initially, panic set in, but then she realized what a relief it was to talk freely to someone without being constantly vigilant with her thoughts, words and behaviors so she wouldn't reveal something inadvertently.

Her behaviors were more closely guarded when she was spending time with Layne and Andy, or even Layne alone for that matter. During those times, Emma was diligent about keeping herself in check...and it was challenging to say the least. The revelation that her mother knew how she felt about Andy enabled her a bit of freedom when speaking with her. She didn't have to watch each and every word that came out of her mouth for fear that she would speak too highly of him or say too many nice things. Anything she said to her mother would be completely honest since she didn't have to hide her true feelings.

Emma phoned her parents and planned another visit to see them only two weeks after her last visit. Hearing the excitement in her mother's voice when she called about the visit made the guilt wash over her once again. She knew her mother would plan another feast for her visit and Emma told herself she'd arrive in plenty of time to help with the preparations.

On Sunday morning she pulled into her parent's driveway a bit before 10 am. Since it was only May, the summer humidity hadn't taken over yet and she noticed her parents had most of the windows open to allow the cool morning air into the house. She used her key to let herself in and immediately smelled her mother's homemade chicken soup. She released a small sigh of frustration as she realized that since her mother had already begun cooking, any offer to help Emma made would be dismissed with a toss of her mother's hand – and rightly so. Emma had never quite gotten comfortable in the kitchen although not for lack of effort on the part of her mother. Emma just couldn't seem to master reading a recipe, measuring ingredients, and combining them to make something delicious. So, after numerous attempts to teach her to cook, Marjorie simply gave up and would bat away any offer of help proffered by Emma – more often than not, Marjorie was holding some sort of cooking utensil that Emma was completely unfamiliar with and would bat her away with it playfully.

Although Emma would offer to help, both she and her mother knew she was perfectly content to sit in the kitchen for a couple of hours with the scent of her mother's chicken soup wafting around her. Just the thought of it made her mouth begin to water.

"Hey, mom." She said, as she walked into the kitchen and gave her mother a kiss on the cheek. "It sure smells good in here."

"I thought a nice batch of chicken soup would be perfect for today. I think it might rain."

Emma smiled. Her mother had always allowed the weather to dictate her menu. If there was a chance of snow or sleet, chances are Marjorie would be making a batch of chili; when it was sunny and warm, she would opt for something on the grill like steaks and baked potatoes; and of course, a rainy day meant soup or stew of some sort.

"Is dad around?" Emma asked.

"I sent him to the store for a fresh loaf of bread."

"Oh. Well, can I help with anything?"

Marjorie wiped her hands on the dishtowel beside the sink and walked over to the stove. "Not until your father gets back. You can be in charge of keeping him out of the kitchen. You know how he loves to add salt to my soup when I'm not looking."

Emma chuckled. "Okay, mom. You got it." As she sat down at the table, she noticed a handwritten note lying on the table. She recognized the handwriting which prompted her to ask about the note's author. "How's Mrs. Billings doing?" She recalled that during her previous visit, her mother had sent over food to the family. A delivery of Marjorie Stewart's home cooked nourishment normally meant someone was battling an illness of some sort. In this particular situation, the recipient had been battling ovarian cancer.

Marjorie sighed and turned to look at her daughter. "Oh, honey. She's not doing so well. She got her test results back and she found out that the cancer has returned. She always knew there was a chance of this happening but she was so close to the five year mark that I think it came as a bit of surprise to her. She really thought she'd beaten it."

"Gosh. I'm really sorry to hear that." Emma knew that her mother and Marlene Billings were very good friends, despite their nearly 25 year age difference. The Billing's had lived down the street from the Stewart's for years. During Marlene's initial diagnosis of cancer six years earlier, Marjorie had cooked for her entire family while she went through chemotherapy and radiation treatment. Emma knew her mother was terribly saddened by the recurrence of the disease. "What's her prognosis?"

"Well, they're going to start chemotherapy next week but you know how the doctors are. They won't tell you anything." Marjorie snorted her disgust and turned back toward the stove.

From outside, Emma heard the crunching of gravel and knew that her father was home. After a few moments, the front door opened and Walter came in carrying what Emma assumed was a loaf of bread in a plastic shopping bag. He placed it on the counter and leaned over to kiss his wife. Instinctively, Marjorie leaned into receive the kiss on her check without even looking up from the pot of soup. Emma knew this routine had been performed thousands of times over the years and for not the first time, Emma felt a pang of longing for that comfort and stability that two people share once they decide to spend their lives together. Emma found herself thinking of Layne and whether or not she'd ever felt that with Andy and if she did, how it was she lost it. Before she could spend any amount of time on that particular thought, her father's booming voice broke her concentration.

"There's my little girl!" Her father's face broke into a huge smile as he walked over and embraced her in a hug. "I knew someone special was coming today! Your mother has been up since the crack of dawn getting everything ready."

"Walter, that is not true!" Marjorie shook a dishtowel at him and tried to appear to be angry.

"Well, maybe not the crack of dawn, but right after." He winked at Emma and hugged her again. "And since I'm not allowed anywhere near the soup, I'm going to check the score of the game."

"Which game is he watching?" Emma asked, after her father had disappeared into the living room.

"Lord only knows. That man watches anything that involves a ball being tossed, hit, thrown or carried. Who can keep up?"

She stirred the soup once more and lifted the spoon to taste. Satisfied, she placed it back onto the spoon rest and came to sit beside Emma at the table.

"I'll let the soup simmer for a bit. We can eat whenever you'd like. Right now, I'd like to talk to my daughter." She paused for a moment and looked at Emma as though inspecting her for damage. "How are you, sweetheart. Are you eating right? Getting enough sleep?"

"Mom, of course I am. You don't have to worry."

"Yes, I do. It's my job as your mother to worry."

"I'm eating right and getting enough sleep so you don't need to worry, at least about that. Okay?" Emma smiled gently at her mom, knowing how much her mother did, in fact worry about her. Part of it was that Emma was an only child but some of it was due to the fact that Marjorie knew what no one else did – that she was in love with her best friend's husband. She thought about Layne for a moment, as she always did when the thought of Andy came into her mind, and then decided to talk to her mother about Layne's recent admission.

"Mom?"

"Yes?"

"Did you ever feel like you made a mistake marrying dad?"

Marjorie was absently fingering the napkins on the table but stopped abruptly to look at Emma when she heard the question.

"A mistake? How do you mean?"

Emma, somewhat embarrassed by the question – although she wasn't exactly sure why – looked down at the table. "Oh, I don't know...like you shouldn't have married him?"

"Heavens, no! From the moment I met your father I was waiting for him to ask me to marry him and then once he did, I never regretted accepting."

"Not even for a minute?"

Marjorie reached over and patted her daughter's hand. "Not even for a minute. Now that's not to say there weren't times I didn't want to strangle him, but not once did I wish I didn't marry him." Marjorie looked at her daughter and narrowed her eyes. "What's this all about, sweetheart?"

Emma paused, unsure how much to divulge, and then realized that her mother was probably the only person she could talk to about her feelings. "It's Layne," she blurted. "I'm worried about her. She...she told me that she thinks she made a mistake when she married Andy."

"Oh, dear." Marjorie sat up straight and placed folded her hands in her lap. "And when did she tell you this?"

"Just this week."

"Well, did she say why she feels that way?"

Emma nodded. "She says she feels like she's 'missing something'." She made quotation marks in the air with her hands.

"That girl is never satisfied, is she?"

Emma sat up abruptly and then leaned forward, somewhat surprised at her mother's tone. "What do you mean?"

Marjorie looked up at her daughter, who was now staring at her with an expression of sadness and confusion. She felt a wave of remorse wash over her as she realized that Emma was wondering what would prompt Marjorie to utter a sentence laced with such sarcasm. It was completely out of character for her because of that, she knew Emma would wait until an explanation was delivered. There would be no diverting her attention away as she knew Emma did several times each day with the children in her class. That was the one downfall of having a teacher for a daughter...they were well-versed in all the parental tricks.

What Marjorie needed to explain to Emma was she loved Layne like a daughter. But loving someone like they are your own means that you are able to see them for who they are, faults and all. And Marjorie did see Layne's faults, even if Emma did not.

Marjorie had never uttered a word about any of Layne's behaviors that had rubbed her the wrong way. As a matter of fact, she was certain that if she had mentioned any one of the numerous things that made her wary, Emma would have defended her to the end. And if she were being honest, Layne's behavior was so subtle that Marjorie wasn't even sure if she could put into words what had occurred that made her feel the way she did. On several occasions, Marjorie didn't even feel as though something were amiss until a day or two later. A thought would enter her mind that something just hadn't gone as it should have.

There was never a feeling that Layne had done anything maliciously. No, that wasn't it at all. For Marjorie, it was more a feeling that something just wasn't right and as Layne and Emma had grown, she'd noticed that feeling lurking around more and more.

Taken individually, each incident that caused Marjorie concern was nothing to get upset about. As a matter of fact, they were hardly worth mentioning, which was why she hadn't mentioned a single thing. It was only when you looked at the relationship between Emma and Layne over the course of years that you began to see a pattern emerge.

Layne took care of herself, no matter what. It didn't matter what the situation was, big or small, she took what she wanted in any given situation and left Emma with the remains – this was the best way Marjorie could describe it.

Over the years, Marjorie had watched as Layne would, albeit in the most subtle, yet devious way, take what she wanted for herself and leave Emma with the scraps. There were numerous outfits, prom dresses, boyfriends – the list went on and on – that Marjorie knew Emma would have chosen were it not for her desire to make everyone around her happy, and most often 'everyone' was Layne. Marjorie would watch silently as Emma fingered the delicate fabric of some article of clothing. She would also watch as Layne would notice the same article of clothing and then express an interest in it herself. Once that happened, Emma would simply back off and let Layne make the purchase. It was much the same for just about anything. Since Emma had never complained or even noticed how the course of those events had turned out, Marjorie never mentioned a word. Layne was someone who only wanted something when someone else wanted it first...and that made Marjorie just a little wary of her, especially when her daughter was involved. Of course, Emma never gave Layne's behavior a second thought. If Layne was happy, Emma would be too.

Marjorie smiled as she thought of that. Her daughter's main focus was to please others, which was probably why she chose to be a teacher. She was always helping her kids, staying late, meeting with parents, providing tutoring…the list went on and on.

She exhaled slowly, trying to determine how best to explain to her daughter that her best friend had the very bad habit of taking advantage of those around her. She reached over and patted her daughter's hand. "Emma, you're such a good soul."

Emma, who was familiar with her mother's very high opinion of her, rolled her eyes and giggled. "Oh, boy. Here we go."

Marjorie's expression remained somber. "I'm serious, Emma. You are. You're a good person with a good heart. I just wish Layne could see you as I do."

"Oh, mom. She does."

Marjorie shook her head. "No, dear. She doesn't. She only sees herself. And this entire situation is just another example of that."

"I'm not following."

"Layne has no idea what's involved in making a marriage work. She probably never did. As a matter of fact, she most likely got her ideas about marriage from some romance novel. The result is that she thinks that her marriage is somehow less than or not as good as someone else's. What she doesn't realize is that no marriage is perfect. It's hard…very hard. Aside from raising you, it's the hardest thing I've ever done. But if you love the person you're married to, you work through all those little irritations that try to drive a wedge between you. And if she thinks her marriage isn't good enough, then she'll go looking for something better. Once that happens….well, that marriage will be in real trouble."

Emma stared at her mother, trying to make sense of everything she'd been told. As it sunk in, her eyebrows came together in a frown. "I had no idea you felt that way. Why didn't you ever say anything?"

"Because it never mattered…until now. You never seemed to be upset or even irritated with anything Layne ever did. You always let her lead and you seemed happy to follow. But now? Now she's involving you in her marital problems simply because she's not sure she made the right decision? That is not okay with me. Not when I'm afraid you're the one who's going to be hurt."

"Oh, mom. I'm not going to get hurt. I'm just going to be here to support Layne…just like I always do."

"Just like you always do," Marjorie repeated. She patted her daughter's hand; then leaned over to kiss her on the top of the head. *And that's exactly what I'm afraid of,* she thought.

Just then, her father poked his head around the corner. "Marji? Can we eat now? I'm starving!"

Marjorie rolled her eyes and whispered. "You'd think I never feed him." Then she walked to the cabinet and pulled out the soup bowls. She held them in front of her, reaching towards her husband, whose entrance had swiftly ended the sober mood that only moments ago, was filling every crevasse in the kitchen. "Come help me set the table, Walter. We'll eat all that much quicker…that is, if you can manage to lift the bowls what with your depleted strength from the lack of food you're provided."

Walter chuckled and winked at Emma as he reached out to take the bowls from his wife.

Chapter 7

The following Friday, Emma and Layne sat in the corner of Willie's, a local cafeteria-style restaurant that catered to an ever growing population of construction workers, policemen, and utility workers. Layne in her pencil skirt and three-inch heels stood out among the crowd while Emma, in her shorts and t-shirt splattered with paint droplets (complements of the morning's art lesson) could almost blend in with the crowd of workers who had been outside for most of the day and who's clothing reflected their efforts.

Not surprisingly, it was Layne who normally suggested this place, and Emma had often thought she did so because some part of her liked not only being the best dressed woman in the room but also the attention she got when that was the case. It wasn't that Layne needed help with her self-esteem; it was more that she spent a good amount of time getting ready each day and wanted people to notice her efforts. Emma, on the other hand, knew any clothing she wore to work could, at any moment, be destroyed so she only wore items that were nearing the end of their wearable life. And since most days the only people she saw were 6 years old and barely knew what makeup was, she chose not to bother with it.

Sitting across from Layne now, Emma smiled as she looked down at her messy t-shirt and suddenly remembered it was, in fact, Layne who had called last night to make plans to come here today, probably after she had picked out her outfit- an outfit which displayed her figure perfectly yet looked completely professional. She wore a white blouse that was sheer and wispy, revealing a matching camisole underneath. Her auburn hair was loose and fell to the middle of her back in gentle curls. Her skirt was a grey pinstripe that Emma knew was the bottom half of a suit she rarely wore. Layne had completed the outfit with very high heeled, black peep-toe shoes and a strikingly bold necklace that looped several times around her neck. Emma once again looked around the Willie's and noticed several admiring glances focused on her friend and she knew that

Layne, without a doubt, was somehow aware of each and every one of them.

Willie's had always been a favorite of theirs, but because of the fat content of every item on the menu, they found that as they aged out of their teens and their metabolisms shifted into a lower gear, they only allowed themselves to eat there occasionally. Today was such a day and both of them happily munched on a shared plate of chili cheese fries.

Layne stuffed a soggy, cheese-covered French fry into her mouth and licked her fingers. "Mmmm-mmmmm. Why is it we don't come here every week?"

Emma rubbed her stomach, feeling the bloating begin. "Because the French fry you just ate had our daily allotment of calories, that's why." She reached for another French fry. "Oh, to hell with it...," she said, tossing it into her mouth whole.

"God, I love this place," Layne sighed as she looked around the restaurant.

Willie's was a landmark that had been in business for nearly 60 years and Emma and Layne were only too happy to do their part to keep it in business. Not that it needed their help, mind you. Every booth in the room was full and the front of the restaurant was packed with people waiting for a seat to open up.

Emma looked around the room and couldn't help but notice the shabbiness of the decor. The wood paneling of the walls was dingy with only a few outdated pictures hanging on them. Nearly everything in the place was faded and needed replacing but it wasn't the ambiance the clients were looking for when they came here, it was the food. Every item on the menu was either deep fried or simmered in butter. There was nothing fat free, sugar free, lite, or low-calorie. If you came to Willie's, you came to eat. Period.

Emma has spent the past few weeks thinking of Layne and the discussion they'd had about her marriage. Although they talked, texted or emailed at least once each day, nothing more had been said on the subject. Emma, however, still held out hope that Layne would tell her something of the "forget about what I said" sort. Somehow though, she knew that wasn't going to happen. Emma allowed the two of them to devour nearly half the plate of fries before tackling the subject.

"Sooooo...I...uhh...haven't had the chance to ask-" she said, popping another French fry into her mouth. "-you feeling any better?" *Or different?* Emma hoped.

"Better?" Layne asked, clearly not understanding what Emma was referring to.

"About Andy. Are things any better with him?"

Layne thought about the question. "I'm not sure if 'better' is possible. It's not like anything's wrong, you know? But I can tell you that I feel better about all of this. Just talking about it makes a world of difference."

Emma nodded and smiled as she ate another French fry.

"Just knowing that I can text you or email you at any time with whatever random thought pops into my head makes me feel so much better." She took a sip of the soda in front of her. "It's weird, but the more I talk about it, the better I feel. Don't get me wrong, I still feel like something's missing but I think just getting it off my chest really helps."

Emma nodded. "So you still feel the same? That you made a mistake in getting married, I mean." She cringed as she said the words.

Layne chewed on a French-fry while she thought about it; then nodded. "Yeah, I think so. I mean, I hope it will get better but I just constantly wonder why I feel this way, you know?"

Emma nodded indicating she understood. "So, what are you going to do?"

"I have no idea. What are my options, anyway? Leave Andy?" She shook her head. "I can't do that. It would kill him. I guess I've sort of resigned myself to hanging in there to see if my feelings change before I do anything drastic."

"I have to agree with you there. I'd hate to see either of you get hurt." *Especially Andy,* Emma thought; then silently scolded herself for thinking it.

"I have to say that it really helps to just talk about it. I mean, I've been carrying this around with me-" Layne clenched her fist and placed it over her heart. "and it's been killing me. Just talking about it is a huge help."

"I'm glad. I just wish I was more available to talk. It's hard taking calls and texting during the day while I'm at work. I just can't leave the classroom and Janet isn't quite ready to handle all 24 kids on her own."

Layne nodded. "I know. I've actually been able to talk to someone at work a lot too."

"Really? Who?"

"Do you remember the guy I told you about? Brad Somerfield? He has the same job as me but works for Dr. Garrison?"

Emma tried to remember.

"He's the one that I told you looked so gruff, what with the shaved head and goatee and all."

"Oh, right. Right."

"Well, it turns out he's a real softy and he's got an entirely different perspective because he's a guy." Layne looked particularly pleased with herself so Emma felt compelled to respond positively.

"Well that's great that you can talk to someone besides me. I'm glad it helps. Anything to get you back to feeling as happy as you did on your wedding day..." Her voice trailed off as a fraction of the pain she felt on that day swept through her. It still managed to take her by surprise; this pain that would come unexpectedly in waves and nearly knock her to the floor. She closed her eyes and took a deep breath, trying to think of anything else so that the pain would dissipate. She opened them after a few moments and reached for another French fry, hoping that the grease would fill the hole in her stomach. As she lifted the soggy fry to her lips, she noticed Layne staring at her with an odd look on her face.

"What?" Emma asked.

"What makes you think I didn't feel like this on my wedding day?"

Emma's face reflected the shock she felt at Layne's revelation. "What are you saying? That you felt like this *before* you got married?"

She watched as Layne slowly nodded.

"Then WHY did you get married!?" Emma huffed.

Lane tossed her napkin on the table and crossed her arms over her chest, visibly angry that Emma didn't immediately see Layne's side of things. "Oh, come on. All the planning? All those people? I couldn't do that to my parents and you know it."

"Right, because this is so much better." Emma's voice dripped with sarcasm.

"Look, I don't expect you to understand it but there was a lot of pressure on me that day. I couldn't just walk away. And besides, it wasn't like I was sure of what I was feeling. I honest to God thought I was just having a really bad case of cold feet!"

Layne's voice had gotten softer the further she explained herself. She now looked as though she was on the verge of tears. As she looked at the sadness in Layne's eyes, Emma felt her anger dissipate. When she spoke again, her voice was free from the earlier sarcasm. "Oh, Laynie. I had no idea. I wish you would have talked to me about this. I might have been able to help."

Layne sighed. "I just couldn't. I wasn't even sure myself what I was feeling let alone how to explain it to someone else. It's only now that I realize that I wasn't nervous or getting cold feet because I was getting married. I was scared because I was marrying the wrong man."

"Oh, God. You're really sure, aren't you." Emma wasn't asking a question, merely stating the obvious and her tone indicated as such.

Layne shrugged. "I think some part of me always knew Andy and I were wrong for each other but the wedding just got out of control and I couldn't stop it."

"Layne, this is serious. What are you going to do?"

She shrugged. "What can I do? I just keep hoping and praying that the feeling will pass...that things will feel better and I can go on with the rest of my life."

"Do you really think that's going to happen?" Emma asked gently.

"I don't know. But I've got to try, right?" Layne smiled half-heartedly and shrugged, as though there were no other options.

"Yeah....you do. But what are you doing to do to change your feelings? Do you think you'll even be able to do it?" *If that were possible,* Emma thought, *I'd have changed my feelings a long time ago.*

"I don't know if it's possible. But I have to do what I can to make it better. I just don't think I'm someone who can end their marriage. It's not in me to do it. Look, I can spend time with him and see if we can at least enjoy each other's company. I mean, isn't that what marriage is? Just spending time with someone? Companionship?"

"Well, yes. But I'm sure a good part of it is actually enjoying spending time with the person you live with. If you don't even-"

"Ugh! No more!" Layne placed her elbows on the table and let her head rest in her hands, face down. "I can't talk about this anymore. I can't be all worked up when I get back to work. I've got too much to do this afternoon."

Emma nodded, knowing that Layne considered her work her top priority. It just wasn't acceptable for her to be anything other than at her best while at the office. She followed Layne's change of subject and asked about her work. "So, you're really busy this afternoon? What do you have going on?"

Layne picked up her phone and reviewed her calendar. "Ummm..... I've got a meeting with Brad at two and then a meeting with all the office staff at 4. In between all that, I'll be visited by maybe 5 or 6 pharmaceutical reps that will want to show me all the new drugs that are out there." Layne rolled her eyes. "Just another normal afternoon at a physician's office! Hopefully, I'll get home at a decent hour. Andy's rented Avatar and he wants us to watch it."

"Well, that sounds nice. A quiet evening at home...watching a movie....maybe a glass of wine or two..."

Layne rolled her eyes in disgust. "I'd rather do anything than sit home on a Friday night and watch a movie about blue people."

"Come on, Layne! That movie that was great! It won ton of awards too, didn't it?"

"I have no idea. But it's a bunch of blue people...." Layne looked at Emma expectantly, waiting for some sort of reaction. "....on a different planet? I seriously doubt it's anything worthwhile. I mean, it's not like it's Braveheart."

Emma smiled at the mention of Mel's historical epic, which just so happened to be Layne's favorite movie ever. In her opinion, there was simply no other movie ever made that held a candle to Braveheart. Emma, however, held a different opinion of the movie in that she liked it but preferred the romance aspect of Avatar as opposed to the amount of violence found in Braveheart. Emma raised her eyebrows and let her smile get a little wider. "You know, if I recall correctly, Mel did paint his face blue in that movie...."

Layne dismissed the suggestion with a wave of her hand. "Well, that was different..."

"Oh? How so? I mean, blue is blue..."

"*Braveheart* was historically accurate. Avatar is not only based in the future but one some planet that doesn't even exist!"

Emma, who had seen the movie several times, chuckled. "I'm

telling you. You're going to love it. The effects are incredible."

Layne folded her arms on the table in front of her. "Well, then. Shall we place a wager on this?"

Emma nodded enthusiastically. "Absolutely. Lunch. Next week. If you love it, then you're buying...and I'm choosing a steakhouse!"

"No way. I'm going to hate it and you're buying me the best seafood this town has to offer."

"We'll just see about that." Emma looked down at her watch and gasped. "Shoot. I've got to get going. I'm going to be late." She tossed a ten dollar bill on the table and stood up. "Call me tomorrow. From home. I'm going to need to check with Andy to make sure you tell me the truth about Avatar."

Layne put her hand to her chest in shock. "Are you saying that you don't trust me?"

Emma laughed as she walked towards the door. "Not a chance, Mrs. Harper. Not a chance!" She waved over her shoulder and pushed open the door.

Layne picked at the remaining fries on the plate and thought about the rest of her day. She was actually looking forward to the meetings she had set up for this afternoon. As a matter of fact, she looked forward to every part of her day right up until she pulled into her driveway. It was then that the discomfort settled in her belly. She began to wonder what she was going to do to change things and if she couldn't, how exactly could she make it through that night, and then the next, and the next...

She picked up the last French fry and swirled it around on the plate, trying to scoop up all of the remaining cheese. She tossed it in her mouth and savored it, knowing it would be some time before she would allow herself to eat here again. She pulled out her compact and smiled into the tiny mirror, making sure her teeth were clean, then re-applied her lipstick and touched up her makeup by applying some pressed powder to her skin. She looked in the mirror, pleased with what she saw in her reflection. What she saw was someone who had it all together.

Of course, the impeccable clothes and the flawlessly applied makeup were just a diversion from the truth. For located just underneath the surface of the façade she had created was a woman who knew beyond a shadow of a doubt that she had made the biggest mistake of her life…and had no idea what she was going to do about it.

Chapter 8

Layne had been staring at those eyes all day long. She wasn't sure exactly what was going on with her, but she couldn't seem to tear herself away. Now she found herself once again staring into those eyes but this time, the arms that belonged to those eyes were wrapped around her holding her tight. She knew, without a doubt, he was going to kiss her and she also knew she wasn't going to do a damn thing about it.

He moved closer, his eyes focused on hers. She was captivated by the golden flecks in his eyes. Why hadn't she ever notice that before? She found she was unable to look away as his lips moved closer and closer to her own. As his lips met hers, she found herself responding in a way that was both unfamiliar and exciting. Her pulse quickened as she felt his soft lips on hers, gently nipping and then nudging them open. As his tongue slipped past her lips, she was surprised to find that her own longing matched his and she met his kiss with a fervor she didn't know she possessed. As her tongue met his, she had another thought. *It's never been like this before...*

Then she was lost.

She found herself reaching her arms around his neck to pull him closer to her in order to deepen the kiss. She molded her body to his and heard him moan in response. His arms grew tighter, pulling her closer to him. He began to kiss her hungrily, pushing against her and probing his tongue deep inside to mesh with hers. Her body trembled in response and she pressed her hips against his. Almost as quickly as the kiss had begun, he pulled away and buried his face in her hair.

"God, Layne. You don't know how long I've wanted to do this."

Layne held on to him, feeling unsteady on her feet. She knew the right thing to do was let go of him and walk away. The only problem was that every fiber of her being told her to stay right where she was. She couldn't walk away...she just couldn't.

She looked up into his eyes and felt a wave of guilt come over her. Slowly, she removed her arms from around his neck and wrapped them in front of her torso, subconsciously shielding herself from another passionate assault – one that she wasn't sure she'd be able to prevent from going further.

Layne hugged herself tighter and took a deep breath before speaking. "Brad, what are we going to do?"

She was looking up at him expectantly; waiting for him to provide some magical answer which would solve the problem they now found themselves in. He knew she was wracked with guilt; he could see it in her eyes. He wanted desperately to ease her pain but he couldn't. She was looking for answers and he didn't have them. He had no idea what to say to her. He only knew that he desperately wanted to kiss her again.

Only a few moments before, her body and been soft and fluid; now, as he reached for her to pull her towards him and comfort her, he found her to be rigid and tense. He wrapped his arms around her now stiff form and pulled her as close to him, resting his chin on the top of her head. "I have no idea, Layne. No idea at all."

* * *

Emma's comforter was wrapped snugly around her creating a pocket of warmth that had produced the best night of sleep she'd had in some time. She was sleeping so soundly, in fact, that while she heard the shrill of the phone ringing, she incorporated the sound into her own dream. After several persistent rings, she woke, looked at the clock, and began to panic. The glowing numbers on her alarm clock told her it was well past midnight – much too late for a social call. Emma swallowed hard and lifted the receiver, bringing it slowly to her ear, afraid of who was on the other end and what they might say.

"Hello?" She whispered.

"Hey. It's me," a familiar voice whispered.

Emma pulled the phone away from her ear with a jolt as a voice filled with tension came through the receiver. While this particular voice was nearly as familiar to her as her own, at the moment it carried with it a sense of unease and terror that caused tension to form in Emma's stomach.

"Layne." She blurted. "Where are you? Are you all right?

It's....," Emma glanced at the alarm clock beside her, "It's two o'clock in the morning."

"I'm in my car outside your apartment. I know it's late but I really need to talk to you. Can I come up?" Layne's voice broke on the last word and it reminded Emma of a child who was desperately afraid they weren't going to get what they were asking for.

Emma responded as she would to one of her own students; careful to keep her voice calm and steady. She had found that when she did this, her students would read her emotions and most situations would be diffused quickly and without any collateral damage.

"Of course you can. I'm walking to the front door right now."

Layne sniffled. "Okay. I'm sorry about this; I just really need to talk to you."

Emma smiled. "Don't apologize. Just get up here so I can make sure you're okay. I'm hitting the buzzer now."

"Thanks."

Emma placed the phone onto the end table and began to worry once again. Layne had never been one to show up in the middle of the night since she was someone who firmly believed in the merits of beauty sleep and strove to get eight hours each night. Something had to be seriously wrong in order to warrant an impromptu visit at this late hour.

Emma pressed the door buzzer and held it until she heard Layne's footsteps come up the stairs to her second floor apartment. She peered through the peephole and saw Layne's normally immaculate face smeared with makeup. Her skin was red and blotchy and her cheeks were streaked with black mascara. She opened the door and gasped as she took in her friend's appearance, which she was now looking at head on instead of through a tiny, glass hole.

"Laynie! What is wrong?! You look awful!"

"Gee, thanks. Now I feel much better." Her hands subconsciously went to her face and made an attempt to wipe the black smudges away from under her eyes.

"Well, at least you have your sarcasm so I know there's not been a death or something. Come in here and sit down." Emma grabbed Layne's forearm and practically dragged her over to the couch. "Do you want something to drink? Water? Ice tea? Something stronger?"

Layne shook her head. "I think I've had enough to drink this evening."

"Uh-oh. Why do I have a bad feeling about this?" Emma sat down heavily on the opposite end of the couch.

Layne fell back against the couch and threw her arm over her eyes before speaking. "Oh, Emma. Brad kissed me!"

"Whaaaat?!??! Wait a minute. Who's Brad?"

"A guy I work with," Layne replied.

Emma was shocked. "Why would you let some guy you work with kiss you?"

"I know, I know. It's horrible. But that's not the worst part." Layne looked up at Emma with a mix of sadness and fear. Then she whispered, "I think I might have kissed him back."

Emma, dumbfounded, sat there silently staring at Layne. The look on her face was one of confusion and fear. It was as though she was seeing some sort of apparition and she was unsure of what the expected response was supposed to be. Luckily, Layne continued without noticing Emma's response... or lack of it.

"It happened so fast. First we were talking...and then he was looking at me....and then his arms were around me....and then he was kissing me! Oh. My. God. Does this mean I cheated on Andy? I can't believe I could be so stupid! How could this happen? I'm married, for God's sake! What the hell was I thinking?!?!?" Layne flopped back on the couch and resumed her position with one arm covering her eyes.

Emma knew she needed to come up with something to make Layne feel better but she found that at the moment she had lost all grasp of the English language. Her mouth was opening and closing as though she were about to say something but she couldn't find it in her to form any words. She sat there and stared at Layne, trying desperately to come up with something – she'd settle for anything even remotely coherent – to say. She was shocked, to say the least. Never in a million years did she think something like this would happen. It just wasn't in Layne to cheat on someone, if that's what this was. At the moment she wasn't sure where she stood on the subject.

Emma rubbed her face with her hands, trying to clear her thoughts, which admittedly, were clouded because of her feelings for

Andy. She realized she couldn't understand how Layne could kiss anyone other than Andy, because of how she herself felt about him. As she acknowledged those feelings once again inside of her, she felt a bubble of anger well up inside of her. Layne held Andy's heart in the palm of her hand. If he were to find out about this, or about any of Layne's concerns about their marriage, he'd be crushed.

Layne had confessed she was confused about Andy and her marriage in general. Was this her way of testing things out? Emma didn't know the answer to that question but what she did know for certain was that this was a dangerous territory for Layne to wander in to. If went too far into this forbidden land, someone was bound to get hurt and most likely, it was going to be Andy.

But she couldn't think about him right now. Her best friend was lying on her couch practically hyperventilating. She needed to help her. Somehow, she had to figure out a way to remove Andy from this situation. Of course, that was nearly impossible, but for the moment, she needed to focus on Layne. The only question was, how was she going to do that? She certainly couldn't give the "it's going to be okay" speech, because this wasn't, by any stretch of the imagination, 'okay.' Part of the problem was that she couldn't imagine being married to Andy and wanting to kiss someone else. But that was it, wasn't it? For Emma, the sun rose and set with Andy. For Layne, lately it seemed as though Andy was somehow an irritation. Layne clearly felt differently for him that Emma had always thought. Of that she was certain. After all, if Layne looked at Andy the way Emma did, another man wouldn't even enter the equation.

Emma realized that suddenly, things had shifted in her mind. For so long, she thought of Layne and Andy as the perfect couple. She felt a sinking feeling in the pit of her belly. If Layne didn't feel about her husband the way Emma thought she did, then it would only make sense that she feel attraction for another man. For the first time since Layne spoke of her fear that her marriage was a mistake, Emma thought it was a distinct possibility, which meant things were only going to get worse.

Emma leaned forward and took a deep breath before speaking. "Okay." Layne turned her head slightly and looked at Emma from underneath her forearm. "You kissed another man."

Layne nodded slightly to acknowledge the statement.

"This wasn't planned or anything, right?"

"No, of course not! It just sort of happened….but…" Layne looked away guiltily.

"But what?"

"It's just that…I liked it." Layne removed her arm from her eyes and Emma saw a smile form as Layne obviously relived the experience.

"What exactly are you saying here?"

"Something… happened when he kissed me." Layne stared off into the distance dreamily.

"Oh, god…" Emma, unsure of what else to say, stared at Layne and waited for her to continue.

"Now don't look at me like that! " Layne pointed her finger at Emma's face and swirled it around to take in her entire expression.

Emma sat back and raised her eyebrows. "What? How am I looking at you?"

"Like you're disappointed." Layne said, with some finality.

"I don't know what I am," she mumbled as she stood up.

"Now where are you going?" Layne asked, somewhat exasperated.

"I need to get something to drink," replied Emma.

She made into the kitchen and opened the fridge. She noticed she had a half-empty bottle of chardonnay on the shelf and for just a moment, thought about pouring herself a glass. Once it dawned on her that it was well past midnight and she'd pay for the wine with a headache in the morning if she were to drink at this late hour, she opted for a bottle of water that was on another shelf. She grabbed the bottle and opened it, taking a long drink, then went back in to the living room to find Layne face down on the couch, hair splayed out all around her. Emma sat down on the ottoman and placed the bottle of water on the end table.

"Okay, tell me what happened." Emma said.

Layne took a deep breath and exhaled into the couch cushions. She pushed herself into a seated position, grabbed a throw pillow and hugged it to her stomach.

"Remember I told you about the staff meetings I have on Fridays?" Seeing Emma nod, she continued. "Well, we all met today, like we do every week. Today, the meeting went longer than the usual day and a half." Layne rolled her eyes. "Since Brad and I are the managers of the two offices, we spent even more time reviewing everything after the meeting. I didn't even meet with any reps today because I was with Brad all afternoon...even after everyone else had gone home."

"Uh-oh..."

Layne nodded her agreement. "I know. Believe me, I know. We were in my office going over some paperwork and we just started talking. Brad asked about Andy – you know, 'How is everything at home?' That sort of thing. So, I started talking about things with Andy and he seemed to be really listening to me, you know? I just kept on talking and talking and before we noticed, it was pretty late. The people who clean the office showed up, so we decided to go down to Murphy's to grab something to eat so we wouldn't be in their way. While we ate, we kept talking until the time came for the band to set up. You know how they do that switch, right?"

Emma nodded. She and Layne had been to Murphy's many times. It was a unique place in that the restaurant served food until 9pm or so and then the wait staff removed the tables in order to make room for a dance floor. It was a restaurant that turned into a club and was a favorite spot among the locals.

Layne continued. "So, we kept talking-God, he's such a great listener – and we decided to have a drink and listen to the band. It was Renegade. Remember them?"

Emma smiled as she remembered the punk rock group that she and Layne were practically groupies for. "Of course. Danny with the orange and purple hair?"

Layne giggled, obviously reliving the same memories. "Yeah, that's them. They started to play and they sounded really great, so we got a couple of drinks and sat and listened. It was very low-key and completely on the up and up. I swear." She raised her right hand and made the scout's honor sign.

Emma nodded, although she wanted to roll her eyes at the cliché of a scene Layne was painting. A meeting that runs late followed by drinks at the local pub? Was she serious? She felt a tiny bubble of irritation inside of her but quickly squelched it.

"So then what happened?" She prompted.

"We had a couple more drinks...and before I knew it, it was midnight! I told Brad I needed to leave so he walked me to my car and the next thing I know? We're kissing!!! I am the worst person in the world!!!" Layne threw herself backwards onto the couch and began to sob.

Surprisingly, Emma actually felt a pang of sympathy for her. She got up from her seat and sat down beside Layne, placing her arm around her shoulders. "Oh, come on now. Surely one kiss doesn't make you the worst person in the world. You made a mistake for cryin' out loud. As much as I hate to admit it, it does happen. The important thing is that you realize you made a mistake. Now, what are you going to do about it?"

Layne had been crying so much that her eyes were red and puffy. Tears had made blackish streaks down both cheeks and her nose was running. As she listened to Emma speak, her sobs began to subside and she began to get herself under control.

"I have no idea," she whispered.

Emma paused before continuing, unsure whether or not she wanted to ask the question. Even more unsure whether or not she wanted to know the answer. "Layne, do you love Andy? "

"Of course I do!"

Shaking her head, Emma prompted again. "No. That's not what I mean." She took a deep breath and then continued. "I mean, do you *really* love him. Do you want to be with him? Forever? Does he make you happy?"

"Well, yes." She nodded, looking somewhat more confident than only moments before. "I do love him."

"Okay, then. This whole kiss thing is just a tiny little misstep. It doesn't have to change anything. You made a mistake and it won't happen again."

Layne sniffed. "A mistake….you're right, Emma. That's all this was." Layne pulled a tissue out of her pocketbook and wiped her eyes.

"So now what are you going to do now?"

"What do you mean?" Layne looked confused.

"Well, if we both agree that this was a mistake and won't happen again," Emma looked at Layne for agreement. Seeing her nod, she continued. "Then all that's left is for you get things back on track at home."

Almost as soon as the word was out of her mouth, Emma noticed her enthusiasm wane. The smile vanished from her face and her shoulders slouched ever so slightly.

"Uh-oh," Emma said. "What's the matter?"

"How do I do that?" Layne asked. "Get things to feel differently with Andy, I mean."

"I, uh…." Before she could stumble her way through a sentence, Layne continued speaking, almost as though she were talking to herself.

"I know this is going to sound awful…so awful….but when Brad kissed me, it was unbelievable! How do I get that with Andy? You know, I'm trying to remember if I ever felt like that and I can't remember if I did! How do I make myself feel something like that?" She stopped and looked at Emma, waiting for a response.

"I don't know, Laynie," Emma replied. "I just don't know…but I do know that you've got to try. If you don't at least try, then nothing will ever change."

Layne looked up at Emma, and for the first time all evening, felt a sense of hope. "You're right. You are."

Emma smiled. "Of course I am! Now, since you're already here, why don't you just sleep here?" Seeing Layne's grin, she grabbed her arm, pulled her off the couch and pushed her down the hall towards the spare bedroom.

Chapter 9

"What the hell were you thinking?!" Emma hissed. One week after Layne had shown up at her apartment in the middle of the night, she found herself standing in the middle of Layne's kitchen with a death grip around her upper arm. Once again, Emma was the victim of a matchmaking attempt. And this time, as she'd done so many times in the past, Layne had missed the mark by a mile.

"Shhhhhhhh....He might hear you!" Layne said as she peered around the fridge and into the living room where Andy sat making every attempt to entertain the latest in Layne's blind date attempts for Emma.

"I hope he does hear me. Maybe he'll tell everyone he knows not to come to dinner at Layne and Andy's house!" Emma noticed that Layne's arm was bright pink around the area her hand was clenched. She dropped her arm and watched Layne rub the soreness away.

"Oh, come on, Emma. You can't seriously be mad. I honestly thought Malcolm would be a good match for you." Layne waved a hand in the direction of living room, where Malcolm sat waiting for his date to return. Emma felt a twinge of guilt as she realized that he had no idea the two women were talking about him and sizing him up like a cow headed to the slaughter

Emma fixed a deadly stare at Layne after taking a long, hard look at the person waiting for her in the living room. "Really..." She deadpanned. "You thought a twenty-two year old, recent college graduate would be a perfect match for me? He still lives at home with his mother, for God's sake!"

"Well, I know that!" Layne huffed. "But think about all the money he's saving by living there."

Emma tried to think of a snappy comment but then realized that Layne actually had a point. "Okay, I'll give you that. But honestly, I'm twenty-eight years old. I'm not about to date someone who just graduated from college! What in the world would we talk about?"

"I don't know. I'm sure you'd think of something. He's really funny and kind of reminds me of Patrick Dempsey when he was younger...you know in that Can't Buy Me Love movie?"

"Ha! I'll bet he doesn't even realize McDreamy acted in anything before Grey's Anatomy."

"Okay, okay," Layne said, putting up her hands in a show of defeat, "I just want you to meet someone. I worry that you're lonely."

"Lonely?" Emma raised one eyebrow and smirked. "Layne, you don't give me a *chance* to be lonely what with all these blind dates you continue to set me up on!"

Layne had the decency to look somewhat sheepish and apologetic at the almost complaint. "Yeah, I guess I do set you up a lot. But that's only because I worry about you!"

"Well, you don't need to. Sheesh! I get enough of that from my mother. I don't need you worrying about me too!"

Layne smiled. "All right...all right. No more blind dates unless...."

"Oh, god. Unless what, exactly?"

"Unless I think the two of you would be perfect together!" Layne clapped her hands together like a young child who has just unwrapped their favorite present.

Emma laughed out loud. "Because you think you've been so good at it so far? Ha! That's a laugh!"

"Oh, shut up," Layne said, as she reached for a dishtowel and tossed it in the general direction of Emma's head. She ducked, although she didn't need to, given the fact that Layne couldn't hit the side of a barn.

Emma opened up the fridge and took out the open bottle of wine. She refilled their glasses and then sat down at the kitchen table. After furtively glancing into the living room to be sure Andy wasn't within earshot, she spoke. "I've been meaning to ask you how things are going...you know, since last week."

"Oh, gosh! I'm glad you brought that up." Layne pulled out the chair opposite of Emma and sat down. She took a small sip of her wine and then leaned forward as though about to reveal some deep, dark secret. "I need you to cover for me tomorrow afternoon," she whispered.

Emma raised an eyebrow. " 'Cover for you?' Why? What's

going on?"

"Oh…I'm uh…meeting Brad tomorrow afternoon." Layne said as she absently fingered the rim of her glass.

Emma's face registered shock and surprise. "What?!?!" She hissed. "What are you thinking?!!?"

"Shhhhhh. Calm down, will you?" Layne leaned over in her chair to peer into the living room, checking to make sure no one heard Emma's outburst. "Look, it's not what you think at all. I promise. Brad's been out of the office all week on vacation. He flew to New York to spend time with his sister and her family. He's been texting me all week and I haven't responded. I figured I at least owed him an explanation and maybe even an apology. I just need to meet with him and tell him that what happened last weekend was a mistake and that I'm sorry, but from now on, we need to be co-workers and that's all. I just think he'd take it better face to face. Texting it seems so rude, you know?" Layne lifted up her wine glass and took a sip.

Emma had to coax the muscles in her face to spring into action and close her mouth, which was hanging open. "Are you kidding me!?!?. You really feel like you owe him something? I mean, he knew you were married but he still tried to kiss you."

Layne leaned back in her chair and fingered a loose strand of hair before tucking it behind her ear. "Well, when you say it that way it does sound pretty bad. The thing is, I keep thinking about how much time he's spent listening to me whine about my marriage and I wonder if I led him on or something. And let's not forget that I did kiss him back."

"Okay, I see your point." Emma admitted. "But I don't think you'd lead him on."

"Not intentionally, no. But what if I gave off signals or something? I just want to make sure we're clear. No hard feelings." Layne placed her palms down on the table in front of her and then inspected her cuticles.

"I don't know about this, Layne." Emma sighed softly. "It just seems sort of…I don't know, devious?"

Layne had been focused on pushing back the cuticle on each finger but stopped and looked up abruptly. "Oh, come on. Pleeeeease do this for me?" She brought her hands together in front of her chest, lifted her eyebrows and pouted her lips into a frown to complete the begging process.

"Oh, for cryin' out loud. I hate it when you beg!" Emma threw her hands up in the air, exasperated. "Fine. Anything to get you to stop making that horrible face. Ugh.."

Layne clapped her hands in front of her chest and bounced up and down in her seat, pleased to have gotten her way. Emma, who was beginning to feel even more uncomfortable with Layne's relationship with Brad, (and she hated using the word *relationship*) shook her head from side to side while she watched Layne hop around in her seat. "I can't believe I let you talk me into this. Now, will you please stop hopping around like that?"

Properly chastised, Layne settled into her chair. "Thanks, Emma. You know I really appreciate this. I'll just tell Andy that we're going shopping tomorrow afternoon. Just so that he doesn't worry," she added, almost as an afterthought.

"Where are you going to meet Brad? Just so I know in case anything happens..."

Layne smiled at Emma patronizingly. "Nothing's going to happen. But just so you know, we'll meet at Murphy's, have a bite to eat, and then I'll head home."

"Are you sure you really need to meet with him?" Emma asked. She watched Layne's eyebrows rise in response to her question and was quick to explain. "It's just that I feel like we're sneaking around or something. And I hate having to lie to Andy."

"I know you do. But don't think of it as lying...think of this as me doing what I need to do to fix a mistake. And I need your help to fix this. You're my best friend. Who else can I ask to help me with this?" Layne was looking at her with such desperation that Emma felt certain that Layne truly wanted to end this and work to save her marriage. Emma felt the tension in her stomach abate slightly as she realized that this meeting with Brad was the one thing that Layne needed to do in order to get her marriage back on track. Then, this would all be over and things could go back to normal with Layne happily married to Andy and Emma pining for him in silence.

At that moment, Andy poked his head into the kitchen. "Layne?"

At the sound of his voice, Emma looked up and her heart did its usual flip flop and she felt the color rise to her face. After nearly three years, he still had the same effect on her.

He was dressed in khaki shorts and a t-shirt that was fitted closely to his torso. Emma knew that Layne, who practically dressed Andy each day, had selected the shirt in order to display his physique in the most flattering silhouette – a fact which did not escape Emma.

She allowed her gaze to rest on him for only the briefest of moments, putting forth much effort to be discreet. She glanced at him while taking a sip of wine and then pretended to look at the clock over his head in order to allow her gaze to linger just a bit longer. Past experience told her that spending too much time looking at Andy was not a good thing to do as it only took a few moments for her to undress him or fantasize about what it would be like to curl up on the couch beside him. Before long, she'd be completely engrossed in her thoughts and have completely lost track of the conversation going on around her. She removed the hand that had been holding her wine glass and discreetly placed it over her cheek in order to hide the color she felt certain was there.

Emma watched as Andy ran his index finger between his neck and the collar of his shirt, trying to loosen it. She'd known him long enough to realize when he was uncomfortable in a situation and tonight that was clearly the case. In addition to the continuous tugging at his shirt collar, his discomfort was displayed on his face in the tiny lines that formed between his brows when he was anxious or concerned as he was now. She found this characteristic endearing and rather liked that his emotions were on display. She wondered if Layne felt the same way and whether or not it was one of the things that drew her to him, as it did for Emma.

It occurred to her then that she and Layne had never spoken of the character traits that had drawn Layne to Andy. There were no stories of his funny laugh, his sense of humor, or even little things that annoyed her yet somehow she managed to find endearing. Their discussions focused more on analyzing his behavior or discussing where the relationship was headed and finally, the wedding plans.

She looked at Andy again and saw his brows come together again and felt a pang of sympathy for him. Did Layne even notice his discomfort? Or her own for that matter? She smiled as she looked down at her glass of wine as she realized that even if Layne did realize they were uncomfortable with these set-ups, Layne would persist, since she seemed determined to find a mate for Emma. Tonight was proving to be a perfect example of that.

"You're, uh, not going to leave me out here on my own all night, are you?" Andy said to Layne.

"Oh, for goodness sakes. We'll be there in a minute." Layne said, rolling her eyes at Emma. "We were just finalizing our plans to go shopping tomorrow. Right, Emma?" Layne glanced at Emma and then discreetly nodded in Andy's direction, indicating to her that she should confirm their plans.

"Yeah, that's right." Emma tried to sound enthusiastic but instead her statement came out as though she were someone confirming her date with a firing squad. Luckily, Layne was too nervous to notice anything out of the ordinary. And of course, Andy was a man and therefore completely oblivious to the inflection in anyone's tone of voice as an indicator that something may be amiss. For the first time in her life, Emma was pleased that men were, for the most part, obtuse when speaking to a woman.

Andy winked at her and Emma felt a shudder rip through her as she focused her gaze back to him. "Promise me you'll keep an eye on this one," he said, placing his arm around Layne's shoulders and pulling her closer to him. "I don't want our debit card to melt from over-usage."

Layne elbowed him in the stomach playfully and he doubled over, faking an injury. "Watch it, or I'll be forced to hit the Kate Spade outlet," she said.

Andy threw up his hands in mock surrender and backed out of the kitchen, laughing as he went. "Okay, okay." After a moment, he poked his head back through the doorway and stage-whispered. "Now would you two come in here and help me out? This guy doesn't get any of my jokes! I'm dying out here!"

Emma shot Layne a deadly look. "See? Too young. Doesn't get our humor."

"Come on..." Layne said, as she pulled Emma into the living room.

* * *

Emma sat in the living room for as long as humanly possible. After listening to Malcolm go on about the merits of Rap music and end every sentence with 'dude', she'd just about had it. After yet another story of how he drank someone 'under the table,' she stood and rubbed her temples, feigning a headache and excused herself.

She had spent the better part of an evening trying to find some redeeming quality in Malcolm and had come up empty. She felt certain that it was only a matter of time before a real headache snuck up on her so she decided to leave before it actually happened. She had spent what she felt was a reasonable amount of time with Malcolm but now she had reached her limit.

"Sorry, guys. I think I need to call it a night." Out of the corner of her eye, she saw Layne raise an eyebrow, which told Emma she may have fooled Andy and Malcolm but she hadn't for a minute fooled her best friend. She focused on locating her keys in her pocketbook in an attempt to avoid eye contact with Layne. After several minutes, she located them in one of the zippered pockets and she had to squelch a sigh of relief at being able to leave. She looked up at Layne, gave her a quick smile and then moved toward the front door.

Layne called out after her. "So, I'll see you tomorrow?"

"Yeah. Just call me." Emma replied, without breaking stride on her way to the door.

Andy got up to walk Emma to the front door. When they were out of earshot, he whispered, "You don't really have a headache do you?"

Emma looked up at him, half expecting to see him angry that she was leaving. Instead, she saw the corners of his mouth lift up ever so slightly as she made eye contact.

"I didn't fool anyone, huh?" She said, grinning.

He chuckled. "All that matters is you fooled Malcolm. And I'm sure you did. But don't worry about it. Layne should stop setting you up like this."

Emma shrugged. "It's okay. She likes doing it and hey, you never know, right?"

He laughed out loud. "I think you give her too much credit. In all the times she's tried to set you up, has she ever been even close to your type?"

She pretended to ponder the question. "Well...now that you mention it...no."

"See? She's horrible at this! But you're a good sport." He opened the door to let her walk through. "Drive safe, okay?"

"I will. Thanks."

She turned and walked down the front steps toward her car. She very nearly turned back to see if he was still standing there but she forced herself to keep walking forward. Once she reached her car, she got in and put the keys into the ignition. Glancing up, she saw that the front door was closed. It was then that she realized she'd been holding her breath. She exhaled slowly, trying to control the thudding of her heart. While she knew it was silly and meant nothing other than friendship, Emma felt a certain amount of warmth knowing that she and Andy had shared a moment together, however insignificant it had been. Unfortunately, it was moments like these that prevented her from falling out of love with him. He was just too damn nice! He had always treated Emma with such respect and compassion that she knew she had no hope of ever getting over him.

"Ugh…" She exhaled loudly and rested her forehead on the steering wheel. "You are completely insane, Emma. Completely insane."

Emma started her car and drove home slowly. Truthfully, she was a bit nervous about the events planned for the next day, although she wasn't exactly sure why. After all, if anything were to be discovered, it was Layne who was risking everything, not her. She was simply providing the alibi in the event one was needed…and she hoped it wasn't. The last thing she wanted to ever do was to admit to Andy that she knew his wife had met another man and she'd helped in any way. She knew he would view her involvement as a betrayal as well. The thought of seeing Andy's face if that ever happened made her shiver. While she knew she'd never be *involved* with Andy the way she would have liked, she couldn't bear to think of a time when they might not even be friends.

Chapter 10

The next evening, Emma sat in her living room watching reruns of Grey's Anatomy. "No way does Malcolm look anything like McDreamy. Layne was completely off base with that one."

As if on cue, the phone rang. Emma glanced at the caller ID before answering and smiled. "So, how'd it go?"

"Hey, Emma. It's Layne."

Emma smiled. Layne would often announce herself as though it was 1985 and caller ID didn't exist. Normally, she'd poke fun at this quirky habit but tonight, she sensed something slightly different in Layne's tone and opted to keep her mouth shut.

"What's wrong?" She blurted.

"Nothing. Why?" Layne asked, a little too quickly.

Emma sighed, wondering how long Layne would insist that there was nothing amiss. She always found it amusing that Layne had no idea she was such an open book; unable to hide any of her emotions.

"Come on, Layne. It's me remember?" She glanced at the clock on the wall. "And it's almost nine o'clock. What happened with Brad? What took you so long? I thought you were just going to meet him and it would take a few minutes?"

"I thought so too." Layne's tone had changed from worry to sadness and Emma noticed the change.

"Okay. What happened?" Emma said gently.

Layne exhaled loudly. "I'm not really sure. Can I come over?"

"Of course."

"Okay. I'm pulling in now."

Emma chuckled softly, realizing Layne had been on her way over when she called. A few moments later, she heard the buzzer sound in her apartment telling her that Layne was outside waiting to be let in. She pressed the button to unlock the door below and waited for her at the top of the steps. Layne normally bounded up the steps in a matter of seconds but tonight the climb took much longer. When she reached the top of the steps, Emma had to stifle a gasp when she caught a glimpse of her. Normally, she was flawlessly put together. Each and every hair would be in place and she'd be wearing an outfit that was perfectly designed for whatever activity she was doing. Tonight, Emma barely recognized her.

Her hair, which normally hung down to the middle of her back in loose curls, was a frizzy, tangled mess. Her face was pale except for the black mascara that was smudged underneath her eyes. Emma tried to think of a time when Layne had ever looked this…disheveled and the memory Layne two weeks ago came to mind. Emma found she had a sick feeling in the pit of her belly and began to wonder if her appearance tonight was at all related to what had happened two weeks ago. She found she was immediately on edge. Emma was closer to Layne than anyone and knew how much time and effort she put into her appearance. It was Layne's attention to detail when it came to her own appearance that made the absence of it all more pronounced.

"You okay?" Emma asked, unable to keep the fear from her tone.

Layne nodded. "Yeah, I'm fine. I think so, anyway."

She stepped aside to let Layne into the apartment, inspecting her closely as she passed by. She watched as Layne flopped down onto the couch and leaned back, staring up at the ceiling. "I think I might need a glass of wine."

"Uh -oh…," Emma said, as she closed the door behind her. "This can't be good…"

Emma walked into the kitchen and pulled a bottle of merlot from the tiny wine rack she had sitting on the counter. The rack held only six bottles but it was the perfect size for her apartment. She tried to keep it full with a variety of wines so that if she felt like having a glass with dinner, she'd have several bottles to choose from. Tonight, she opted for the merlot since she hadn't planned for company and it didn't need to be chilled.

After pouring two glasses, Emma stuffed the cork back into the slim neck of the bottle and then carried the glasses into the living room, placing one in front of Layne. She sat down on the loveseat and placed her glass beside her on the end table. Normally, the two of them would chat incessantly but for whatever reason, tonight, no one spoke for several moments. Emma simply sat there waiting for Layne to speak, knowing that she would do so when she was ready.

Finally, Layne sat up and reached for the wine glass in front of her and took a sip. She placed the glass back on the table and leaned back, resuming her earlier position.

"I really thought today was going to be easy."

"I'm guessing it wasn't?" Emma asked.

"Not at all."

"Well, what happened?"

Layne sat up straight and looked Emma in the eye. She took a deep breath and then blurted, "I think I'm falling in love with him."

"Very funny," Emma said dryly. Not hearing a response from Layne, she sat upright stared at her friend. "You *are* joking, right?"

Layne's expression was steady as she looked Emma directly in the eyes. "I don't think I am."

After that brief moment of strength, Layne dissolved before Emma's eyes. She watched as Layne's head dropped into her hands and her shoulders hunched forward. She then watched at Layne's shoulders began to shake and although there was no sound, Emma knew she was sobbing.

She felt her jaw drop open and sat there staring at Layne, stunned into silence. Initially, she had seen a display of strength – defiance even- but now Layne was crumbling right before her eyes. She was a complete mess. Emma wasn't sure what to do and as a result of her confusion, she sat still near her friend momentarily stunned into immobility. After a few moments, Emma was able to get over her shock. She reached over and placed her hand on Layne's shoulder.

"What are you going to do?" She asked gently.

Layne shook her head from side to side and managed to lift her head up in order to look Emma in the eye. "I have no idea. All I know is that I *have* to spend more time with him…I just have to!"

Emma watched as Layne wiped the tears from her eyes and smeared her mascara further across her cheeks. She was such a mess, which was so out of the ordinary for her, that Emma couldn't help but feel bad for her. Feeling bad for her though, didn't mean that she was going to give Layne carte blanch to do what she had suggested. If anything, what Layne needed was for someone to give her a dose of reality.

"I hate to be the voice of reason, here, but you can't spend time with him. In fact, you should do your best to avoid him at all costs."

Layne gasped. "Why would I do that?"

Emma raised her eyebrows. "Why would you do that? Well, for one reason, you're married and if you want to stay that way, I don't think you should spend any time with Brad. It's not a good idea *at all* to spend time with him if you have feelings for him. I say avoid...avoid...avoid."

Layne shook her head. "I don't think I'll be able to do that," she whispered. She rubbed her face with her hands as though she were tired simply having the conversation and then looked at Emma from between her fingers. "Look, just hear me out, all right?"

Emma heard something in Layne's tone that sounded...well, a bit desperate. Upon hearing it, her curiosity was peaked and she leaned back wanting to hear what Layne was about to say. "Okay," she said.

Layne paused before speaking and looked at Emma for a few moments, scrutinizing her. Emma thought she was trying to determine how best to say things and what her reaction might be. Finally, she began.

"You know I've been feeling...I don't know, like something's not right with me and Andy."

Emma nodded.

"I'm not sure what it is that's missing. But it worries me. I mean, I shouldn't feel this way about my husband, but I do. Ever since I've been talking to Brad, I've felt so...different."

At the word 'different' Emma began to feel a bit of apprehension. She leaned forward just a bit in order to give her undivided attention. "Different? Like how?" She asked.

"I can't explain it really. I just know that when I'm with Brad, I feel like I've never felt before. It's the whole she-bang...butterflies, racing pulse..everything!"

Emma grinned. "Did you just say 'she-bang'?"

"Oh, shut up," Layne replied, grinning. "I guess what I'm saying is...Brad gets me like Andy never did. When I'm with him, I feel...I don't know, happier than I've ever been. It's like I didn't know anything was missing and then when we're together, I realize he was missing. All of a sudden, I don't care what I'm doing as long as I'm doing it with him. If I'm in a meeting, I hope he's going to be there. And if he is? I don't want the meeting to end." She paused, apparently unsure of how much to reveal. With Emma remaining silent, she went on.

"Emma, I walk the halls hoping to run into him. I stop by his office to ask questions that I *know* the answer to just so I can speak to him. If we're going out to lunch, I wait to find out if he's going before I say that I'll go. If he doesn't go, I stay in the office and hope that we'll have a few minutes of uninterrupted time to talk."

Emma was stunned. In all the time that Layne had been with Andy, she'd never spoken of him like this. The entire relationship had been very logical and almost mechanical. What sat before Emma now was a woman who was very nearly swept away with passion. She took a deep breath and exhaled slowly. "Wow. I had no idea. I mean, I knew you had feelings for him but I guess I thought it was sort of a passing thing or something."

Layne nodded. "I know. I hoped it was…but I don't think it is."

"Look, I hate to be a downer here, but you are married. I mean, you can't just ignore that."

"What if I married the wrong guy?" Layne's voice was so soft and hesitant that Emma had to lean forward to hear.

"Is that what you think?" Emma asked.

Layne shrugged in response. "I don't know. I just keep thinking about that kiss. I felt something there that I've never felt with Andy."

Emma nodded. "Maybe you felt that way because it was the newness of it. It was someone new and different…"

Layne shook her head vehemently. "No. It was more than that. I *never* felt that way when I kissed Andy. Doesn't that tell you something? Like maybe, just maybe I'm supposed to be with Brad."

Emma exhaled slowly. "You really think there's something there, don't you?"

Layne nodded. "And if I feel like this, don't I owe it to myself to find out what this is all about?" She gestured to her chest. "I've got to find out what all these feelings are before it's too late."

"Too late? Too late for what?"

She shrugged. "I guess the rest of my life. What if I'm not meant to spend my life with Andy? Shouldn't I find that out now before we spend 5, 10, even 20 years together? Isn't it better to know now?"

Emma shook her head from side to side and rubbed the back of her neck, trying to relieve the tension she felt there. "I don't know,

Layne. I mean, I hear what you're saying but I you made this huge commitment to Andy. Shouldn't you do everything you can do to make it work? Spending time with someone else when you have feelings for them...it's like you're asking for trouble."

Layne sighed. "I know that. Of course I know that. But Emma," Layne took one of Emma's hands in her own. "When Brad kissed me...I can't even explain what I felt. It was like...all that corny stuff you read about or see in the movies? Well, it felt just like that! Don't you think there's something to that?"

Emma gently removed her hand from Layne's. "Maybe there is something to it...I don't know. But you're married. That's got to count for something. Doesn't it?" She looked at Layne for some sort of agreement.

Layne nodded in response. "It does. Of course it does. But I also have to do what's best for me. If I did make a mistake and married the wrong man, I've got to know. I can't just walk away from the way I feel for Brad."

Emma's expression softened a bit. "You really care for him, don't you?" She asked.

"I really do. More than I thought possible. Which is why I *need* to spend some time with him. See if what I'm feeling is what I think it is." Layne was looking at Emma and practically begging for her approval with her eyes. Emma found that she had to look away. She wasn't ready to agree to anything just yet.

Layne, it seemed, could sense Emma wasn't ready to give her approval just yet so she continued talking, trying to convince her of how she felt.

"We talked today for such a long time and it made me think that what I've been feeling for him might be something serious. Honestly, I've tried to ignore how I feel. I really have. But I just don't think I can do it any longer. Look, I know this sounds....well, corny, but I just can't imagine *not* spending time with him. I feel like...like...God, I can't believe I'm going to say this, but....I feel like I can't even breathe if he's not around me. It's like I *need* him to be near me in order to live. Do you have any idea what that feels like?"

Emma knew exactly what that felt like all too well. She looked down into her lap, unsure of how to respond. Clearly, Layne's feelings for Brad had progressed past the point of some passing crush or flirtation. Emma felt a cold chill run through her.

Layne sat on the other end of the couch, silently waiting for Emma to nod or indicate some type of agreement with what she was saying. It was one of those times she wished Emma were married or in some sort of relationship so she'd know what it was like to feel so much for someone that just thinking about them took your breath away.

"What exactly are you saying?" Emma asked, although she was certain she already knew the answer.

"I want to spend some time with Brad. I need to do this to see if whatever this is," Layne waived her hand over her chest, "is real."

Emma stared at Layne and could see how much she felt for Brad. The emotion was all over her face. It dawned on her that she'd never seen her look this way when she spoke about Andy. "Jesus, Layne. What the hell happened today, anyway?"

"We talked and talked....for hours. It's like I'm completely myself when I'm with him. We can talk about anything and the thing is? I'm completely happy doing it. I thought it was just me that felt like this and I would have been able to handle it-"

"Oh god. Don't tell me...." Emma knew where the conversation was headed and it was exactly what she'd feared.

Layne continued, not even pausing as Emma spoke. "- but it's not just me. Brad feels the same way. He told me today. And Emma? I can't tell you how that made me feel. I was....ecstatic! I've never felt anything remotely like that with Andy. Doesn't that tell you something?"

Emma stared at Layne for a moment before speaking. "I just don't know what to make of this. I mean, on the one hand, I see where you're coming from. But on the other hand, you're married. It's like you're testing things out to see if things are greener on the other side of the fence. There's a part of me that thinks you should just suck it up and work on your marriage – you know, you made your bed and all...."

Layne stared at the far corner of the room and absently chewed on the side of her finger. "Well, when you put it that way, it does sound kind of shitty." Emma watched as Layne, deep in thought, kept gnawing on the side of her finger. She alternated ripping off a piece of skin and then wiping it off her tongue with her other hand. Emma felt certain if Layne were left to sit there any longer, she'd start to bleed.

"But," Emma continued. "There's another part of me that just wants you to be happy. I mean, I can see the emotion all over your face..." She sighed. "I don't know, Laynie. I hate to put my stamp of approval on this but honestly? I've never heard you talk about Andy this way before. It makes me think that you might really feel something for Brad."

She looked up at Layne, who was looking at her expectantly. "I cannot believe I'm saying this but...what are you planning?"

Layne looked shocked. "Planning? Well, I hadn't really thought about it. I guess I thought you'd be so mad you wouldn't even listen to me. I should have known better. You've always been there for me...no matter what." She beamed at Emma for a few seconds, thrilled to have her support. Then she scrunched up her forehead as though deep in thought. "Hmmm...now that I can think about it.... I guess I just want to spend a little time with him outside the office to get to know him."

"A little time outside the office? That sounds like dating to me. I don't know about this. It all just seems so....wrong!" Emma still wasn't ready to give her full-fledged support to this. It almost felt as though a part of her family were falling apart, so close was she to Andy and Layne. She always thought they were so perfect together and now Layne was telling her it was all a mistake? And Emma hadn't even allowed herself to ponder the fact that she'd spent the better part of six months telling herself that Andy marrying Layne was for the best, since they were meant for each other. What was she suppose to tell herself now? It was too much for her to take in at once.

Layne's forehead was creased with worry. She absently smoothed the lines away with her finger before speaking.

"I know it's wrong. But what am I suppose to do? How else can I figure all of this out?" Layne cried. "I'm between a rock and a hard place here – I'm married but I'm certain I'm falling in love with someone else. Before I end my marriage and cause Andy any pain, I've got to see if this- whatever this is with Brad – is really something. It sucks that I'm going to sneak around but I really don't know what else to do!"

"I guess I can see where you're coming from..." Emma said. She could feel the tension snake its way up her back and settle on her shoulders. She closed her eyes for just a moment and tried to picture something pleasant. The only image that came to mind was that of Andy on his wedding day, looking handsome in his black tuxedo. She felt her chest constrict as she realized that the entire day might very well have been a farce, yet he had no idea.

Layne continued. "It'd be one thing if I had these feelings for Brad and everything was just fine and dandy at home. But it's not. You know I've felt for awhile now that something was missing between me and Andy. I realize this is just semantics but I'm not falling for Brad because I'm looking for something better. I'm falling for him because I think I might have married the wrong man. Please, Emma. I've got to figure this out."

As much as she hated to admit it, what Layne was saying did make some sense. Not much sense, mind you, but enough for Emma to actually consider what she was asking. She wasn't sure exactly how this had happened, but somehow, Layne had put forth an argument that almost....*almost* justified her spending time with another man. Emma still didn't like it – she didn't like it *at all* - but what if Layne were right? What if she had married the wrong man? Should she be forced to spend the rest of her life with him?

Of course, in her heart she knew the answer to her own question. Layne needed to leave Andy if he was the wrong man and not "test out" things with Brad before making any decision. This was all backwards.

Emma knew, based on her experience with Layne that once she set her mind to something, there was no deterring her. Layne would always do what she wanted, regardless of the opinions of those around her. It was becoming quite clear to Emma that this was one of those situations. She felt sick to her stomach as she realized that no amount of arguing would get Layne to change her mind.

As much as she hated to do it, she knew she was going to agree to help Layne, and she did just that. Just as the thought entered her mind, the tension wrapped around her shoulders and a sick feeling settled in her stomach. Somehow she knew neither of these feelings was going to go away until Layne figured out just what the hell she was going to do with the rest of her life.

Chapter 11

After Layne left the apartment, Emma locked the door behind her and then collapsed onto the couch. What had she gotten herself into? She didn't want any part of this but knew that Layne would badger her until she agreed. Emma just hoped that her part in all of this was minimal. She knew, however, that even having the tiniest of roles in this deception would cause the guilt to eat her alive.

And what was going to happen once Layne figured everything out? Emma wasn't sure what she hoped for. On the one hand, she wanted Layne to be happy but on the other hand, if she found happiness with Brad, then Andy would most assuredly be devastated. She wasn't sure she could bear to see him hurt. The idea that he was happy had been what had kept her going these past several months. If Emma couldn't be with Andy, the fact that he was with someone who loved him was all she could ask for. To find out that it was all a mistake? Well, that information was nearly suffocating her. She knew she had to somehow put all of this out of her mind or she'd spend the next...how long would this be? A week? A couple of days? A month? She groaned and thought, s*urely, it can't take that long for Layne to make up her mind?*

It better not, she thought, as she walked down the hall and into her bedroom.

The next morning, Emma got up early and prepared for her week as she'd done numerous times in the past. Today, however, her mind wasn't focused on her class and what was on her planner for the week. Instead, she was focused on the events of the previous night and found she was unable to focus on anything else for any length of time. Somehow, she was able to go through the motions at school but wasn't able to put her heart into it. She let the children spend much longer in "circle time" and "centers"; times where her instruction wasn't entirely relied upon.

She kept wondering how exactly she got herself into this mess. But there again, she knew the answer to her own question. She would do practically anything for Layne, even if this latest request was pushing the limits.

She was, after all, her best friend.

Emma continued to be plagued by guilt and had no desire to return to her empty apartment that night. To her, it felt like a crime scene. The bodies had been removed but she felt the orange tape was still splayed across her living room. Besides, she desperately needed someone to talk to and an empty apartment was not going to help. The only person she felt could discuss this with was her mother so she headed over there after the final bus left the parking lot. Of course, her mother was more than thrilled to see her and gave her tight squeeze when she walked through the front door.

"Emma! What a nice surprise!"

"Hey, mom." She held on just a second or two longer than normal but that second was long enough for Marjorie to realize that something was amiss. She pulled back slightly and looked at her over the rim of her reading glasses. After inspecting her for a few moments, she frowned, sighed heavily and then removed her glasses from her face and let them hang from around her neck on the beaded chain. "Sweetheart, what's the matter?"

Emma sighed. "Geez, mom. I just walked in and you already think something's wrong?"

"I'm right, aren't I?" Marjorie asked, smirking.

"Of course you are!" Emma replied, feeling a bit exasperated. "But can't you try to hide the fact that I'm an open book for just a minute or so?"

Marjorie quickly hugged her daughter again. "Now what would be the fun of that?" She pulled away and inspected Emma closely. "It's nothing too serious, I hope?"

Emma leaned back against the wall, suddenly tired. "I just need to talk. Do you have some time?"

"Sweetheart, I always have time for you. Now, come into the kitchen. Your father and I were just going to have grilled cheese sandwiches and tomato soup. Would you like me to make you one?"

"Do you have goldfish?" Emma asked, remembering a childhood favorite of hers.

Marjorie turned to face Emma, hands on hips. "Now, when have you ever known me to serve tomato soup without goldfish crackers?

Hmmmm?"

Emma giggled. "You're right. How stupid of me to ask."

"Hmmmph. Now sit down and tell me what's on your mind."

Emma sat down at the table and rubbed her face with her hands. "I don't even know where to begin."

"Why don't you start at the beginning?"

"Well, you already know the beginning. The beginning is Layne feeling like she married the wrong guy."

"I see." Marjorie had pulled the items she needed out of the cabinets and was preparing the soup and sandwiches.

"Things are….a bit more complicated now." Emma heard her mother release a small sigh.

"What is that girl up to now?" Marjorie asked.

"You know how I told you that Layne was feeling like something was missing between her and Andy? "

Marjorie nodded.

"It really helps her to talk about it…you know with me and stuff." Emma absently fingered the salt and pepper shakers in front of her. "She's also been talking to a guy she works with. Brad something-or-other. Anyway, they hung out a couple of weeks ago – I guess they were talking in the office and decided to grab some dinner or something. One thing led to another and he kissed her.

"Oh, dear…"

"Wait. It gets better." Emma replied dryly. "She apparently kissed him back. She showed up at my apartment to talk to me about it and I thought we had it all straightened out. She was going to meet him face to face and tell him that the kiss was a mistake. I felt like things were back on track and she was going to work on her marriage."

"I'm guessing that didn't go as planned."

Emma shook her head. "No. It sure didn't. She met with him yesterday to tell him that what happened was a mistake and that they should only be friends but now she says she has feeling for him. And he has feelings for her. She says she's never felt like this before! Not even with Andy!"

Marjorie flipped the grilled cheese sandwiches and Emma felt her stomach growl as she heard the sizzle of the butter crisping the bread in the pan. "I was afraid something like this was going to happen."

"You were afraid this would happen?" Emma's voice had raised a full octave.

Marjorie nodded. "I'm afraid so. I had hoped that she'd figure things out by talking to you but it seems like she had other plans."

Emma was quick to defend. "I don't think she *planned* for this to happen."

"No, no. I don't mean that, dear. I just mean that sometimes your heart has other plans for you. As much as I hate to admit it, sometimes it just happens."

"How do you 'just happen' to have feelings for someone that's not your husband?" Emma huffed.

Marjorie looked at her daughter and paused, unsure how to respond. "I really don't know how it happens. I just know that it does. Unfortunately, that is."

"I can't *believe* I didn't see this coming! And now, I'm in the middle of it. Layne is pretty much going to date Brad. I'm not at all comfortable with it, but she's my best friend. I need to support, her, don't I? "

Marjorie sighed. "Oh, sweetheart. I wish I had the answer for you but I don't. I know you want to help Layne figure this out and that's admirable, but given how you feel about Andy...well, I just don't know if this is a good spot for you to be in."

"No, it's not....not at all." Emma replied.

"If Layne were married to anyone else, I think you'd struggle with it. But this? This is just torture for you. I don't envy your position at all."

"So what do I do?" Emma cried.

Marjorie waived her spatula at her daughter. "You're the only person who can answer that question. Only you know what you will and will not do. Now, I know Layne is your best friend and you want to help her but you're going to have to decide how much help you're willing to give her at the expense of what you believe in and despite your feelings for Andy." Marjorie clucked her tongue. "I just can't believe that girl is putting you in this position. If she only knew how you felt about him…"

"But she doesn't mom. She has no idea. And although what she's asking me to do is awful, I wouldn't be the first person to do this for a friend, right?" Emma raised her eyes and looked to her mother for any sort of confirmation. "It's just that much harder because it's Andy. I'd hate to see him get hurt by any of this."

"Well, if you reach the point where you can't handle it, then you'll have to tell Layne. If she's truly your friend, she'll stop putting you in this position. Of course, she shouldn't have put you in this position in the first place."

Emma smiled. She knew that she had at least one person in her corner. Marjorie slid the sandwiches onto a platter and poured the tomato soup into large mugs. She reached in to the cabinet and pulled out a large box of goldfish crackers. She placed the box in front of Emma and winked. "They're all yours."

Emma smiled as she tore into the crackers and tossed a handful of them onto her soup.

* * *

Normally, an afternoon with her mother – especially one where she got to eat grilled cheese and tomato soup – would miraculously erase any worry she had. Today, however, that was not the case. It seemed the more she thought about Layne, the more conflicted she became. On one hand, she felt as though she should support her best friend. Who else was Layne going to confide in and discuss her confusion with? Maybe Emma would do or say something that would encourage her to work harder on her marriage.

On the other hand, she knew beyond a shadow of a doubt, that what Layne was doing was terribly, terribly wrong and Emma was guilt-ridden because of it. The entire situation was never far from the forefront of her mind and she found that it began to make her sick to her stomach every time she thought about it. She kept wavering between the two sides of her conscience. Supporting your best friend was the number one rule in her book. On the other hand, how could she have a part in something so deceitful?

Emma had determined that the only was she going to be able to get through this without feeling like she had the flu each and every day was to cling on to Layne's analogy in that Layne truly felt as though she had married the wrong man and was trying to figure her life out. She realized her entire train of thought was borderline ridiculous, but if that's what it took to enable her to sleep at night, then so be it.

In order to keep her mind off the situation with Layne, she did her best to fill her mind with anything and everything else. Each day, she went to work full of ideas for the day's activities and each night, she would plan and research ideas for the next. Her planner had never been so up to date and brimming with new ideas.

The only downfall to this was that her cell phone still pinged each time she got a message from Layne telling her that she would be with Brad in the evening. This happened every day that week. By the end of the week, Emma was certain that this entire fiasco would come to an end and she found herself waiting for the phone call telling her that everything would go back to normal...whatever normal was going to be, that is.

Instead she heard nothing. Friday after work, she checked her cell phone repeatedly, making sure she hadn't inadvertently deleted a text message. It wasn't until nearly six o'clock that Emma's phone finally pinged with a text message informing her that Layne was going to spend some time with Brad that night.

Emma sighed quietly as she deleted the message, not even taking the time to respond. She settled in for the night, knowing that it would be best if she wasn't out and about. She would hate to run into Andy and then be forced to come up with some excuse as to where Layne was. She wasn't one of those people who was could like easily or quickly so it was just easier for her to stay in and avoid the possibility altogether. Luckily, she had gone to the grocery store on her way home and picked up a bottle of wine and a chef salad. She opened the bottle of wine and poured herself a glass, settling herself on the couch in front of the television.

Much, much later, the bottle was nearly empty and Emma was dozing on the couch when the buzzer to her apartment woke her. She sat upright, bleary eyed and looked around, trying to figure out what exactly it was that woke her. Once again, the buzzer sounded and Emma heaved herself off the couch and stumbled over to the speaker. She pushed the button to use the intercom.

"Er..hello?"

"Emma?" It was a familiar voice as Emma breathed as sigh of relief. "Can I come up?" Layne asked.

Emma responded by pushing the button that unlocked the door. After a few moments, Layne appeared at the top of the stairs. Her eyes widened as she saw Layne approach the door to the apartment but waited until she closed the door behind her to say anything.

"Layne. What in the world…"

Emma looked her up and down and took in the disheveled appearance of her friend. Her lipstick was smeared across her cheeks, her hair was matted to the back of her head, her shirt was partially untucked from her pants and the buttons to her shirt were mismatched. Emma couldn't help but ponder the fact that this was now the third time Layne had shown up at her apartment looking like she'd just woken up. She couldn't help but wonder if Layne had lost her mind since she wouldn't even retrieve the paper from her front yard looking the way she did now. Yet here she was, showing up at Emma's apartment? Emma couldn't wait to hear this story.

"What happened to you?" Emma asked.

At that moment, Layne burst into tears.

"Okay, okay…" Emma's concern was now approaching full-on panic. Seeing her best friend collapse into tears caused Emma's mind to race with horrific possibilities of what might have happened. She placed her arms around her friend and tried to squelch the fear that was nearly suffocating her. "It's going to be all right. Just tell me what happened. Did he hurt you? Are you okay? Do I need to call the police?"

Layne wipe her tears away with her sleeve. "Emma, calm down. I wasn't attacked, for God's sakes. Why would you think –" She turned away from Emma to put her pocketbook down on the table near the front door and caught a glimpse of herself in the mirror. "Oh my God….I had no idea…" Her hands went up to her hair and tried to smooth the wild strands.

"You didn't realize you looked like this?"

"No. I mean, I thought I was a bit…er.. unkempt but now I can see why you thought…."

"Layne, what happened?" Emma asked. She moved to sit down on the couch and motioned for Layne to do the same. Once they were settled, Layne took a deep breath and began.

"Well, I was on my way to meet Brad at Murphy's. He called to say he was running late and asked if I would mind meeting him at his house."

Suddenly, Emma had a very clear picture of where this story was headed and she knew she was not going to like it. Still, she remained silent while Layne continued.

"So I went to his house. We've been seeing each other all week and I thought nothing of going to his house. Actually, I thought it might even be better since I might be more relaxed and not looking over my shoulder the entire time."

Emma frowned, guessing the reason Layne refused to look her in the eye but kept her mouth shut.

"Anyway, I went to his house and we decided to order pizza. We opened a bottle of wine and just sat in the living room talking. Emma, he's so wonderful. The more time I spend with him, the more I'm falling for him. I never knew I could feel like this! Do you have any idea what that's like?"

Emma knew she had felt that way for nearly three years but could only shrug in response to the question.

"It's stupid, really. We're just sitting there eating pizza and I'm having the time of my life! Emma, I am completely in love with him." Layne looked up at Emma and the emotion she saw on her face nearly made Emma gasp. "I'm just *drawn to him* in a way that I never was with Andy."

"Oh. My. God."

"I know! I can't help it. Every moment I spend with him I fall for him more and more. He feels just awful about the entire situation- you know, me being married and all."

"Well, isn't that chivalrous of him." Emma asked in a tone that was laced with sarcasm.

Layne looked at Emma sternly and then got up and began to pace the tiny living room, absently chewing on a hangnail. Emma had a sudden flash back to the previous week when Layne had first confessed her desire to spend time with Brad while chewing on the skin around her fingers. Once again, she made a mental note to vacuum after Layne left.

"Look, I know you don't agree with any of this but I can't help the way I feel. I never thought was possible to feel this way. Am I making any sense at all?"

Everything had become crystal clear to Emma. She knew exactly where Layne was headed. All the pieces fit together perfectly. The matted hair, the disheveled appearance, the guilt she obviously felt... She didn't need to ask the question since she already knew the answer. Speaking it out loud was merely a formality.

"Oh. My. God. You slept with him." When Emma spoke, it was

more of a statement than a question.

Layne slowly exhaled and then nodded. "Yes, I did," she whispered. A tear made its way down her cheek as she admitted to not only having feelings for another man, but having sex with him even though she was married.

Emma leaned back against the couch, suddenly exhausted. "I...uh...I..." Her mouth moved but no words came out.

"Say something, Please?"

"I'm not sure what I'm supposed to say. Just give me a minute." Emma pressed her fingers to her temples and massaged them. This was all too much for her to absorb and now her head was pounding and it felt like it had been placed in a vice that was slowly being wound tighter and tighter. She wasn't sure what was expected of her now. Was she supposed to be happy for her friend who had found what she thought was missing in her life? Or was she supposed to do the "right" thing and persecute Layne for cheating?

And now, she was involved, whether she liked it or not.

She continued to massage her temples, willing the pressure to subside. After several moments, she felt the tension ease a bit. She removed her fingers from her temples and slowly rubbed her eyes, as though willing herself to wake up and realize this was all just a horrible nightmare.

"So...what are you going to do now?" Emma asked.

Layne flopped down on the couch next to Emma. "I have no idea. I just know that I feel something for Brad that I've never known before. I don't know how to explain it, really. It's like I was fine when without him but then when he's with me, I can't believe I could even breathe before he was beside me."

When Emma heard the passion in Layne's voice, she looked up. Layne was sitting on the couch, staring at some point across the room. Her mouth was formed in a delicate smile and Emma watched as her hand came up to touch her lower lip, obviously remembering the touch of another. Emma looked at her best friend, the person she'd known for most of her life and realized that she'd never seen her look this happy. She tried to recall the expression on Layne's face when she told her she would be getting married, when she walked down the aisle, or when she spoke her vows. Oddly enough, Emma only remembered a smile that in hindsight, almost seemed to have been forced. The expression on Layne's face at the moment was one of pure contentment and happiness. Of course, she'd seen that look on her own face many times...

Emma hated the fact that Layne had betrayed Andy but she also knew there was no way she could have prevented herself from falling for Brad. If anyone was familiar with that concept, it was Emma, who'd tried for nearly three years to stop loving her best friend's husband. God knows she'd tried everything in her power to make herself stop loving him but it was impossible. The heart had a mind of its own.

"Emma?" Layne asked hesitantly, tearing Emma away from her thoughts.

She was leaning back on the couch, staring up at the ceiling. "Laynie....I don't know what I'm supposed to say here." She lifted her head to look at Layne. "You really love him, don't you?"

Layne looked up ever so slowly before responding. "Yes," she replied. "I do."

"Well, then." Emma took a deep breath and slowly exhaled, rubbing her eyes as she did so. She looked at her best friend, trying to figure out what to say next. After several moments, she began.

"This is a lot for me to take in. I was there the night you and Andy met, I was there for practically every date, I was the maid of honor at your wedding and now you're telling me that it was all one big mistake."

"I know-" Layne began. Emma silenced her with the wave of her hand.

"Let me finish." Seeing Layne nod, she continued. "You're my best friend in the whole world. If you tell me that you made a mistake, even one as huge as marrying the wrong man, I have to help you. I'd do anything for you."

Once the words were out of Emma's mouth, Layne felt the weight of the world lift off her shoulders. "I don't know what to say."

Emma only nodded. "You don't have to say anything. Just know that this is hard for me. You're my best friend, but Andy's my friend too. This is betraying him. *We're* betraying him...and I hate that. You've got to know that."

Layne nodded.

"I'll help you....figure this all out...but please, *please*, fix this." Emma's eyes begged Layne to listen to her. "You've got to end things with Andy if you're going to be with Brad."

"I will," she replied. "I promise."

"So, what are you going to do?" Emma asked.

"I have no idea. The last thing I want to do is hurt Andy...." Her voice trailed off. Emma, knowing her best friend all too well, had a feeling she knew where Layne's thoughts were headed.

"But..." Emma prompted.

"But, why do I feel this way? I'm married, for God's sake. This is not supposed to happen!" Layne cried. She picked up her hand and began chewing absently on another cuticle. Emma thought that pretty soon, she was going to be bleeding from more than one finger, given the amount of time she'd spent gnawing at the delicate skin around her cuticles.

"Look, I don't want you to think that I'm telling you what to do but you've got to figure this out...all of it. I don't believe for one minute you meant to do fall for Brad. None of us really have any of us have control over our emotions-" *Unfortunately,* Emma thought. "But now that you know your marriage was a mistake, you've got to fix it."

Layne had taken her hand out from between her teeth and wiped it on her jeans, ridding it of the saliva. She looked up at Emma hesitantly. "So you don't think badly of me for feeling this way?"

"No, I don't." Her voice sounded more confident than she actually felt. She felt awful, if she were being completely honest. And things were only going to get worse. That she knew with absolute certainty.

Emma continued. "You can't predict how you're going to feel. It's not possible. Just think about it. Imagine how easy life would be if we could simply choose who we should love. No one would ever disappoint their parents!" She smiled, trying to get Layne to do the same.

"I guess you're right. But I still feel horrible about this." Her finger had somehow found its way back between her teeth and Emma watched as Layne tore off a piece of skin and picked it from her tongue.

Emma did her best to ignore the fact that by the end of the night, there might very well be an entire finger chewed up and scattered throughout the carpet of her living room. She automatically glanced toward the closet where her vacuum was held, itching to take it out of its spot and turn it on.

"You should feel horrible; that's what's going to push you toward fixing all of this. Now, what are you going to do?" Emma leaned back and waited patiently for Layne to speak.

Layne let out a sigh of exasperation. "I have NO IDEA! What I really need is some time to figure things out. Dammit! Why couldn't I have met him three years ago!!?!? Then I wouldn't be in this mess!"

Neither would I, thought Emma. *Neither would I.*

Layne stood up and paced around the living room, trying to determine how to handle the situation. After a few moments, she stopped and snapped her fingers. "First things first. I've got to take care of how I look. I really don't want Andy to see me like this. Can I take a shower here?"

"Of course." Emma nodded.

"Great," she said, as she rummaged through her pocketbook to locate her keys. "I managed to leave the house a bit early so I was able to pick up a few things at the mall. I'm just going to get those out of my car and put them on. This way, Andy won't notice anything out of the ordinary. Besides, he never notices what I'm wearing." Layne stopped in front of the mirror beside the door and looked at Emma in the reflection. "Can I use your makeup?"

"Sure," Emma replied.

As she stood there watching Layne prepare herself to head home, she couldn't help but notice that she seemed to process each step smoothly. Layne made sure she had new clothes, would make sure that her hair was perfect, and finally make sure that her makeup was flawless, all in an attempt to ensure Andy never thought anything was amiss. She watched as Layne paced around the room, putting all the pieces together and as she did so, Emma became more and more uncomfortable. Layne was systematically making sure that every aspect of her appearance was as it should be and Emma couldn't help but be amazed at the amount of thought that went into ensuring each and every detail was taken care of. She seemed so comfortable, methodical even, in her planning. She'd gone from distraught woman to master planner a little too easily for Emma's comfort. Layne could sense that something was bothering Emma but luckily, she thought she was still struggling with the fact that Layne had actually cheated on Andrew. She had no idea that Emma was concerned with how well she was able to cover up her indiscretion. Layne looked at Emma for a brief moment and then came over and sat down beside her. She took her hand in her own and patted it with her free hand. "I know you don't like this and I don't like it either. But I just need a little time to...figure things out how to tell Andy. Can you understand that?"

Emma's throat had gone dry. All she could manage was a tiny nod.

"I promise. Just a little time. Okay?"

"Okay," Emma whispered.

Layne gave Emma a hug. "I'm going to head out to my car and get those clothes. I'll be right back."

Layne went to get the clothes she would change into. Emma sat on the couch and stared at the door as it closed. She couldn't help but feel a bit dirty dealing with all of this. She made yet another mental note to shower after she vacuumed.

Things like this never ended well... for anyone involved. She worried mostly for Andy since he was the one who would end up losing the most. Of course, her feelings for him made her ache for the pain she imagined he'd go through and she wanted to avoid that at all costs. She couldn't bear the thought of him being hurt.

"This is not going to be easy," she said, suddenly exhausted.

Once Layne returned, she took a shower and got herself dressed. When it was time for her to head home, Emma had to admit that she looked refreshed; as though none of the day's events had ever happened. Layne had re-done her hair and makeup using the supplies she found in Emma's bathroom and both of them felt certain that any trace of the earlier indiscretion had been successfully erased. Layne was performing a final inspection of her hair and makeup before heading out when Emma felt another twinge of guilt.

"Um...Layne?"

"Yeah?" She turned away from the mirror to look at Emma.

"How much time do you think you'll need to figure all this out? I mean, I know it's hard for you and all...but I'm going to have a really tough time going to your place knowing about...all of this."

Layne smiled at Emma then reached over to give her a quick hug. "I know you are. The thing is...I just don't know how much time I'll need. It's not like this is familiar territory to me. I'm going to do a lot of thinking about all of this because I don't know what to do." She sighed. "I guess I'll just take it day by day. That's really all I can do."

Emma nodded, more out of habit than for any sort of agreement. Layne leaned over and pulled Emma into another hug, this time holding her a bit longer.

"I really don't know what I'd do without you." Layne whispered. Then she pulled away and headed out the door.

Emma closed the door behind Layne and then sank against it. She was, without question, in the most uncomfortable position of her life. She only hoped that this entire situation would be resolved quickly and with minimal damage to those involved.

She just wasn't sure what amount of damage could be considered "minimal" in this type of situation.

Chapter 12

Over the next week or so, Emma became somewhat obsessed with checking emails, texts and phone messages. She felt certain that at any moment, Layne would call and tell her that she had asked Andy for a divorce. Once that happened, although it wouldn't be an easy time, at least Emma would feel some relief from the stress that had now permanently settled in her neck and shoulders. At least the knowledge that Layne had asked for a divorce would put an end to the sneaking around that Emma was so uncomfortable with and everyone could just get on with their lives.

The decision never came. And Emma couldn't help but wonder why.

Layne had seemed so certain - so absolute even - in her feelings for Brad that Emma couldn't understand why she was having such difficulty making the decision to begin a life with him. When Emma spoke with Layne, which wasn't much these days, she was even more certain of her feelings for Brad but seemed to hesitate when the subject of her marriage came up. As a matter of fact, the only time Layne exuded any sense of indecisiveness was when Emma pursued a line of questioning that had anything to do with her marital status and what she was going to do about it. She couldn't help it – she'd begun to think Layne liked being exactly where she was and had no desire to change things.

Of course having never been married or even in anything even remotely considered a serious relationship, Emma truthfully had no idea what Layne was going through. She knew that ending a marriage was one of the most difficult things to do but it certainly couldn't be any easier to go home each night and lie to the man you're married to. Surely that had to cause some amount of stress?

Over the course of the next few weeks, Emma watched-well, heard since she never actually *saw* Layne- as the two of them fell more and more in love. Each and every time she spoke to Layne, the conversation was about Brad and what they had been doing, how much she felt for him, and what their future held. There were times that Emma felt she were speaking to someone she barely knew, so different were these conversations than any she'd ever had with her about Andy.

During each and every conversation, Emma would probe (gently at first, then with more persistence as time went on) to find out what and when, exactly Layne was going to end things with Andy, since she was sure that was going to happen. At first, Layne avoided giving any specifics. She would respond to Emma's inquiries with hesitation and indecisiveness. After a few weeks, her responses changed subtly. Now, it seemed, Layne was concerned for Andy and how he might respond to his wife's leaving him. After two months, the excuses were simply non-existent, with Layne instead opting for avoidance. When asked when she might take steps to end her marriage, Emma was greeted with "soon," or "I haven't found the right time." Emma felt as though she were the mistress in the situation asking for her lover to leave his wife as the responses Layne gave were so clichéd. And, like any mistress, it didn't take long for Emma to realize that unless something convinced Layne she needed to leave her husband, it wasn't going to happen.

What Emma didn't understand was how Brad could continue with things the way they were. Not once had Layne mentioned Brad asking the questions that Emma for so long had been seeking answers to? Wasn't he at all impatient to begin his life with the woman he so desperately loved or was he simply fine with this purgatory Layne had created for the two of them?

As the days turned into weeks, Layne's relationship with Brad continued to get stronger. She spent as much time with him as possible and Emma noticed that time spent with Brad was more of a routine rather than something that was out of the ordinary. Lunch meetings that started as a continuation of work discussions became an every day event and before long, Layne was heading over to Brad's place after work for dinner. It seemed as though she never went home. And each and every time Layne was with Brad, she told Andy she was with Emma.

Emma waited for what seemed like an eternity for Layne to speak to Andy. When it didn't happen after three months, Emma began to worry it might never happen.

She could read Layne like an open book and knew by looking at her that she was more in love with Brad than she ever could have hoped to be with Andy. What she couldn't figure out was how Layne managed to not look that way when she was at home with Andy. It was so blatantly obvious to Emma that she couldn't imagine Andy not seeing it. *Andy,* she thought. While she was happy for Layne, she was miserable thinking about how Andy would feel when he found out that his wife was leaving him. She worried for him – more than she should, but it was unavoidable. Given how Layne felt about Brad, there was no way this was going to end pleasantly for Andy.

Emma did think about the entire situation often, though, and couldn't help but feel taken advantage of to a certain extent. During the time Layne was with Brad, she had told Andy she was going to spend time with Emma. Obviously, this was not the case. This alone made her feel on edge because she was not a very good liar and never had been. Whenever Layne spent time with Brad and Emma was the cover story, she felt certain she'd mess things up somehow. She worried about answering her cell phone only to find Andy on the other end of the line or if she stopped somewhere on her way home from work, she'd inadvertently run into Andy or one of his close friends and it would get back to Andy that Layne was not with Emma on that particular night. As a result, Emma barely left her apartment for fear of discovery. It seemed that she was the one who bore the brunt of all the worry when it came to this situation – she worried about Andy, who was bound to get hurt, she worried about Layne and whether or not she would get caught somehow, she worried about Brad, who might never have the woman he so desperately wanted to be with and finally, she worried about herself revealing something inadvertently to Andy or anyone else for that matter.

On top of all the stress associated with covering for Layne was the constant swirl of emotions she felt whenever she thought of Andy. She loved him, without a doubt and that inevitably led to feelings of anger that were, much to her surprise, directed at Layne.

It took some time for her to realize this, however and initially it started with feelings that were less than irritation. The feelings could hardly even register as annoyance. It wasn't until much later that Emma would recall that as was the first moment that she felt more than anxiety about the situation. She felt annoyed. And not just with the situation…with Layne.

The moment in question was something so insignificant that Emma could hardly understand why it had such an effect on her. But perhaps, that was what the issue was. The *insignificance* of what Layne had said on one particular evening nearly three months after first acknowledging her feelings for Brad.

Layne had called Emma after spending an evening with him. He was bringing her to Emma's apartment and she was calling to ask for a ride home. When Emma questioned why, Layne had remarked that her car had been making some sort of "funny noise" so Brad was going to take it to be checked out the following day. He was going to drive Layne's car in and while on his way in to work, have it looked at by a mechanic friend of his.

The entire conversation would have been normal and ordinary had it not been for the fact that Brad was not, in fact, Layne's husband. In Emma's mind, it should have been Andy who was taking care of Layne's car and the fact that Layne was asking Brad to do it implied more to Emma than any words of love could ever have. Layne was relying on Brad to take care of things for her, her car being the first of many. To Emma, this indicated that Layne was depending on Brad as more than just someone she 'wanted to spend some time with.' The more Emma thought about it, the more upset she got. Clearly, Layne had decided that Brad was the man she should be with – taking care of of something so ordinary and insignificant was such a clear message to Emma, yet Layne hadn't done anything about the fact that she was married to another.

Once this realization dawned on Emma, she became more and more frustrated with Layne until frustration turned to anger, which was where she found herself now. She realized she would have to talk to Layne about it in order to get some sort of resolution. She knew that if Layne would just pin down when she was going to speak to Andy, she'd feel better. Once that happened, she'd be able to see the light at the end of the tunnel. Unfortunately, Emma had been unable to speak to Layne either in person or on the phone. Despite numerous voice mails, emails, and text messages, Layne, for whatever reason, had not responded to any of them. She knew she'd have to resort to calling her cell phone at a time when she was with Brad. A phone call that was normally reserved for emergency use – if Andy were to show up at Emma's place looking for Layne, for instance. Emma knew that Layne would answer simply because of that reason.

One evening after work, Emma made the call and Layne picked up on the second ring, sounding breathless and worried at the same time. "Emma? What's wrong?"

"Nothing's wrong. I just wanted to talk to you."

Emma could sense her relief through the phone before she spoke a word. "Whew. For a minute there, I thought Andy might be at your place or something. Sheesh! You scared the crap out of me!"

"Sorry. Didn't mean to. I just needed to talk to you. I've been texting and calling but can't seem to catch you." Emma forced lightness into her tone.

"Oh. I guess I've just been busy. Between work and spending time with Brad, I guess I don't even have time to answer texts. What's up?"

Emma took a deep breath before speaking. "Nothing, really. I'm just wondering when we can get together. I haven't seen you in so long; I think I've forgotten what you look like!"

Layne chuckled on the other end of the phone. "Well, I'm pretty tall...auburn hair...."

"Ha, ha, ha!" Emma replied, allowing the sarcasm to creep in slightly.

"I'm just kidding. I know I haven't been around much lately...it's just that things have been so hectic with all that's going on." Layne had the decency to sound properly apologetic.

"Yeah, you've been pretty busy."

"I know! Every day I come in to work and Brad has something different planned for that night. Today is the first day all week that we've just hung out at his place."

"Wow! So things are still going well? No bumps? No hurdles?"

"Nope," Layne replied. Emma heard some shuffling through the phone and assumed Layne was moving out of Brad's hearing range. Sure enough, when she spoke again, her voice was hushed. "I really can't believe how great we get along! It's incredible. It's so different than being with Andy. I was always bored or irritated...well, you know...but when I'm with Brad, I'm just happy. *This* is what it's supposed to be like."

"I really can't believe it. I mean, I thought you and Andy were the perfect couple. But if Brad's 'the one,' then I'm thrilled for you,

I really am." Emma was sincere and smiled as she spoke.

"He is. I'm sure of it. I've never felt anything even close to this before."

Emma pressed the phone a little more closely to her ear as she thought of Andy and what was surely going to happen. As the image of him floated in front of her, she felt the color come to her cheeks. She shook her head and tried to focus her attention back to the conversation at hand. Although she didn't want to, she knew she needed to press the issue of when Layne was going to move towards getting this entire situation settled. Emma was becoming more stressed with each passing day and needed to know that some sort of closure was on the horizon.

"So, what now?" Emma asked. "Laynie, what are you going to do?"

Layne was silent for several moments before releasing what Emma momentarily thought was a well-rehearsed sigh. She quickly banished the thought. "I have no idea. It's all just too much for me to deal with right now, you know? It's just so....overwhelming. "

Emma pursed her lips at Layne's dramatics. She could almost picture her holding the back of her hand against her forehead, Scarlett O'Hara style. "I'm sure it is, but you've got to deal with all of this. You can't go on like this forever."

Another sigh, this one not quite as rehearsed. Emma was beginning to feel a bit of wariness in the pit of her belly. "No, I guess you're right. I just need some time to figure out the best time to tell him. It's not going to be easy, you know."

"I know it won't. But you've got to do it. Layne, you've got to tell him you're leaving him."

"I will, I will. I just need a little more time. You've got to see how difficult this is for me. I really don't want to hurt Andy but I'm going to. I just need to work up to it."

Emma sighed softly. "I know. I don't want to see him hurt either, but unfortunately, it's got to be done. The sooner you do it, the sooner it will be over...for everyone."

"I know you're right, Emma. I just can't deal with this right now. I mean, I'm here at Brad's place but I'm out on the deck talking to you about my husband! I can't think about Andy right now."

Emma pulled the phone away from her ear and looked at it,

somewhat surprised at Layne's tone. She sounded....well, annoyed and Emma wasn't sure exactly why.

"Ummm…Okaaaayyy."

"Look, I'll talk to him, I will! I just can't think about all of this now, all right?" Layne snapped.

Emma knew when to back off and this was one of those times. She told Layne she'd talk to her later (Although she wasn't sure exactly when that might be) and quickly got off the phone, since she was feeling more uncomfortable the longer the conversation went on. After ending the call, Emma laid back on the couch, thinking about what she now referred to as 'this situation.' She couldn't help but feel as though she was taking care of the entire situation when it came to Layne and her boyfriend- if you could even call him that. What should she call him, anyway? Lover? Partner? Infidel? She knew she needed to stop this train of thought before she let herself get out of hand. Her emotions were quickly getting past the level of irritation and moving well into anger.

Emma felt, to a certain extent, like the parent in this situation. She was the one who was doing all the worrying and making sure that everyone was taken care of. And all of that worrying made her think of her own mother, who famously worried about Emma all the time. On a whim, she got in her car and drove the thirty minutes to her parent's house.

As she pulled in the driveway, she noticed her mother in the back yard tending the garden. Marjorie was dressed in full gardening regalia, from a large-brimmed hat that was decorated with flowers in extremely vivid colors right down to the matching clogs. She was kneeling down with her back to her daughter but turned and stood when she heard the slam of the car door.

"Emma? Why didn't you tell me you were coming? I would have made something for dinner. Your father and I were just about to order some Chinese takeout."

Emma couldn't mask her surprise. Even growing up, her mother hadn't so much as ordered a pizza for any of Emma's slumber parties. There was nothing but home-cooked meals in the Stewart household and now her parents were eating Chinese takeout?

"You and dad are ordering takeout food? Is something wrong? Are you okay?" Emma felt a sudden surge of panic at this change of routine.

"Now stop worrying," her mother chastised. "Even I get to have a night off once in awhile. You should try it, dear. It's actually quite delicious."

Emma rolled her eyes, feeling relief wash over her. "Mom, I've had Chinese takeout. I can't cook, remember?"

"I know, dear. Believe me, I know. After all, I'm the one who tried to teach you."

Emma smiled, thinking of the numerous times her mother had tried to teach her the basics of cooking. Marjorie had started with the most basic of tasks and Emma had failed at nearly every one of them. It wasn't that she lacked the skill to cook; rather it was that she lacked the attention span to complete a task once she started it. Emma had been known to set a pot of water boiling on the stove and then leave it unattended until it completely destroyed the pan. Or, she'd attempt to bake cookies (the store bought, drop and bake kind) and forget they were even in the oven. Now that she lived by herself, she stuck to mainly sandwiches, cereal and ready-made foods that could be prepared in the microwave. The timer on the microwave turned out to be a very handy reminder, Emma quickly found out. Plus, there was the added benefit of the machine shutting off once the time was complete. As it turned out, the appliance that her mother hardly ever used was the one that Emma couldn't live without.

"Have you ordered yet?" Emma asked.

"No. Run in and tell your father what you'd like. I'm sure he heard you pull in."

Marjorie turned back to tend to the vegetables while Emma went inside to tell her father what she'd like for dinner. When she came back outside, she found her mother sitting on the back porch, surveying her garden and looking particularly pleased with herself. Emma sat down beside her and looked out at the garden as well.

"It looks like everything is coming in really well."

"It sure is. Thanks to Mr. Wilkins down the road."

"Mr. Wilkins? The farmer? What'd he do?"

"We made a deal, he and I." Marjorie looked devilishly at her daughter. "I bring him one of my chicken pies every so often and he keeps me supplied with manure."

Emma coughed a little as she realized what her mother meant. "You mean cow poop?"

"It's the best fertilizer for a garden, dear."

"I know that but don't you have to...you know...spread it around ...like with your hands?"

"Well, yes. But I am wearing gloves when I do it."

Emma's jaw opened in shock. Her mother was more than seventy years old and spreading cow crap around her garden with her hands. Would there ever come a time when she would cease to be surprised by her mother? She didn't think so. It was then that she noticed a rather pungent odor surrounding them.

"Mom, that smell...it isn't...."

"Manure. Yes, dear. It's manure. I spread some just a couple of days ago."

Emma stood up. "I think I need to go wash my hands." She turned and walked into the house, followed by the sound of her mother's laughter.

"This is not funny!" Emma yelled over her shoulder.

When she came out of the bathroom, she found her mother sitting at the kitchen table, barely stifling a giggle. All gardening paraphernalia, including the flowery hat, had been left out on the back porch.

"I thought you might be more comfortable in here."

"Thank you veeeeery much," Emma responded dryly, as she sat down at the kitchen table.

"Your father ordered the food a few minutes ago so we have some time to chat before it's delivered."

"Good. I was hoping I'd get the chance to talk to you."

"Is everything okay?"

Emma realized her mother was worried that something might be seriously wrong so she was quick to calm the fear she saw in her mother's eyes. "I'm fine mom. It's just that this thing with Layne has gotten...well, it hasn't progressed as I would have liked."

Marjorie patted her daughter's hand and nodded. "Well, then. I want to hear all about it."

Emma nodded. "Thanks, mom." She paused for few moments, realizing that what she was going to tell her mother might change her opinion of Layne and she didn't want that to happen. "I don't want you to think badly of Layne, all right?"

Marjorie placed her hand under Emma's chin and lifted her face up, turning it from side to side to inspect. "I can see by the look on your face that it's pretty bad, isn't it?"

She shrugged. "I don't know if bad is the word I'd use. More like horrible, awful, stressful, unbearable....need I go on?"

"Oh, dear." Marjorie sat silent on the other side of the table with her hands folded neatly in front of her. "Tell me what's been going on."

Emma continued. "They're together all the time! They're with each other all day at work and then Layne is with him most nights, which means that I'm afraid to go out in case I see Andy or someone who might speak to him. I'm terrified that I'll blow this for Layne and it's stressing me out!"

Marjorie sat still, listening to her daughter release everything she'd been holding inside of her.

Emma, not entirely comfortable talking to her mother about her friend's sex life, stumbled a bit as she continued. "Layne apparently realized she had feelings for Brad and they've....uhhh.....gotten closer?... over the past couple of months."

"Sweetheart, you don't have to sugar-coat it. I'm aware that people have sex. I had you, remember?"

"Mom, please!" This entire conversation was uncomfortable enough without her mother adding to it. "So, they got closer...." Emma looked pointedly at her mother, who nodded, sensing her discomfort. "And now she sees him all the time but she tells Andy she's with me! I feel horrible mom. I'm torn between supporting her – or whatever the hell it is I'm doing – and telling her what an idiot she's being!! I'm worried I'm going to do something to screw this up either by answering my phone or being out someplace when I'm supposed to be with Layne and I'm stressed all the time! And I haven't even gotten into the fact that she's cheating on the guy that I'm completely in love with, which makes me so angry, I could punch something!"

Marjorie remained silent and still save for the fact that her hand had slowly moved from its place by her side to covering her mouth, as though she were physically trying to prevent herself from speaking. Her eyebrows came together in a frown as she watched her daughter become more and more agitated, yet she knew that what was best for Emma was to just get it out. She stood there, watching her daughter's pain, knowing there was nothing she could do to help her. This was one of those times when she was powerless to help her daughter. In fact, the only person that would be able to help Emma was the one person who was hurting her.

Emma continued. "I feel like I'm lying to Andy if I see him and don't say anything but Layne is my best friend! Aren't I supposed to help her? But then I think, 'Andy's my friend too' and isn't this betraying his friendship? What would he think of the fact that I knew about all of this? God! Why can't she just tell Andy, already! She loves Brad, mom. She loves him more than she ever loved Andy but she just won't tell him she's leaving him! How much longer can she go on like this!?!" Emma threw her hands up in defeat and then collapsed onto the table, her head resting on her arms. "AAArgh!!! Where do I go from here? What do I do?!!?!?"

Marjorie reached over and gently stroked the top of Emma's head. "Layne is in love with this Brad character?"

Emma's voice was muffled when she spoke. "I'm sure of it."

"Oh, dear. This is quite a mess that girl has made for herself." Marjorie tsk-tsk'd, which was a sound Emma had heard numerous times growing up. Any time she had disappointed her mother, there was no yelling, no screaming...only that sound and often times Emma would rather have heard her mother yell. Somehow, the calmness in which it was delivered made the receiver feel all the more guilty.

"She keeps saying she needs some time to figure things out. But the thing is, I don't know how much time I can give her. I mean, I want to help her- she's my best friend – but this is a nightmare! "

Marjorie sighed. "Yes...yes it is." There was a moment of silence before she spoke again. "Do you think she's going to leave Andy?"

Emma looked up at her mother and nodded. "Eventually, anyway. I just have no idea when that might be. Mom, am I doing the right thing?"

"I don't know if there's any 'right' thing to do in this situation. But I do think you're doing the best under the circumstances."

"What do you mean?"

"You're doing your best to support Layne and I'm going to assume you've told her how all of this sneaking around makes you feel."

Emma nodded.

"Well then. That's all you can do. Until you've reached your limit, that is. And not telling Andy? That's a mine field all its own. You certainly don't want to be the messenger there."

"I know. I couldn't bear to see the look on his face if he were to ever find out."

Marjorie patted her daughter's hand. "That would be difficult. Sweetheart, I don't like this any more than you do but I'm proud of the way you're handling yourself. Just remember, Layne is the one who's doing the cheating, not you."

"I know. I just don't know how much more of this I can take. It's a horrible feeling; this being in the middle."

"Only you'll know when you've reached your limit. And once you do, you've got to tell Layne that you've had enough. If she's truly a friend, she'll understand. And in my mind, she should understand what she's putting you through now, whether you're in love with Andy or not."

Emma smiled at her mother, already feeling better for having been able to confide in someone. The burden of holding this secret inside had been eating away at her. Just then, they heard the crunch of gravel on the driveway indicating their dinner had arrived. "Thanks, mom."

Marjorie leaned over to give her daughter a hug and then stood up. "I'm so proud of you."

"Proud of me? For what?" Emma was genuinely confused.

"For handling yourself the best way you can in a difficult situation like this. I just wish Layne knew how much of a burden this is for you. Unfortunately, I don't think she'll ever realize what you did for her."

Marjorie shook her head and then walked to the front door to get their dinner.

Chapter 13

Emma felt only marginally better after speaking with her mother but even that respite didn't last very long. Truth be told, it lasted barely an entire day. It lasted, in fact, until Emma took a phone call on her way home from work the following day.

She answered her phone without even so much as a glance at the caller id, which of course, in this current age of technology, is an unforgivable mistake. She assumed it was Layne, asking her to do cover for her while she went someplace with Brad. Unfortunately, her assumption couldn't have been further off.

"Hey," she said.

"Emma! It's been so long! How ARE you?"

Expecting to hear Layne's voice, Emma pulled the phone back and stared at it when she heard the uncharacteristic pleasant tone of the caller. Immediately, her guard went up.

"Vicki....hi..." Her tone was vacant from the normal, friendly tone she customarily used. Instead, it had been replaced with one of wariness. It was a tone Emma normally reserved when she didn't want to be bothered. For instance, when a parent would interrupt the mere 15 minutes she had each day for planning. Didn't they realize that these precious few moments were all she had? She even had to eat her lunch with her class. Every year, parents failed to grasp the fact that she was happy to meet with them either before or after school. The school day? Well, that was off-limits.

Emma steeled herself for the unknown, since one never knew what was going to come out of Vicki's mouth. "How are you?"

"I'm good, really good. Listen, did you ever make an appointment with my dermatologist? She's wonderful, really she is. I'm certain she could really help you out with your freckles."

"I really don't think...I mean...I'm fine with my freckles." Emma replied, already annoyed.

"Of course you are! Good for you, loving who you are. But if you ever feel the need, to say, improve? Well, just give Dr. Provost a call."

"I will," said Emma, knowing she never would. She then sat there, phone to her ear, driving home in silence, waiting for Vicki to ask what Emma was certain the point of the call was. Surely Vicki didn't only call to once again refer Emma to Dr. Provost. Even Vicki wasn't that bold.

Finally, she spoke. Emma could picture her filing her nails or tapping a pencil, anything to make the request sound offhanded and casual when in fact, the request had probably been rehearsed several times. "So...I was wondering if you'd do me a favor."

Here we go, Emma thought. Being the polite person that her mother brought her up to be, she wasn't able to simply say no. Instead, she'd listen to Vicki's request and then see if it was within her realm of possibility before making any decision.

"If I can," Emma replied. "What do you need?"

"Well....I was wondering if you'd ask Layne to do something for me."

The request seemed simple enough. "I would, but you probably see her more than I do. You work with her, remember?"

"I know. But this is sort of...well, uncomfortable and I think it might be better if you had your hand in it."

"Hand in what, exactly?" Emma asked.

"Fixing me up with someone. See, there's this guy in the office and Layne works with him a lot and I thought if she said something to him, you know, suggested that he ask me out, maybe it would work. She's quite the matchmaker, you know."

"I know. Believe me, I know." Emma couldn't help but smile, thinking of George and Malcolm and a host of other men Layne had tried to set her up with. "But why not just ask him out yourself? Why get me involved?"

"I could never do that! I mean, ask someone out? Nope. Never." Emma could practically hear Vicki's head shaking from side to side. "Besides, you know how guys are. If a friend suggests something to them, they tend to do it. I figured if Layne were to suggest it to him, he might actually do it."

"Okay, that makes sense. But what do you need me for?" As much as Vicki annoyed Emma, her curiosity was piqued.

"I've tried, but I can't seem to catch her. Either we're too busy at the office or she's running to a meeting with Brad. I figured when you see her, she's not stressed. If you put the idea in her head, she might go for it. What do you think? Would you talk to her for me?"

"I don't know, Vicki. I doubt she'd go for it. Besides, she likes to be the one to play matchmaker, not me."

"But that's just it! She LOVES to play matchmaker. I just think she's too stressed at work to think about fixing me up with anyone. Normally, she would have come up with this all by herself since we're the only two single people in the office. I just don't feel like waiting for her to get the idea. I want to nudge her along a bit."

As she listened to Vicki speak, it began to dawn on Emma exactly what Vicki was suggesting. She also knew this was going to be bad…very bad and Emma began to feel herself become even more stressed than she ever thought possible. She hoped she was way off base with her assumption but she knew deep in her heart she was right, unfortunately. She took a deep breath before asking the question, almost relishing the moment before her assumption was confirmed. "Who did you say this guy was?" She cringed as she waited for the answer – the answer she knew before Vicki even uttered his name.

"Brad Somerfield. He's the manager of the sister office."

"Oh, right." *Oh, God.* Emma struggled to speak since her mouth had gone dry. Vicki was suggesting that she get set up with Brad? There was no way Layne was going to set up Brad with Vicki. Besides the fact that he was taken -well, sort of - Vicki was the last person in the world Layne would trust to spend an evening with Brad.

The more Emma thought about it, though, the more she realized that Vicki was right. Layne was a serial matchmaker. The moment she met someone and saw the absence of a ring on the third finger of their left hand, she would begin to rifle through the rolodex in her mind that held the names, phone numbers, and email addresses of all the single people she knew in an attempt to filter out who would be the best possible match for the person in question. It would only make sense that she make an attempt to set up the only two people in her office who were single. Now that she thought about it, Emma couldn't believe this conversation hadn't happened two months ago. She felt deflated, knowing that Vicki had a very valid point.

"Look, I can't promise anything, but I'll talk to Layne." Emma said this with more confidence than she felt since she had no idea what she was going to say to Layne. She quickly realized this was going to be another conversation that she did not want to have with her best friend.

"Great!" Vicki replied. "I can't wait to hear what she has to say!"

Before Emma could reply, Vicki had hung up, which was just as well. Emma had nothing to say. She tossed the phone into the passenger seat, hoping it would bounce and fall out of her reach. Then, she could at least postpone calling Layne until she arrived home. That didn't happen. The phone bounced off the passenger seat and into the back of the seat, then landed in the center of the seat, well within Emma's reach. She glanced at it and noticed it was face up, as though mocking her. She stuck her tongue out at it, knowing she was being ridiculous and not caring. She was mad as hell and she needed to take it out on someone or something...like her cell phone.

"Dammit," she muttered, reaching for the phone. She scrolled through her list of contacts to find Layne's number. As she did so, she realized that normally she'd simply click on her 'recent calls' and dial Layne. Since Layne hadn't called her in sometime, her number wasn't located there, a fact that saddened Emma and made her miss how close they once were.

Emma tried to think of the last time she'd spent any time with Layne where it was just the two of them. Of course, she knew it would have been one of the times Layne showed up at her apartment after spending time with Brad early in their relationship. She was losing touch with her best friend and Emma felt it was through no fault of her own. Layne was spending all her time with Brad and leaving Emma with the scraps.

This has to end, Emma thought.

She called Layne's number and was surprised when she answered on the first ring.

"Hello?"

"It's me," Emma replied. "Are you sitting down?"

"I guess you could say that. I'm driving, why?"

Emma took a deep breath before beginning. "Vicki just called me. And you're never going to guess what she asked me."

"Vicki? From my office?"

"The one and only." Emma replied, rolling her eyes.

"Well, what did she want?" Layne asked, somewhat impatiently.

"She wants me to talk you into setting her up with someone. Apparently, it seems as though everyone in the office is married or with someone which *obviously* makes her a perfect candidate for…are you ready for this? Brad." Emma let his name roll of her tongue and waited for Layne's reaction. She looked like a terrified child waiting for the loud bang at a fireworks show.

"Really? That's actually sort of funny. I mean, she's not exactly his type."

"No, she's not." Emma said, dryly. This calm reaction from Layne was confusing Emma but she still had a good amount of apprehension while waiting for her to fully grasp what Vicki had suggested. She was on edge waiting for Layne to lose it.

It didn't happen. What did happen, Emma never saw coming.

"You know…" Layne suddenly had a thought come to her mind. "Vicki does have a point there. I mean, I do occasionally set people up."

Emma laughed, but only half –heartedly, as she was still on edge waiting for the storm. "Occasionally?"

"Okaaaaay, I'll go with frequently," Layne replied. Emma could practically picture her waving her hand around dismissively. "Anyway….Vicki's idea actually isn't too bad."

"What?!?!" Emma gasped. "You're actually going to set her up with Brad? Have you lost your mind?"

"Not entirely, no. Listen to me for just a second. I said that her idea was a good one – setting Brad up with someone, that is. I'm a serial matchmaker. It's what I do." Layne chuckled. "So…it only makes sense that I would try to fix him up with someone. The only thing is, I can't really fix him up with Vicki now, can I?"

"No. That would just be weird. But what are you going to tell her? I mean, you can't just tell her you're not going to do it without some reason." Emma was finding it very difficult to drive home and was glad she was nearly there.

"Oh, I have a reason. I'm going to tell her that I've already set him up with someone else and I need to see how that goes." Layne was smiling at her own ingenuity and feeling quite pleased with herself.

"Right. Who in the world are you going to-" Emma stopped, suddenly realizing what Layne had planned. "No!! Absolutely not!!! No way! No how!"

Emma pulled into her parking lot and screeched around the aisle, trying to reach her apartment and park her car. She pulled in to her regular space and slammed on the brakes, causing her body to jar forward and then back against the seat. She slammed the car in park and pounded her fist on the steering wheel angrily.

"This is a STUPID idea, Layne!"

"Come on. It makes perfect sense to fix you up with Brad. You know I have to! It's not like me to see a single guy and not try to set him up!" Layne's voice was surprisingly calm, which only made Emma angrier.

"That may be true, but this is….it's borderline *incestuous!*"

"Oh, don't be so melodramatic," Layne huffed.

"Melodramatic?!!? Are you kidding me? Look, I really don't think this is a good idea." Emma was well past the anger point. Layne, ever the polar opposite, was remaining quite calm during the entire exchange. As a matter of fact, it didn't even occur to her that any part of this conversation was even a tiny bit abnormal.

"Sure it is. It is absolutely what I'd do with any other single man that I meet and Andy knows it. It only makes sense that I'd have you over to meet Brad."

"Look, I know you set me up all the time, but this is ridiculous. I really think you're playing with fire here." Emma was doing her best to drive home while talking to Layne but the conversation was making it more and more difficult.

"We've got to do this. Can't you understand that? If I don't, Andy will ask me why I haven't tried to fix you up with him!"

"Can't you come up with something? Tell him I got sick of your set-ups or something?"

"Yeah, right. He'd never believe that. He knows you go out with whoever I fix you up with." Layne chuckled at her own joke, infuriating Emma even further.

"First of all, I do not. And second of all, I really do not want to be fixed up with guy you're cheating on your husband with. It's just creepy. I'm in this whole thing deep enough without actually *dating* him."

Layne was silent for a moment before speaking, as though she were thinking the best possible thing to say in order to get her way. "Emma, please? You've just got to do this for me. Please, please,

please? We've got to go about our normal lives until all of this is settled and right now that means I've got to fix you up with Brad. Please? Just do this one thing for me."

Emma felt her resolve weakening just a bit and let out a small sigh. Layne heard it and went in for the kill.

"You know how important Brad is to me. I really want you to meet him and this is the best way! You can learn all about him while you're on a date with him! Please, Emma. Oh, please do this for me. We'll just all have dinner just like any other time. Okay?"

Emma felt worn out from the conversation and didn't have the strength to argue about it anymore. "Fine. I'll go on the stupid date. But we're not meeting at your place. That would just be too weird...and wrong. Horribly, horribly wrong."

"Fine. Just so long as you meet him." Layne sounded impatient, which under the circumstances, Emma felt was completely inappropriate and succeeded in irritating her further. Layne continued. "We'll meet at Murphy's. Then if you and Brad hit it off, we can stay for the band."

"Okay, now you're just being ridiculous." Emma didn't even try to mask her irritation.

"We've got to act like we normally do, remember?" Layne's tone was similar to the one used when Emma during the school day when she needed to repeat herself numerous times. It was a patronizing tone with a mix of impatience and irritation thrown in.

"I remember." Emma said, suddenly feeling like a child who was being scolded for a reason they weren't aware of. "But just so you know, *you're* telling Vicki."

Emma felt the need to at least assert herself with something and this was all she could come up with at the moment, so befuddled was she. It was a small victory, but a victory, nonetheless, and it made Emma feel just the tiniest bit better – now she only felt like a small rug as opposed to a doormat.

"Fine, Fine...I'll talk to her tomorrow and set things up for Friday night." Layne replied.

Emma pushed the end button on her cell phone and threw the phone down onto her front seat. It was only Tuesday yet she felt as though this was the longest week of her life. It did not escape her notice that Layne didn't even ask whether or not she had plans for Friday night. Typical, she thought. Layne just assumed Emma would be sitting home doing nothing. The fact that she was correct in her assumption was irrelevant; she was still annoyed.

Emma hunched forward and placed her forehead on the steering wheel. Layne was actually going to set up a mock blind date with Brad. What in the world was she thinking? How was she supposed to act while on a date with the man Layne was cheating on her husband with? Was she supposed to act as though she liked him? Or should she act as though indifferent?

Emma resigned herself to the fact that she would be spending Friday night with the two men Layne was currently involved in. Of course, if she thought about it too much, she found that she could easily make herself sick to her stomach. Better to not think about it, she thought.

* * *

That Friday after work, she did her best to make an attempt to treat this date as she would any other. She selected an outfit that complemented her petite figure and took extra time to put on her makeup. Once she had finished, she looked in the mirror for a final inspection.

And realized she couldn't move.

She just couldn't do it. This was well beyond what she was willing to do. There was no way she was going to leave her apartment to do on a "date" with the man Layne was having an affair with.

Suddenly filled with strength she didn't think she had, she picked up her cell phone and called Layne.

Breathless, she answered on the first ring. "Hey! What's up?"

Emma took a deep breath and let it out slowly, gathering strength as she did so. "I'm not going."

"What are you talking about? Going where?"

"To Murphy's."

"Of course you are. Don't be silly. Andy and I are just heading out the door now."

"I'm serious Layne. I am not leaving this apartment." Though Layne couldn't see her, Emma crossed her arms over her chest in a show of defiance, cradling the phone in the crook of her neck.

There was a long pause before Layne spoke again. When she

finally did speak, her voice was softer, as though she knew that bullying wouldn't work any longer. "Emma, come on. We're all going to meet at the restaurant and have a nice evening. You said you would. "

"Look, I know what I said but I changed my mind. I'm sorry, but I just can't do it."

"Well, you can't back out now..." Layne said, trying to talk some reason into Emma.

"Sure I can. Actually, I just did."

Emma heard a deep voice in the background and assumed it was Andy. The sounds got muffled and she imagined Layne had placed her hand over the receiver in order to speak to him. After a few moments, the sound was restored and Layne's voice came booming through the phone.

"Emma," she hissed. "You CANNOT do this to me! I told Brad we would all meet there. He's probably on his way. It's just rude to do this now!"

"You know what, Layne. I don't care if it's rude. I'm sure he'll understand, given the circumstances." Her voice softened. "I'm sorry. I don't mean to do this but I just can't pretend to go on a date with him. It just wouldn't be right."

"Emma, please. Please do this for me."

"I'm sorry, Layne. I just can't." She ended the call and sat down on the couch, feeling exhausted yet lighter than she'd felt in months. Of course, she knew it was only a matter of minutes before Layne showed up at her apartment and made every attempt to guilt her into going on this "date." Emma closed her eyes and leaned back against the cushion, knowing that this particular confrontation was not going to be pretty.

Chapter 14

As the seconds ticked by, Emma felt her resolve becoming stronger and stronger. She had done exactly what Layne had asked of her for nearly six months but now, she had reached her limit. Of course, she was torn between two sides of the argument she'd had with herself since this had begun. One the one hand, she'd done everything her best friend needed her to do. On the other, she'd been asked to do something that went against every fiber of her being. Where did one draw the line? She had always thought she was someone who would do anything for her best friend but now she wasn't so sure. Apparently, she wasn't one of those people that would help someone dig the hole to bury a body. Absolutely not, she thought with a chuckle. She wouldn't even pretend to go on a date with the man her best friend was having an affair with!

Emma glanced at the clock on the wall. It had been nearly fifteen minutes since she hung up the phone. She figured Layne was already in her car on her way over here. She got up and began to pace nervously around her tiny apartment. She felt her stomach clench as she heard a car door slam. Thinking Layne had arrived, she peered through the living room window. She exhaled slowly when she realized it wasn't her. Emma was completely on edge knowing that she and Layne were about to have a serious discussion about all that had gone on in the recent months.

Emma walked through her bedroom and sat down in the sunroom. This room was her favorite in the apartment, and her main reason for selecting this particular unit. It was a tiny room by anyone's standards – only four feet by eight feet - and all of the second floor apartments had one. But what appealed to Emma about this particular apartment was that the sunroom overlooked absolutely nothing.

The building her apartment was in had been tucked in the corner of the apartment complex, almost as an afterthought. As a result, the rear of the building, and her sunroom, overlooked a vacant lot. To most, this would have been an eyesore, but for Emma, who spent most of her days with twenty-four rambunctious children and spent much of her time at home recovering from those days, needed a place in which to think and just, well…be still. The location of this apartment was perfect. This sunroom was the one place she knew she could sit and hear nothing…and it was pure bliss.

She sat there now, thinking about Layne, Brad, and Andy – especially Andy - who was completely oblivious to all that had been going on with his wife during the past few months.

Layne's relationship with Brad was serious; of that Emma had no doubt. Over the past few months, she'd spent more and more time with him and Emma had noticed something different in Layne. As much as she hated to admit it, Layne seemed happier than she'd ever been before. If that was the case, though, then she needed to change her situation so she could be with Brad all the time, and not just in hiding. As it was, she'd shown no indication of wanting to change things. It seemed to Emma, at least, that she was perfectly content to continue to masquerade around with Andy acting as though she had the perfect marriage while spending time on the sly with Brad. Emma had waited as long as she could for Layne to decide what she was going to do and being asked to pretend to go on a date with him was the breaking point for her.

Emma hadn't been comfortable with any part of the situation she now found herself tangled in. But she had to draw the line at participation at this level. Pretending to go on a date with Brad in front of Andy was one level beyond where she had any desire to be. What she couldn't understand was how Layne didn't seem to understand Emma's problem with it. It just seemed as though Layne seemed too wrapped up in trying to conceal Brad and the time she spent with him. If Layne were convinced that she was destined to spend her life with Brad, shouldn't she be less worried about losing the man she was certain was the mistake in her life? And while she didn't want Andy to be hurt by any of this, she certainly would have expected Layne to at least take some steps to separate herself from Andy in order to make room for Brad in her life. Shouldn't she be more focused on the future than on salvaging what was left of her past? This led Emma to believe that Layne was going to continue along this path for as long as she could, which was why Emma now sat in her sunroom, trying to determine what she was going to say.

One thing was certain, though. Emma was through with all of this.

Once she came to this decision, she knew she had to talk to Layne. That, unfortunately, was the difficult part. Layne, on occasion, had a tendency to only see what she wanted. In this case, she would only see that Emma would no longer help her. And of course, this meant that Layne would also conveniently forget that Emma had done just that for several months now. Emma was trying, without success, to figure out how convince Layne that while she was her best friend and loved her like a sister, she couldn't support the affair any longer. How to accomplish that and at the same time, salvage the friendship was the question she did not have the answer for.

She knew it would be nearly impossible.

In any event, she'd had enough. She was tired of being the scapegoat and while she had never been comfortable in her role, she was now completely fed up and knew things had to change. It had become clear to her this week that Layne, without some sort of nudge in the right direction, would continue to go on as though she had all the time in the world. Well, Emma was more than ready to nudge, push, jab, or throw Layne in order to get her to fix this situation.

And so today, she found herself sitting in her sunroom, staring at the barren concrete, trying to determine what exactly she was going to say to her best friend. One thing she knew for certain was that this was not going to go well at all.

The battery operated clock above the door frame was ticking loudly and seemed to reverberate throughout the room. As she looked up at the clock, she realized that Layne should be here any moment so she walked into the living room to peer out into the parking lot. Layne had just pulled in and was checking her makeup in the side mirror. Emma watched as she adjusted her hair and checked her teeth before walking over to the outside door of the apartment. Layne pushed the buzzer and held it in so that the annoying sound played continuously in Emma's apartment.

"Let me guess, Layne. You're pissed," Emma muttered to the empty room as she walked across the living room to push the button and allow Layne entry into the building. As she reached the top step, Emma opened the door.

"Hey."

"Just what the HELL are you doing?" Layne fumed.

"Uh..okay. Why don't you come in? I'd rather not talk about this in the hall."

Layne stared at Emma for a few seconds and then, seeing the good sense behind Emma's suggestion, walked into the apartment and tossed her pocketbook down on the couch. She turned to face Emma and crossed her arms over her chest.

"Okay. I'm in. Now WHAT is going on with you? I thought we were going to go out and have a good time and you cancel at the last minute? Emma, that's not like you."

"Look, I'm sorry I cancelled but I just can't do this anymore."

"Really." Layne raised one eyebrow as she stared at Emma.

"Yes, really. And why are you looking at me like that?"

"I'm just trying to understand why you have this change of heart now when none of this seemed to bother you before."

"You think this didn't bother me?!? How can you say that? I've told you over and over just how much that has bothered me."

"Well, I certainly didn't see it that way. I thought you were supporting me while I tried to figure out what to do with my life. I didn't realize it was such an *inconvenience* for you."

Emma ignored the sarcasm and spoke calmly, trying to explain just how she felt. "It's not that it was an inconvenience. I just never got comfortable with the fact that you were cheating on Andy. It just...didn't sit right with me."

Layne continued to look at Emma, turning her head from side to side as though inspecting her. "Okay, spill it." Layne leaned forward and gave Emma her full attention.

Emma looked at Layne and paused for a moment before speaking. "I thought I would be able to do this but I just can't. That's all."

"But why now?"

"I don't know. I guess it just seemed a little too 'in Andy's face' for me."

"You're worried about Andy, aren't you?

"Well, yes, but-,"

Layne waived her hand to dismiss what Emma was about to say. "Look, you don't have to worry about Andy; he's a grown man. He'll be fine after all of this. And I promise I'll make it up to you." She walked over to the couch and sat down, crossing her legs as though this entire conversation were somehow normal.

Emma sighed and sat down in the chair across from Layne. "Look, it's not that. I just feel like I'm letting you carry on this...relationship with Brad. It's like I'm condoning it and I just don't feel right about it."

Layne absently picked at the seam of her jeans. "I know you don't like this but I just need a little more time. I promise, Emma."

Suddenly, Emma realized that her tone sounded rehearsed somehow. It was as though she'd heard the same line over and over again and Layne wasn't even trying to sound convincing. Anger welled up inside of her and she took a deep breath to try to calm herself, once again afraid of saying something she would regret. She shook her head. "I can't, Layne. I can't do it anymore. I can't keep lying to Andy. It's just not right."

Layne stared at Emma with a confused look on her face. "I didn't realize you were so bothered by this. I mean, I knew. But I guess I didn't think it was this much of an issue for you."

"Layne, you know me better than anyone. You know how I feel about this...you've always known. I'm in the middle of you and Andy with all this sneaking around and I'm always on edge, afraid I'm going to say something about a time when we did something or a time when we were suppose to be doing something. I'm so afraid I'm going to let something slip out that I just stay away from your place so I don't run into Andy."

"You don't have to stay away."

Emma shook her head. "See, that's just it. I do have to stay away. That's the easier alternative for me. At least that way, I don't have the stress of watching every single thing I say. If I were to say anything to him, I'd feel like I'm lying to him, which I hate!"

Layne crossed her arms over her chest and gave Emma the tiniest of smiles. Emma felt herself get angry since she felt that Layne was entertained by her outburst. "You're really upset by all of this aren't you?"

"Of course I am! This is a horrible situation for me!" Emma leaned back and tossed her hands into the air, frustrated with having to explain her emotions.

"You know, it's not exactly been fun for me."

Emma was stumped for a moment. "What are you talking about?"

"It's been hard on me too! I mean, I've had this pressing on me for months now. I've been confused about everything! I've got this merger at work and my home life is completely out of sorts. I've been trying to work on things with Andy and try to get to know Brad. Now, I've got to meet his parents....It's all so stressful what with the-"

Emma felt herself bristle, hearing Layne speak. She knew she had to cut her off before she completely lost it. "So....you're telling me that this has been stressing you out? You can't be serious."

"What's that suppose to mean?"

"How can this be stressful for you?"

"Well, for one thing, I don't want Andy to find out. I mean, I've got to make sure I cover all my tracks..." She stopped when she saw the look on Emma's face. "Look, I don't mean it like that. What I meant was that I don't want Andy to find out on his own. I want to be the one to tell him so that he doesn't get hurt."

Emma's eyes narrowed. "So what you're saying is that the stress you feel is from making sure you don't get caught."

"Uhhh..." Layne, unsure of what to say, had a blank look on her face.

"Forget it," Emma said, dismissing Layne's words with a sweep of her hand. "Don't say anything. I really don't want to hear any more about how this whole situation has been stressful for *you.*"

When she heard the inflection of Emma's voice as she spoke the word 'you,' Layne raised one eyebrow. "Now what's THAT suppose to mean."

"It means I'm wondering how you can sit there and tell me how stressed you've been like you're a victim or something! Come on! It's me you're talking to. We both know that you are not a victim here and if I were being truly honest-"

"Yesss... go on." Layne sat back against the couch and crossed her arms once again over her chest.

Emma looked at Layne's body language, all calm and somewhat haughty, and knew she was going to lose it. "If I were being truly honest, I would tell you that from where I'm sitting, it didn't look stressful at all! As a matter of fact, I might even go so far as to say that you made it look easy. For you to sit there and talk about how much stress you've felt during all this is just a slap in the face to me, Andy, and even Brad!"

Emma's hands were flailing around excitedly. "Oh, but wait. Forget about Andy. He doesn't even know what's been going on so I guess he's exempt from all this. I guess he'll get his share of stress once you tell him you're leaving him."

Layne sat there silently, listening to Emma's while she ranted and she was becoming quite uncomfortable. Truth be told, it had been easy for her. Easier than she thought it would ever be and Emma had hit a nerve when she said it. That just goes to show how close to two of them were and how well they knew each other. Layne was shocked to realize she had made it look easy. Easy enough, that is, for Emma to mention it. As she sat there, she wasn't sure what to say in response to Emma's outburst. She looked down at her jeans and played with the perfectly torn hole in the thigh while trying to come up with something to explain why it had seemed so easy to her. But she knew better. And Emma knew her better than anyone. "It's not…I mean, I don't…"

Emma exhaled sharply. "What is it, Layne?"

"The thing is…" She looked Emma in the eye. "The thing is…."

Emma heard the hesitation in Layne's voice and didn't like it. "Layne…." The word itself was a warning. "Why do you sound like that?"

"Like what?"

"Like you have something to tell me." Emma eyes narrowed and fixed on Layne. She watched as Layne shifted her position several times, trying to get comfortable. Finally, Emma couldn't stand it any longer. "For God sakes, Layne, what is it?"

"I don't know if I can do this to Andy."

"Do what? Tell him? Leave him?"

"All of it. Any of it." Her voice was barely a whisper.

Emma's lips formed a thin line, then she spoke softly , yet forcefully. "Well, you're going to have to. You can't go on like this forever…sneaking around and having me cover for you."

"I know… I know. I just need a little more time."

Emma sighed softly. "Layne….you've got to tell him. It's just not fair to keep on like this."

"You're right. I know you're right. I just…don't know if I can do it. Andy's really a great guy."

"Yes, he is a great guy," Emma mumbled. She didn't realize

Layne heard her comment, nor did she see her look up at her with eyebrows raised.

Layne looked back down and continued. "I guess I'm feeling a bit guilty about all of this. It's really not his fault and he's the one who's going to be hurt."

"Layne, this is going to come out wrong but....you choose now to feel guilty? After you've been seeing Brad behind Andy's back for what? Six months now? I'm sorry, but you've got to take care of all of this. It's not fair...to either of them."

Layne looked up again, somewhat surprised at Emma's tone. "You say that like I haven't felt guilty. I have. I've always felt guilty about this."

"Then fix it. Either end things with Brad or end things with Andy." Emma said it more strongly than she intended and Layne looked somewhat surprised.

"You know, I'm trying to do just that. It's just hard for me."

"I'm sure it is hard for you. But compared to the other people involved, your role is easy. You know what you want. You've even gotten to test things out for the past few months. But now you've got to take care of this. Just think about Andy! He loves you and thinks everything is just dandy with your marriage but in actuality, you're in love with someone else!" Emma could feel herself getting angrier and needed to sit in order to calm herself. Layne noticed her anger and looked at her strangely.

"What's gotten into you?" she asked.

"I'm just tired of being in the middle of all of this. It's not easy covering for you all the time. I hate lying to Andy! God, I just hate it!"

Layne began to think there might be something here that she'd missed. Emma was more upset than she'd ever seen her. Of course, she knew that this was difficult for her but it never occurred to her that she was causing this much pain to Emma. Emma looked....distraught. That was the word that came to her mind. And distraught was much too harsh of a word to be used in this situation. Emma should be bothered, maybe, but distraught? It didn't make sense. "I...I guess I didn't realize...I mean I knew you weren't happy about this but I didn't think-"

Emma cut her off, causing Layne's eyebrows to rise in surprise. "No. You didn't think. How could you not see how much this bothered me? I've told you so many times how much this upset me. I practically begged you to talk to Andy and leave him if that's what you want to do. I told you I would support you, no matter what. It's just this…this…purgatory that you're in I can't take anymore. I just don't understand how you can keep going on like this! Just make a decision already!" Emma had jumped up and was now pacing the room.

Layne looked closely at Emma, trying to determine what was causing this change, albeit a subtle one. Although Emma would never have been considered mousy or a pushover, she was definitely someone who had always been easily convinced. Layne always thought she'd make a great juror, so easily swayed was she by listening to another person speak about their views. Now, however, Emma was standing her ground despite Layne's arguments. It seemed that Emma had suddenly realized she had two feet of her own and wanted to stand on them by herself, unassisted. "Look, I know this hasn't been easy on you but don't worry about Andy. He doesn't have any idea that anything is different."

"See? That's just it," Emma huffed, sounding exasperated. "He doesn't have any idea. You spend time with Brad while Andy is sitting home waiting for you. He had no idea that you're in love with another man. But I know it. And I have to lie to him every time I see him! Geez, Layne. Do you have any idea how uncomfortable that is for me?"

"I didn't realize…"

"Of course you didn't. You're so wrapped up in your life with Brad that you never even considered how I felt about all of this or what effect this is going to have on Andy." Emma stopped abruptly, realizing she might have gone too far.

Layne again felt a tingling of something that she was missing, something that was right in front of her but she couldn't figure it out. Had she done something to cause Emma to be so upset? While she knew that she hadn't really been around much because of the time she spent with Brad, both she and Emma knew (she hoped) that if Emma really needed her, she'd be there in a minute. So what was it that had Emma so riled up? She leaned back against the couch and crossed her arms across her chest. "Go on. I think I should hear this."

Emma looked at Layne as though deciding whether or not to

speak. "Fine. I honestly don't understand how you can do this to him and go about your day as though you don't have a care in the world. Andy loves you, Layne. You have the most wonderful man sitting at home waiting for you at the end of every day and it's not good enough. He buys you flowers, and you criticize. He makes you dinner and you tell him it's overcooked. He rents a video for you two to watch and you tell him you're not interested. Jesus, Layne! You have and handsome, intelligent, attractive man who loves you more than anything, sitting at home waiting for you to spend time with him! Any woman would be lucky to have him so I can't understand why that's not good enough for you! "

She sat down, as though exhausted. "I just don't understand you at all. You have what the rest of us want....so badly and you treat it like it's something to discard with the weekly trash. How can you do that to him?" Emma's voice caught on the last word and when she looked up, her eyes had filled with tears. Embarrassed at having shown so much emotion, she wiped away the moisture angrily and looked back down into her lap.

Layne stared at Emma, her eyes squinting as though to see her more closely. She was, in fact looking as her in a way that she never had before. She was looking at her as woman; a woman who had emotions that Layne had never even noticed until this very moment. Emma felt the scrutiny and fidgeted slightly. Layne sat there silently, waiting for the thought to form in her mind. She felt as though someone was turning the lights on ever so slowly and she was finally able to see what she'd missed all this time. It had been right there in front of her and she never saw it. How was it that she missed it all this time? Her mouth formed a tiny 'o' as the answer to all her questions came rushing forward. She gasped as she realized what she'd failed to see all this time. "Oh my God...."

Emma ·flinched at the sudden outburst after so many long minutes of silence. Thinking something was wrong, she immediately asked, "What? What's the matter?"

Layne got up off the couch and began pacing. "How is it that I never noticed this before? I can't believe I never saw it. God, I never even thought about it. I mean, you...and him? It's just...ridiculous, that's what it is."

Emma felt herself go cold with fear. She felt a tingling in her hands that worked its way up her arms and then she felt everything go numb. The fear slowly spread its way through her body making her mouth go dry and her throat close up. She tried to swallow but realized she was unable to move a muscle. She tried to lick her lips to moisten them and then tried to speak. "Uhh..."

Layne turned on her heel and stared at Emma. "How could I be so stupid?"

Emma finally managed to swallow and then found her voice. "Layne? What are you talking about?" She croaked.

"You." She stopped in front of Emma and pointed at her. "It's you. You're in love with him. I'm right, aren't I?"

Emma stared at Layne, trying to hold her gaze steady. She was trying to maintain a look of indifference but her body betrayed her. Thoughts of Andy made their way into her mind and her expression softened for just the briefest of moments. Her eyes took on that far-away, dreamy look of someone who is completely and desperately in love with another.

Quickly, she pushed the thoughts of him away and re-grouped, but it was too late. Layne was now looking at her with the tiny, evil smile of someone who had cornered their prey and was about to rip them to pieces. Emma thought that if it were possible, Layne would have venom dripping from her teeth. She tried to brush off the accusation. "What are you talking about?"

"Don't give me that. I can see it all over your face. You're in love with...Andy?" She laughed out loud then looked back at Emma. "You are! You're in love with him. How could I never see this before?" Layne resumed pacing around the room.

"Layne, sit down. You're-"

"No, no. It all makes sense now. All the guys I've tried to set you up with. You didn't give any of them the time of day. You don't date anyone. You don't even act like you're interested in dating." Layne collapsed back onto the couch. "Oh my god. It's so clear."

"Layne...."

Layne turned to face Emma, who was had remained seated the entire time, unwilling to move any more than she had to for fear of further rocking the boat. For some odd reason, she'd always felt that if you stayed still, things would just pass you by.

"How could this happen? Why would you do this to me?" Layne cried.

"Wh..what are you talking about? Do what to you?"

Layne's teeth were clenched as she spoke. "How could you fall in love with my husband? You're supposed to be my best friend!"

Emma flinched at the accusatory tone. She felt a bit of anger well up inside of her and when she spoke, she couldn't hide the sarcasm. "I would think that you of all people would understand that you have no control over who you fall in love with."

"What is *that* supposed to mean?" Layne crossed her arms over her chest in a show of defiance.

There was something in Layne's posture that tossed Emma over the edge. She looked at Layne and noticed the hands clenching her upper arms, the upward tilt of her head, the lips pressed tightly together and the sense of indignation that surrounded her. Emma shook her head, astounded that Layne had somehow been able to turn the situation around from her own infidelity to Emma's feelings; feelings that were left to smolder inside of her since she'd never acted on them.

Emma's own lips pressed together while she gathered her thoughts. "You're not actually going to stand there and tell me that I should have had some control over my emotions? Isn't that a little like the pot calling the kettle black?"

"This is entirely different and you know it! Andy is my husband! How could you do that to me?"

Layne's sense of self-righteousness infuriated Emma. It was as though her entire relationship and wrongdoing with Brad were somehow erased because of Emma's feelings for Andy. Emma stood up and walked over to Layne, who flinched when she saw the look in her face.

"Do this?" She pounded her chest with her fist. "TO YOU?!?!?! Are you actually going to stand there and accuse me of some wrongdoing with Andy when you're FUCKING someone else!??? How dare you? How dare you accuse me of something while at the same time exonerate yourself from any wrongdoing!!! You are UN-BE-LIEVABLE!!"

They both knew that Emma rarely, if ever, raised her voice, let alone swore like a trucker. Layne stood there, mometarily stunned by the outburst. Because there was no immediate reaction from Layne, Emma bulldozed on.

"So what? I love him. I can't help the way I feel. But let me tell

YOU something," She pointed at Layne. "I have never, EVER done anything about it. I have kept this inside of me, never telling anyone!' Emma's fist clenched again and she pounded on her chest as though to give some indication of the pain she'd endured. "I told no one about this. I couldn't even tell you! My god, the only person who knew was my own mother and that's because she guessed! Not because I confided in her. Do you know how hard that was for me to keep something like this from you?! From everyone!?!?" Emma's voice softened and she began to pace the room. "For three years, I've listened to you talk about your relationship with him, going over every detail of your sex life, every detail of your wedding. Do you have any idea, any idea at all how hard it was for me to listen to you knowing that I would never be with him? Because he loves YOU, Layne. From the moment he met you, I didn't stand a chance. It nearly killed me, but I did it. For you. Because you're my best friend."

Emma paused and looked up at Layne. "How can you accuse me of something that you know better than anyone I would never do! I've done nothing wrong here. And yes, I love him. I love him so much it hurts." Emma's voice broke on the words. "But I stood by you even though I hated what you were doing...even though I knew at some point it would destroy him."

Layne slowly leaned forward, resting her forearms on her thighs. She stared at the floor between her legs while two tears made their way down her cheeks. She wiped them away and then found her voice. "How...how long have you been in love with him?"

It was soft; barely a whisper but Emma heard it nonetheless. She just wished she hadn't since she wasn't prepared to answer that particular question. How long? How could she answer that? Was there a moment when she didn't love Andy? She took a deep breath, knowing that she might as well reveal everything.

"Always...." Emma finally answered. "I've always loved him."

Layne stared at Emma for what seemed like an eternity. Finally, she stood up, grabbed her purse and walked out of the apartment, gently closing the door behind her.

Emma, expecting the door to slam, flinched when she heard the soft click of the lock falling into place. Somehow, the gentle closing of the door was more final than any slamming could have been. At least if Layne would have slammed the door, she would have known she was angry. Anger meant she still cared. The silent click of the door indicated something different; something more irreparable.

To Emma, it signified indifference. And indifference meant there was nothing left.

Chapter 15

Emma's assumption was correct. For all intense and purposes, Layne had summarily ended their friendship. Despite numerous texts and phone calls to Layne, she had yet to receive anything in response. After nearly a month, Emma gave up and ended all attempts to speak with Layne.

If Emma were not so sad about the loss of the friendship, she would have been angry at Layne for how she chose to handle the situation. Emma knew that she would go through all stages of grief and come to a point in time where she was angry with Layne for solely placing all the blame on Emma. For now, though, she was still knee-deep in the depression stage.

What stunned Emma the most was the fact that Layne had seemed so *surprised* to realize that someone had feelings for Andy. It was as if Layne herself had turned a blind eye to the attractive qualities her husband possessed. Andy was a handsome man. He was kind, intelligent, and caring and Emma felt certain that there were many women that found him as desirable as she did. Of course, none of them were best friends with his wife and spent nearly as much time with him as she did. Layne did have a point there, Emma thought. But then again, who can help how they feel? Emma could no more stop her feeling for Andy than she could stop a war from raging on in the Middle East. She was powerless. So she did the next best thing. Suffered in silence. And if that wasn't good enough for Layne? Well, she wasn't about to be the one to grovel for forgiveness.

Yet, she still picked up her phone out of habit to check for the random text message or missed call. There were none. As the days crept by, Emma found that she would check her phone nearly every hour, then only before work and after, and then she found that she'd even forget to take her phone out of its charger on her way to work. After all, the only people who called her besides Layne were her parents, and they knew her work number. Most of her other friends were at work with her and they didn't need to call; they could just knock on her classroom door.

Before she knew it, it had been three months since she'd spoken to Layne, a lifetime really, if you considered how inseparable they'd always been. Interestingly enough, in her own mind, she still thought of Layne as her best friend and when she did so, she would immediately wonder how long it would be before she stopped. Of course, she knew it would take quite a long while to erase a habit she'd had since she was a little girl.

The summer had come to an end and Emma found that she was able to jump right back into the swing of things at work. Her new kindergarteners were excited to be learning and her parents seemed to be a great group this year. Things were going well for her, at least at work. Her personal life still needed a bit of tweaking. She decided to tackle one task at a time, the first being a visit to the grocery store so that her fridge no longer looked barren. Besides, she was finding that eating out nearly every night was adding up quickly and she was running out of co-workers to join her after work for "a quick bite to eat."

She finally resigned herself to making the hugely procrastinated trip to the grocery store. She surveyed the fridge and finding only a jar of mayonnaise, a few packets of condiments and some questionable lunchmeat, Emma decided to make a trip to the grocery store. She closed the door and went in search of her pocketbook. After locating it and making a list out of some necessities, Emma headed out to the nearest Food Lion to stock up on some basics.

She weaved her way through the aisles, grabbing items that she could fix easily, since she wasn't one who enjoyed cooking, especially when it was just for one person. As she rounded the last aisle, she realized she had forgotten to get some apples so she walked back to the entrance of the store to select some. She placed a half-dozen or so in a clear plastic bag and turned to put them in her cart. It was then that she saw him.

Andy. Walking through the front door, carrying one of those hand-baskets people used when you only needed to pick up a few things. Although he looked like he'd lost a few pounds-and didn't need to, in Emma's opinion - he looked the same. It was only because she knew of his situation that she stared a bit longer than necessary, almost as though inspecting him for damage. As if sensing he was being watched, he looked up and saw her staring at him. He hesitated, and for a moment, she thought he was going to walk in the other direction. She gave him a smile to let him know she was friend rather than foe. He smiled back hesitantly at her and then slowly walked over.

"Hey," he said.

"Hey, Andy. How're you holding up?"

He snorted. "So you know then. About the divorce, I mean."

She nodded.

"Yeah, it sucks. Really sucks." He sighed and ran his hand through his hair, leaving it messy and out of place.

"I'm so sorry, Andy."

"I've racked my brain trying to figure out what happened and I can't come up with a thing. I know you two didn't spend much time together right before we split, but did you notice anything wrong?"

Emma didn't like where this was headed at all. "You know, I hadn't seen Layne in probably a month before you two split up. I'm not really sure."

"I'm sorry, Emma. I shouldn't be asking these questions of you."

"It's fine. Really. I know you're upset and looking for answers. I just wish I could give them to you." There. She didn't lie but she didn't betray Layne. It was the best she could do.

"I know." He shrugged. "Well, I guess I'd better get a few things if I'm going to eat at all this week."

Emma smiled. "I know the feeling," she said, pointing to the contents of her cart, which was nearly full with supplies.

He glanced down and made what Emma felt was a good attempt at a smile, but failed. "Well, see ya around."

Andy turned and began to walk away. After a few steps he stopped and turned back. "Hey, Emma?"

"Yeah?"

"It's good to see you."

Emma once again felt a tingle deep in her belly which told her that she was still as much in love with him as she ever was. She smiled back at him, afraid to speak for fear of showing any emotion. She turned her cart and walked to the checkout, furtively glancing over her shoulder to steal a final look at his retreating figure.

She finished her shopping and headed home. As she unpacked

her groceries she thought about her encounter with Andy. Seeing him, while always a pleasant thing, reminded her of what she'd lost with Layne. She hadn't seen her in nearly three months and it still pained her to think about it. They'd been so close for so long that it didn't seem possible that they didn't speak anymore. Friends did grow apart, but that wasn't what happened in this situation. Truth be told, Layne had turned on her. It was like all she could focus on was the fact that Emma had feelings for Andy and chose to ignore that Emma had never done a thing about those feelings. It didn't matter, Emma thought sadly. She knew that her friendship was a thing of the past. Not only because of her feelings for Andy, but because of the things she'd said to Layne and the venom with which she'd said them. Some things were unforgivable.

Emma fixed herself a sandwich and ate while standing at the sink. She went into the living room and turned on the TV, trying to find something to take her mind off the fact that she'd just seen Andy after three months and realized nothing had changed in that arena. She was still completely and utterly in love with him.

After surfing the channels for a few minutes, she gave up and went to bed, knowing that sleep would be the only way to get her mind off of Andy – at least the conscious part.

The next morning, Emma woke early after a fitful night's sleep. She got up and made a pot of coffee, then decided to park herself on the couch for a rather long session of HGTV. She poured herself a cup of coffee and sat down to watch House Hunters. She lifted the cup to her lips and took a small sip, fearful of burning herself. As it turned out, it was lucky she only had a small taste because she immediately spit it back into the mug.

"Ick! This is awful!" The bitterness stuck to the inside of her mouth and nearly caused her to gag. "I can't even make a decent cup of coffee! God, I'm hopeless!"

Unfortunately, Emma now wanted a cup of coffee – a good cup of coffee, that is. Since she was incapable of making one, she decided to drive to the nearest Starbuck's and get herself one made by professionals. She gathered her hair into a loose ponytail and changed into a pair of pants that didn't look like she'd just slept in them. Those, she placed on the bed for that evening. She splashed some cold water on her face so that she'd be awake enough to drive and headed out of her apartment.

Within five minutes, she was walking opening the door of the Starbuck's. There were only a couple of people in line, which was good because by now she really needed some caffeine.

She stepped up to the counter and was greeted by an employee who was much too cheerful. Of course, she knew that there was probably an IV of caffeine for the employees somewhere in the back.

"Hi, there! I'm Brandi-with-an-i'." She pointed to her name tag and Emma saw that it was indeed spelled with an I; a capital I, no less. "Welcome to Starbuck's! What can we get for you today?"

Emma was thinking that Brandi-with-an-I was too chipper for and for a moment thought about trying to locate Layne's friend Malcolm-too-young-for-Emma and offer to fix him up with her when movement in the far side of the store eye caught her attention. She glanced over and saw Andy sitting in the corner reading the paper. He had the paper opened in front of him and was looking down at it, seemingly engrossed in some article.

Of course, she thought. She was a complete mess today – hadn't even showered - and she runs into Andy. Of all people! Absently, she smoothed her hair back, feeling for any loose strands. Did she even look at herself as she left the apartment? And what exactly was she wearing, she thought as she looked down. She breathed a sigh of relief when she remembered that the pants she had put on were clean.

Maybe he wouldn't notice her. She could just get her coffee and leave without being seen, go back to her apartment and make herself look presentable, then come back and "run into him." Maybe she should forgo the coffee and just sneak out the opposite side of the store now and head home…

While she stood there deciding what to do, he put his paper down on the table and took a sip of his coffee. As he lifted his cup to his mouth, he saw her. He smiled and motioned for her to join him. She nodded and motioned that she'd be just one minute. Crap, she thought. Busted.

She focused her attention back to Brandi-with-an-I and said, "Can I have a grande vanilla latte?"

"GRANDE VANILLA LATTE!" She shouted to the barista.

Was that really necessary? Emma thought. He was only three feet away from her. She handed over a five dollar bill, waited for her change, then moved over to wait for her drink. After a few moments, the barista placed it on the counter and smiled at her with a smile only someone completely full of caffeine can do.   As she reached for it, she smiled as best she could without the benefit of coffee in her and then walked over to Andy's table. She sat down, trying to erase any trace of nervousness.

"Hey Andy."

He smiled at her and she felt her insides turn to water. "Long time, no see."

She chuckled. "So, what are you doing here? Besides getting coffee, I mean."

"I come here every Sunday morning to read the paper. I started it right after Layne moved out – I guess I didn't like spending Sunday mornings alone." He shrugged. "Anyway, it sort of became a habit. You doin' okay? You know, since, what, twelve hours ago?"

"Yeah, fine thanks."   She took a tentative sip of her coffee, anxious to feel the effects of the caffeine, but knowing that the coffee was still too hot to gulp.

They sat in silence for a few moments, each unsure how to proceed. Andy spoke first.

"Listen, I'm glad I ran into you today."

Emma's heart did a flip-flop. *Really?* She thought.

"I wanted to apologize for last night. I shouldn't have badgered you the way I did."

Oh. Emma forced herself to smile. "You didn't badger me at all.   It's completely understandable that you'd want to ask questions."

"I really shouldn't have asked them of you. You're Layne's friend and I shouldn't have asked you to betray her confidence."

"You know, I'm your friend too." She gently smiled at him. "How are you holding up?"

"The weekends are sort of rough, you know? No work to distract me and I get to thinking about the good times instead of the bad times. It's funny how being alone will do that to you."

Emma nodded but must have had a sad look on her face because Andy smiled and said, "Sheesh, it's not all that bad. Surprisingly, I am doing well.   I mean, it was hard at first…when she told me she was leaving, I was shocked but then…the more I thought about it, the more I realized it was for the best."

"Really?" Emma didn't even attempt to mask her shock.

He chuckled. "I know. It's strange, isn't it? As it turns out, we really didn't have all that much in common. I guess I didn't see it until she was gone. I kept on doing the things that I always did and realized that it was no different. I had always done things by myself. As it turns out, we really didn't spend all that much time with each other. Don't get me wrong, it was difficult for a bit- I think ending any relationship is – but it wasn't like I thought it'd be."

"How's that?" Emma asked, taking a larger sip of her coffee, which was at least not boiling anymore.

"Well, I guess I thought it'd be much harder than it actually is. Once she moved out, I thought for sure I'd be really depressed; not be able to function and all that. It bothered me but truthfully, I think it was more the fact that I felt like a failure rather than I was depressed because I missed her." He paused. "Geez, that sounds awful doesn't it."

Emma shrugged. "Oh, I don't know. Remember, I've never been married."

He smiled gently. "Touché. I guess I thought ending a marriage was supposed to be one of the most stressful things a person can go through. For me, though, it wasn't. I think if it came as a surprise, it would have been more stressful."

This time, Emma tried to suppress her shock. "Are you saying you knew it was going to end?"

He shrugged. "I don't know if I knew, exactly. But I did have a feeling that things just weren't right. It just wasn't what I thought marriage was going to be like."

"What do you mean?" Emma leaned forward, resting her forearms on the tiny table between them.

"I guess I pictured the two of us doing more things together, you know? But it seemed like Layne always had something she needed to do. She would make these lists all the time of things that she had to get done and it was only after all of that was done that she'd be able to spend time with me at home. It was like I had to schedule time with her or something. And then when we finally just hung out at home, it felt like she couldn't wait for it to end. I think I bored her or something." He chuckled as though trying to tell her that it didn't bother him. Emma, however, knew better.

She found herself staring at him as he spoke and she realized that he was going to be okay. She looked at him closely and then spoke again. "You're really okay, aren't you?"

He looked back at her. "You know, I think I am." And then he flashed her a smile that made her tingle inside.

God, I'm pathetic, she thought, but continued to smile right back at him.

He took another sip of his coffee and folded the paper neatly in front of him, letting her know that he wanted to talk rather than read. "So, what about you? You're still teaching, I take it?"

Emma nodded. "I sure am. Kindergarten. I still can't believe I'm teaching the same grade.

He brought his eyebrows together in confusion. "Why's that?"

She shrugged. "I always thought I'd move to different grades but I never seem to want to make the change. I love getting the kids for their first time in school. I feel like if I give them a positive experience, they'll love school forever. It's silly, I know…"

"I don't think so. We need more teachers like you. Teachers who like what they do and actually like children."

Emma laughed. "I think we've all had a teacher who we knew shouldn't still be teaching. If I ever get there, promise me you'll shoot me."

"I promise." There was a small lull in the conversation and Emma thought that she should leave him, figuring he'd want to finish reading the paper. She was just about to make an excuse to leave when he lifted his head and looked directly at her as though an idea had struck him.

"Hey, you live pretty close by, right?" He asked.

Emma nodded. Andy had actually never been to her place, she remembered. There was no reason for him to. Anytime Layne was over it was so that they could have some girl-time and most recently, it was so she could meet Brad. Normally, Emma went over to Layne and Andy's house for the blind dates. "I live just a couple blocks over there." She pointed out the window.

He looked out the window at where she was pointing. "That's right! You live in the Ardmore apartments. I forgot how close you were to my place."

Emma was momentarily confused, knowing that Layne and Andy's house was on the opposite side of town and took about fifteen minutes to get to since there was no direct route. When driving from Emma's apartment to Layne and Andy's, one was at the mercy of one-lane roads, traffic lights and busy intersections.

"I thought you lived over by the high school."

He nodded. "Used to. Sold the house as part of the settlement."

"Sorry."

He dismissed her apology with a wave of the hand. "Don't apologize. I'm sort of glad to be rid of it. I never had enough time to take care of the yard, the fence, the basement and all the other stuff that goes along with home-ownership."

Emma smiled in agreement. "One of the few benefits of renting...someone ELSE has to fix everything."

Andy lifted his cup and took a long drink. He slowly put it down and looked at Emma as though he had something to say but wasn't quite sure how to say it.

"What?" She asked.

"I was just wondering if you see much of Layne."

The mention of her name made Emma's face cloud over momentarily. She'd mourned the loss of her friendship for quite some time and had only recently felt as though the hole Layne had left inside of her was healing. She also worried that Andy was asking in the hope of finding out what Layne was up to, not because he was curious, but because he still cared about her. The thought of that being the case made Emma's mouth go dry and she found she needed to gulp some coffee before answering. Still looking down at her cup, she replied. "Not so much, anymore. We had sort of a falling out."

He nodded sympathetically. "Sorry to hear that. I thought something had happened. You sort of dropped off the face of the earth I wondered what was going on. I asked Layne but she wouldn't talk about it."

She shook her head. "It was just stupid girl stuff."

"You and Layne were friends forever. I can't believe you couldn't work things out."

Emma nodded sadly. "Yeah..."

"You know..." Andy stopped abruptly.

"What?"

"I was just going to say that it's odd that Layne doesn't see either of us anymore. It's like she ended one part of her life."

If you only knew, Emma thought, but she only looked at Andy and nodded.

"Well, at least we're still friends, right?" He looked at her and grinned.

She couldn't help but smile. "Right!" she replied.

"But as your friend, I have to tell you something." He leaned toward her as though about to share some secret.

She leaned in as well. "Oh, yeah? What's that?"

"Under no circumstances will I set you up on any blind dates. Deal?" He extended his hand to shake with hers.

She laughed, and for the first time in a very long time, felt a little bit like herself. She placed her hand in his and they shook. "Deal."

Emma felt very much at ease with Andy. It seemed that the previous evening's chance meeting had broken the ice and now they were acting like old friends. They sat at their table and talked for well over an hour. Emma spoke of the children in her class and told Andy of one child in particular that she was worried about. Much to his credit, he listened and even asked questions about her class and school, which surprised Emma, though she wasn't exactly sure why. She had always known Andy to be a great listener, and today was no different.

Andy began to chat about his work and what he had been recommending to his clients recently. He was a financial advisor and spent much of his time analyzing the stock market and reviewing his clients' portfolios'. Emma did her best to keep up, but found that the subject matter was way over her head. She tried to follow but found in order to do so, she needed to ask question after question, which she feared might irritate him. Finally, after rattling off several questions, Andy stopped talking and looked at her as though she had two heads.

"What?!" Emma asked, feeling very self-conscious.

"You're asking so many questions." He said, grinning.

"Gosh, I'm sorry." She felt the color rise to her cheeks and silently berated herself for all the questions.

"No. Don't apologize. It's just that no one ever listens to me. I tend to bore people with all my financial talk and I forget that people who don't work with me have no interest in it. It's a nice change of pace."

Emma breathed a sigh of relief. "Oh, well good. Because I have about 100 more. I have to confess...I only got about half of what you said."

He laughed. "Well, that's about half more than anyone else ever gets!"

Andy drank the last of his coffee and placed it down on the table. "I'm glad I ran into you, Emma."

"Me too."

He looked at his watch. "Listen, I hate to leave but yesterday I told my mom I'd head over to her place and help her get some stuff out of the attic. She's cooking me lunch, otherwise I wouldn't-"

"Don't worry about it. Mom's come first. I'll see you around, okay?"

He nodded. "Maybe next Sunday?"

"Sure."

Andy stood up and made his way out. As the door closed behind him, he turned back around and waved goodbye to Emma. She waved back and then watched at he jogged to his car.

Chapter 16

It was silly, really, but having spent just that little bit of time with Andy seemed to set her week off on the right foot. Not only did she enjoy the time she spent with him, but she also felt as though she had re-established some connection to her former life. Even without Layne's presence, the feeling warmed her and gave her a renewed sense of vigor…insight, or….something. Whatever it was, she was in a better state of mind and was able to face things with a positive mindset rather than through the gray cloud she'd been seeing things through recently.

Maybe it was her outlook or maybe she was just having a good week, but whatever the cause, the result was that the week flew by. Her kids seemed to be on their best behavior, diligently listening to her during instruction time and at least for this one week, the gossip at the school was kept to a minimum – a nearly impossible feat when a building holds nearly 100 women whose only break in an otherwise boring and routine day was to create scandal.

Although she was definitely in a better mood since seeing Andy, she convinced herself that it was that connection to her former life that changed her outlook rather than the actual time she spent with the man who had the starring role in all of her fantasies. After all, her time with him wasn't a date; they'd simply run into each other and then sat down at the same table. It was more of a conservation of space than anything else.

Still, she told herself, any time she spent with him was better than no time at all, even if they were only friends. She had always gotten along with Andy and found him to be great company- in addition to being extremely handsome. Coffee on Sunday mornings with Andy suited Emma just fine, thank you very much.

When Sunday morning came, Emma found herself awake earlier than normal out of sheer anticipation, as though she were a child on Christmas morning. She laid in bed for the better part of an hour trying to fall back to sleep but to no avail. Finally, she got up and took a shower, knowing that she was not going to repeat her disheveled appearance from the prior week. The trick, of course, was not giving the impression that she was trying too hard or putting forth too much effort. She needed to treat this as she did any other time she had met Andy before. He had no idea she felt the way she did and the last thing she wanted to do was make their friendship uncomfortable by revealing anything. While she knew she'd probably love Andy for the rest of her life, she also knew she'd rather have him as a friend than nothing at all. And the surest way to ruin a friendship was for one of them to profess their love to the other. There was no way Emma would ever do that. Period.

But...wanting to remain friends in no way was going to prevent her from making herself look as attractive as possible (without *looking* like she'd exerted any effort to do so, of course). For Emma, that entailed choosing an outfit without paint or some other kindergarten damage rather than spending time on her hair and makeup. Because of her freckles and fair skin, she had found out at a very early age that even the slightest bit of makeup that was applied incorrectly had the undesirable affect of giving her a clown-like appearance. As a result, she mainly stuck to mascara and a little bit of lip gloss.

After much debate, Emma decided to wear a pair of olive green Capri pants with a white short-sleeved t-shirt and her favorite pair of Sketchers. She felt the outfit was perfect. Nice, but not too overdone. Sort of a casual but still put together.

* * *

Andy found he was actually looking forward to meeting Emma for coffee, not for any reason other than he enjoyed her company. He always had. When he was married, he'd enjoyed having her over for dinner but he hated the fact that Layne had always tried to set her up with men she'd meet. Emma was attractive, certainly, with her freckles and petite frame, and Andy knew she'd meet someone when the time was right.

Andy looked around the apartment and then grabbed his keys from the table beside the front door. He missed home ownership but since he'd been forced to sell theirs during the divorce, he hadn't had any time to look for a new place. What he'd told Emma last week was in fact, the truth. He never had enough time to take care of the house the way he wanted to and he wasn't about to purchase another one unless he found the time. He wasn't exactly sure what he was looking for so the option to rent for period of time appealed to him.

He bounced down the steps and went out to his car, excited to have something to do on a Sunday morning that involved another human being.

He arrived at the Starbuck's a few minutes before 11 am and looked around for Emma. She hadn't arrived yet so he ordered a coffee and sat down to wait. Luckily, he had brought this morning's paper, so he opened up to review the financial section.

Looking around the coffee shop, he noticed that the only other patrons were an elderly couple. He watched them read the paper together and noticed that there was a rhythmic pattern to it, one that had obviously been developed over many years. For just a brief moment, he felt a pang of envy. He had hoped to have that with someone but it looked like it just wasn't in the cards for him. While he still hoped for that, he realized it probably wasn't going to happen for him a second time around. Sure, he wanted it, but he just didn't think he would ever take that chance again, which was why he was glad it was Emma he was meeting. He wasn't ready to even consider dating again and Emma provided the safe-haven he needed to get out without the added burden of trying to impress. He'd always enjoyed her company and they'd been friends for so long that it seemed only natural that they meet for coffee. This was perfect, he thought. He'd always been very comfortable with Emma and that was what he needed right now.

It was then that the door opened and she walked in. She smiled and waved once she saw him and he smiled back. She walked up to the counter and ordered, then came to sit down with him, her latte in hand.

"Hey," she said, taking a sip of her coffee.

"Hey, yourself. How was your week?"

"Blissfully uneventful… no vomiting, no bleeding and no crazy parents." Emma looked up to find Andy staring at her eyes wide, mouth agape.

"Seriously? It sounds like a war zone."

"Well not every day," she joked. She nodded toward the paper scattered on the table. "Mind if I share?"

He waved his hand as though surveying his kingdom and smiled. "Be my guest."

Emma rifled through the paper and selected a few sections to peruse. He noticed that she did not even glance at the business section, the local news, sports or anything even remotely containing information that would be considered news. Andy watched her from behind the classified section, peeking over the top of the paper and smiling. After several minutes, she looked up at him and raised her eyebrows.

"What?!" She asked.

"Aren't you going to read any of the news? You're only reading the sale flyers and Parade magazine."

"I watch a half hour of news every night and that is more than enough. I've got no desire to spend my Sunday morning reading about the decline of our economy or how some child got run over by a school bus. I'll stick to the sale flyers, thank you very much." She crossed her arms over her chest as though daring him to disagree with her. "All righty-then. I'll read the important sections and let you know if there's anything earth shattering." He chuckled.

"You do that." She uncrossed her arms and picked up the Target flyer to continue perusing the sale items for the week.

They read in comfortable silence for a few moments until Emma pointed out the Best Buy flyer. "Oooh! Look! Best Buy has the new IPOD on sale." She looked up at Andy. "Do you have one? I've been thinking I might like to get one."

"Yeah, I have….that one," he said, pointing to the middle of the page.

"Do you like it? When do you use it? Is it hard to program?"

Andy laughed. "You've never had one?" Seeing her shake her head, he said, "You're kidding! Well, we're going to have to fix that. Here let me see that."

He reached for the circular and looked at the items on sale. "These are pretty good prices. I can take you there if you like. Help you pick one out."

Emma clapped her hands. "That would be great! You sure you don't mind?"

"Not at all. When are these prices good until?"

Emma looked at the front of the circular. "Ummm…Saturday."

"Do you want to head out there Friday night after work? I'm

151

normally home by five or so. I can pick you up at your place and we can head out."

"That would be great! Are you sure you don't have any plans that I'm stealing you away from?"

"Believe me. I have no plans. And I can always look at the TV's."

"Aha! An ulterior motive!"

"Guilty. But look at it this way; you'll get an IPOD and I'll get to scope out the latest selection of flat screens."

Emma thought about that for a moment. "That sounds fair."

They finished reading the paper and drinking their coffee and spent a few minutes firming up their plans for the following Friday night. Emma was feeling more excited than she should and, of course she realized this, but she was unable to prevent herself from being excited at the thought of spending an entire evening with Andy. Even though she knew he had no feeling for her other than friendship, it was something to do other than spend yet another evening at home alone in her apartment. And, as an added bonus, she would be with Andy. The thought made her tingle with anticipation.

* * *

That Friday night, Andy picked up Emma as arranged. Although a bit tired from a week of six year olds, she was excited to be heading out with Andy. Around 5:30, she heard her buzzer. She buzzed him in then opened up her front door when she heard him bounding up the steps.

"Hey," she said.

He walked in to the apartment, looked around and whistled. "Wow. Nice place. This is much better than my apartment."

"I keep forgetting you sold the house," Emma replied, biting down on her lower lip.

Andy grinned and nudged her with his elbow. "Don't look so sad. It really didn't make much sense for either one of us to keep it. Plus, neither one of us could afford it on our own."

She shrugged. "I guess that makes sense. I just feel bad that you had to sell. It seemed like you really liked it there."

It was his turn to show nonchalance with a shrug of his own.

"It's all right. I don't think it would have been healthy to keep living there, you know?"

"I guess you're right."

"But your place is great! Did you do all this yourself?"

"Yeah. I just pick up things here and there. If I like it, I just buy it and figure out where to put it later. Sometimes, though, I worry that I'm going to clutter up the place."

"No, it looks good." He looked around for a few minutes nodding as he checked out the pictures she'd hung. "Really good. Not cluttered at all."

Emma was pleased with his comments and then immediately felt stupid. He was simply being friendly. She needed to remind herself (continuously, if need be) that he was here as her friend and this was not a date. "Well, should we head out?"

"Sure. Let's go," he replied.

They arrived at the Best Buy and Andy led the way to the section of the store where they had the IPOD's. He knew what she was looking for and what she had to spend since he had asked her all the pertinent questions on the drive over. When they were in the aisle, it was simply a matter of choosing a color. She opted for the purple, feeling like a bit of color.

Once that was completed, Andy walked over to the big screen TV's. While she didn't understand a word of what he was saying what with the clarity and size and mega pixels, she sure enjoyed watching him speak. She was able to stare at him and appreciate the view since he was engrossed in the conversation with the sales clerk.

She thought it funny that when Andy was married to Layne and she'd spend time with them, it was hard for her to bear. While this was hard, somehow it was different. It was just the two of them, without Layne as the common ground that brought them together. Tonight, they were here together because the two of them had decided to do so; there was no set-up with some random guy or some fake date with Brad. There was no pressure; just an enjoyable evening, for which Emma was immensely grateful for. She knew if she spent any more time on her couch, her behind would be fused to it forever.

* * *

Andy looked at the TV's and thought how great it would be to have one of these in his home. Unfortunately, he was still living in his apartment. Perhaps when his bonus came, he'd be able to afford to buy a small house but at the moment, he was stuck. Still he could fantasize about watching TV in his own home on something like this, he thought, as he looked at the 51 inch monster in front of him.

He glanced back at Emma, wanting to make sure she wasn't waiting impatiently for him to finish. She wasn't. At the moment, she was inspecting a small(in his opinion) TV that he had to admit, would look great in her living room. He anticipated a trip back here in the future and he found himself looking forward to that. He too, was tired of sitting home by himself.

He turned back to the TV and realized that this particular purchase would have to wait until he had a room to fit it in. He walked over to Emma and asked if she was ready to go.

As they walked to the cash register, he realized he was hungry and really didn't want to go back to his apartment and eat some frozen dinner or yet another sandwich.

"You hungry?" He asked.

"Actually, I am."

"You want to grab something to eat?"

Emma pretended to consider, knowing that she'd pick up trash if she knew she'd be doing it with Andy. "Okay, but it's my treat. You really helped me out here tonight and by the looks of this thing, you're going to be helping me out a bit more. Dinner is the least I can do."

"Whatever you say," he replied, as he grinned at her.

For the briefest of moments, he thought about Layne and their time spent together. As much as he hated to make comparisons, he couldn't help it. When he thought about Emma and Layne and their friendship, for the moment he was stumped as to how they'd gotten to be so close. They were opposite in every way. He was finding out more and more about her without Layne between them directing the conversation. Although he had known her for years, it was always in sort of a secondary way – through Layne, the middleman. He felt as though he were getting to know her all over again without another person filtering things between them.

Layne and Emma were so different. Emma was so much more low-key and willing to just "go with the flow" where Layne required advance notice and preparation time for pretty much everything. It was more than that or the way they dressed. It was something that he couldn't quite put his finger on....just yet, anyway.

After Emma paid for her purchases, she turned to Andy. "So, where do you feel like eating?"

"It doesn't matter to me. Anything in particular you feel like? Italian? Mexican?"

Emma's eyes lit up. "Oooh! Mexican! Let's go to Tequila. It's only a few minutes from here."

He smiled. "All right. Lead the way."

They were seated at the table, nursing margaritas when Emma pulled out her new purchase.

"This is so great! Andy, I can't thank you enough for helping me out with this. I've wanted one but never really knew what to get or what I wanted."

"No problem. Do you have a bunch of CD's you're going to load up?"

Emma nodded. "And now I need to get an ITunes account. You know I've always bought the entire album. It will be nice to only buy the songs I actually like."

"You're really going to like it. I take mine to the gym with me and play it while I'm working out. Great music really makes the time fly."

"I can imagine." Emma looked down at her IPOD and then back up at Andy. "Is it difficult to set up Itunes?"

"Nah. Not too bad. But I can help you with that too."

"Really? You wouldn't mind?"

"Not at all." And he didn't mind at all, he realized. He looked down at his watch and noticed the time. "You know, it will be pretty late when we're done here. Why don't I come to your place tomorrow afternoon and work on it with you. "

"Really? You'd do that for me?"

Andy smirked at her. "Emma, you are one of the very few people I'd do just about anything for!"

She grinned back at him, hoping she wasn't revealing any of the fluttering going on inside of her. "Well, then. Eat up!" She said. "We've got to keep your strength up!" She took a large bit of her quesadilla.

He laughed and smiled at her, feeling very comfortable for the first time in a long time.

The next afternoon, Andy showed up Emma's apartment just as he said he would. She let him in and they walked into the kitchen area, which was where she had her laptop. She'd been working on progress reports for her students and the table was littered with piles of pager.

"Let me just clear this off..." Emma slid her arm across the table and piled all the papers into a messy pile. All this really did was move the mess into one even messier pile, but at least they had a place to work. She opened up the laptop and he sat down in front of it. She pulled a chair over and sat down beside him.

He opened up the IPOD package and took it out, attaching it to the computer. As it began to charge, he clicked onto the internet and got onto the ITUNES website. He began to type in the information required to set up her account. Some of the information was basic – her name, address, and date of birth – other information was much more personal, like her mother's maiden name. Emma watched him enter the information without even glancing in her direction. She was astonished and surprised that he knew all of this information about her.

"How do you know all this?" She asked, as he began to enter more information than she thought he knew about her.

He stopped typing and looked at her strangely. "Emma, I've known you for more than three years. Of course I know all this stuff."

"Well, sure...But my mother's maiden name? My High School? When did I ever mention that? And why would you pay attention to those useless pieces of information?"

Unsure of how to respond, he looked back at her and shrugged. After a few moments, he responded. "Emma, I pay attention to everything you say."

Still joking, she replied, "Now why would you do that?"

He was staring at her with an expression of pure seriousness. "Does that surprise you?"

Seeing the look on his face, she erased the smile from her face and suddenly became uncomfortable. She thought she knew where she he was headed with this conversation but wasn't sure she was ready to go there; not with him, anyway. "Er...no. It's just that...I uh..."

He smiled at her knowingly. "You didn't think anyone paid attention to you because you were always with Layne."

Emma looked up in surprise, astonished that he had been able to pinpoint what she'd always felt but never knew how to verbalize. It didn't bother her – well...once she'd gotten used to it. And truthfully, she was comfortable in the background. But was she? Or was it just that she'd grown accustomed to it because it was easy to stay there and simply give all the attention to Layne, who needed it almost as much as she needed food or water. "That's about right." She frowned. "But how would you know that? I mean, I barely realized it myself."

He turned to her and chuckled. "I was married to Layne, remember? The one thing I know all about is being in her shadow."

She chuckled and found some comfort in knowing that another person had experienced what she had. It also made her feel a bit better knowing that she wasn't completely off base for thinking it in the first place. Andy looked at her for a moment longer, then turned and continued registering her IPOD.

Once he had finished, Emma got some of her CD's and they began loading them onto her computer. Andy showed her how to make playlists of different types of music so she could listen to what she was in the mood for. Once he had finished, Emma felt confident she'd be able to work all of it.

It was nearly two hours later when he'd finished setting everything up and Andy decided it was time for him to head home. Although Emma was thrilled to have the use of the IPOD, she was sad to see their afternoon come to an end. As though he'd read her mind, he suggested they meet up later in the week. "Any chance you want to catch a movie this week? I've been thinking I might like to see the new Leonardo DiCaprio movie."

Emma felt warm and tingly but did her best to ignore it. "Sure,' she said, nonchalantly. "That sounds good. Wednesday night?"

"I'll swing by around 6:30 to pick you up. That work?"

She nodded.

He nodded in the direction of the kitchen. "So, try out the IPOD and let me know how it works for you."

"Okay, I'll do that. Thanks again for helping me with all of this. I really appreciate it."

"Of course! That's what friends are for! I'll see you Wednesday, all right?"

Emma smiled and nodded. "See you then."

She shut the door behind him and slid the deadbolt into place. Friends, she thought. She waited for the pang of depression to hit her but it never came. She thought about it for a moment and realized that she was truly fine with just being friends. She enjoyed spending time with Andy, regardless of what they were doing. Their time together was very relaxed yet fun and it seemed so natural since they'd known each other for so long. They'd already been friends but with Layne as the sort of mediator. This was new and it was nice. She was learning about Andy from her own experiences instead of through Layne. And truth be told, she was enjoying it. Yes, she thought. Being friends suited her just fine.

Chapter 17

When Wednesday rolled around, Emma was excited. But something had changed for her...something so subtle that it even took her some time to realize it. For the first time since she'd met him, she was enjoying getting to know him without focusing on her feelings. While she knew, without question, she was still in love with him, she rather enjoyed just spending time with him - not because they had to or because Layne insisted on it, but because they wanted to.

Andy showed up at Emma's apartment on Wednesday evening and they headed out to the theater. Andy had purchased the tickets earlier on Fandango.com so they were able to walk right in – not that there was much of a line since it was the middle of the week. Emma slowed down a bit as they walked through the lobby, inhaling the scent of the popcorn.

"Andy, wait," she said, grabbing his elbow. "You're not going to actually watch a movie without popcorn, are you?"

He laughed. "I guess not," he replied, as he followed her to the counter.

"One large popcorn...and could you layer the butter, please?"

"Boy, you don't hold back, do you?" He asked, eyeing the attendant pouring the golden syrup over an enormous bag of popcorn.

"Nope. If you're going to splurge, why not go all the way?" The attendant placed the popcorn on the counter and she selected a piece that was coated in butter flavoring and tossed it into her mouth. "Yum. Now what do you want to drink?"

"Well, since we're going, as you said, 'all the way,' I'm guessing water is out of the question?"

"You guessed it." She turned to the attendant. "Can we have two large cokes, please?"

Emma pulled out her wallet and shook her head at Andy when she noticed him reaching for his. "Nope. I've got this. You bought the tickets."

He reached for one of the cokes and mock saluted her. "Yes, ma'am."

By the time the movie had ended, each of them had eaten their fair share of popcorn. Their cokes were nearly empty and they were nearly sick because they were so full. As they were walking out of the theater, Andy rubbed his stomach and moaned.

"How do you manage to keep all of that down?"

"Practice. Loads and loads of practice," she replied, grinning.

"Good, god. I was going to suggest we grab something to eat but I don't think I could fit anything else inside of me."

Emma giggled. "There's nothing like a popcorn dinner!"

He raised one eyebrow at her. "Popcorn dinner? You have a name for what we just did? That's just not right." He shook his head from side to side. "Come on. Let's get you home."

He unlocked the doors using the remote and they both climbed in to Andy's Accord. As they drove home, they discussed the movie they'd just seen – Inception.

"So, was it a dream or not?

He shook his head. "I have no idea. I can tell you though, I'm exhausted! I had to stay on full alert just to follow what was going on!"

"Really? I thought it was just me and I wasn't able to follow."

"I think there were loads of us who weren't sure what was going on." He paused for a moment. "Great movie, though. Right?"

She nodded her agreement. "Absolulety. One of Dicaprio's best."

They pulled into the parking lot of Emma's apartment complex too quickly, it seemed to Emma. Andy drove around a bit and finally located a spot not too far from Emma's building.

Since Sunday, Emma had managed to load several of her CD's onto her computer as well as purchase a few songs from ITunes. She was excited to show Andy how far she'd progressed considering she hadn't even owned an IPOD last week. "You want to come up?" She asked, grinning. "I'd like to show you something."

He grinned back at her. "Well, I'm intrigued…" He turned off the car and pulled the key out of the ignition. "Let's go," he said, as he opened the door.

Emma got out of the car and headed up to her apartment, loving the feel of Andy walking beside her. It was perfect, she thought. They were so at ease with each other and they got along so well, each one willing to do something for the other. This was what friendship was supposed to be like, she thought. She couldn't help but feel a twinge of bitterness at how she'd been treated the last few months by Layne. But she couldn't focus on that right now. She slid her key into the lock and opened the door.

"Let me show you this," she said, as though about to reveal something spectacular. She walked into the kitchen and reached over her laptop to grab her IPOD. She handed it to Andy. "Go ahead," she prompted. "Turn it on."

Andy smiled as he looked at Emma, who was bouncing up and down on her two feet as though she was a four year old who needed to use the bathroom. He pressed a button on the IPOD and watched it light up. He toggled through her selections and figured out what she was so excited about. She'd not only added CD's from her collection to her IPOD, but she'd managed to download a number of songs and then organized them into playlists. "Whoa. You did all this?" Seeing her nod, he continued. "I'm impressed."

Emma now appeared to demonstrate a bit of humbleness mixed with embarrassment. "Well, I can't take all the credit. I had a great teacher."

Now it was Andy's turn to look embarrassed. "I think it was because I had such an attentive student."

She grinned even wider. "Okay, we're both fabulous. All these complements are making me thirsty. You want a glass of wine?"

"Absolutely," he replied.

"Go sit down if you want. Take the IPOD. You can review all my hard work."

He chuckled. "I don't know if I'd call downloading a few songs 'hard work,' but I'll let you get away with it...this time."

"Gee, thanks," she said with just a touch of sarcasm. "I've a bottle of merlot. I hope that's okay."

"Sure," he said. "I'm not picky." He sat down on the couch and leaned back and continued to review her music selections. "Now what's this?" He asked. "Rest?"

She sat down on the other end of the couch and handed him a glass of the merlot. "Oh, that. It's for the kids. I figure if I have a child who just needs a little bit of down time, I'll let him listen to that playlist for a bit. It's very soothing music; ocean waves and birds chirping – that sort of thing."

"Does that really work?"

Emma shrugged. "I don't know. But we'll find out the first time I try it!" She grinned.

Andy took a sip from his glass. He was surprised at how comfortable he was here. Her apartment was so welcoming. It was clean and neat but not to the extent that you felt as though you couldn't relax. He couldn't quite put his finger on what about this place made him feel so at ease. It was, after all, just an apartment. There wasn't anything out of the ordinary that struck him as soothing. Sure, she'd painted the walls a shade darker than the "builder beige" he assumed it had been when she moved in but that was the extent of it. He'd noticed himself relax from the first time he'd entered her place but now, as he sat there next to Emma on her couch, he wondered if perhaps it wasn't the apartment that made him feel so at east. For the first time, he began to wonder if Emma herself was what made him so relaxed. He thought about the time they'd spent together. It wasn't all that much, to be honest, but he felt more comfortable with her than he'd felt in a long time. There was something so…different about spending time with her lately and wondered what had caused the change.

He continued to search through the music she had stored on her IPOD but found himself casting the occasional glance at her out of the corner of his eye. It seemed as though each time he glanced at her, he found something that he'd never noticed before…the pattern of the freckles across her nose…the way her smile spread all the way up to her eyes…the way she tucked her hair absent-mindedly behind her ear. She seemed different somehow and he kept stealing glances at her in order to determine what it was. Had she cut her hair recently? Maybe lost some weight? He shook his head, trying to forget about it for the moment. Instead, he focused on the tiny piece of electronic equipment in front of him.

His attention didn't stay focused very long on the purple apparatus he held in his hand since he was still distracted by the feeling that something was…well, different about Emma. Again, he glanced at her out of the corner of his eye but couldn't figure out what it was. He shrugged involuntarily, trying once again to rid himself of the nagging thought.

He realized that he'd been staring at the same song title on the IPOD for some time when he realized Emma had asked him a question.

"What?" He tried to mask his embarrassment at being lost in thought. "Sorry, I was trying to remember where I'd heard this song before."

"I was just wondering if you wanted another glass of wine." Emma looked at him expectantly, waiting for his answer. He just stared at her with a blank look on his face; almost as though he didn't understand the language she was speaking. It was then that it happened. He felt a twinge of something deep inside of him and knew that in that instant, things were different somehow. As he looked at her delicate features and the spray of freckles on her face, he began to think about one thing...and one thing only.

Kissing her.

The moment the thought entered his mind, he knew that he would do just that. Almost involuntarily, he found himself leaning towards her with his eyes locked on hers. Emma was looking back at him and he noticed how blue her eyes were. How had that detail escaped him up until this very moment? He found it difficult to look away and felt his body moving toward her slowly. Had he been less confused by his thoughts at the moment, he would have noticed that Emma's expression was one of confusion and surprise. But he didn't notice. His body was on auto-pilot, thinking of one things only – that of kissing her.

He reached up gently and tucked a loose strand of hair behind her ear. She shuddered slightly, but he felt it and knew in that instant if he were to kiss her, she would kiss him back. Knowing she would respond to him was all encouragement he required. He neared her lips and gently closed his eyes. Then, something broke through them. Emma was shivering, or so he thought.

"What's that?" He asked.

"What?" Emma pulled back and looked around dazed. "What's what?"

"There! That buzzing!" Andy looked around the room, trying to determine where the sound was coming from.

"What? Oh...." Emma leaned back and pulled her cell phone out of the pocket of her jeans. *Dammit*, she thought. *This better be important.* She grabbed the phone out of her pocketbook and flipped it open without looking at the caller id.

"Hello?"

Andy leaned back while Emma answered the phone. He reached for the glass of wine in front of him but flinched when her cell phone hit the table. He looked up at Emma and gasped. She was now as white as a ghost.

Then she burst into tears.

"Emma? What is it? What happened?" Andy's voice had gone from concern to near panic since he couldn't seem to get a response out of her.

It took several moments but Emma finally managed to look up at Andy. She wiped the tears from her cheeks with the back of her hand. "That was my dad. He thinks my mother had a heart attack."

He stood up, grabbed her purse with one hand and Emma's hand with the other. "Come on. Let's go."

Numbly, she followed as he led her outside to his car.

The tears streamed down her face as they drove the twenty minutes to the hospital. Andy pulled in front of the hospital and she jumped out. "I'll meet you in there!" He yelled, as she ran into the emergency room.

She located a nurse who told her where her mother was located and then found her father outside the room, waiting while the doctor's spoke with her mother.

"Dad? Where's mom?" Seeing him point to the room beside him, she asked. "Why aren't you in there?"

He looked at her and she saw the smile. "She kicked me out. Told me to come out here and wait for you. Marjorie's not ready to give up control just yet. Even when having a heart attack, she's got to be running the show." Walter turned and hugged his daughter. "We're not losing her yet, baby girl."

At the sound of those words, Emma nearly collapsed. Her mother was her backbone and they had become closer and closer lately. Emma simply couldn't bear it if she were to lose her.

As her father released her, he looked up and saw Andy walk up behind Emma. He quickly glanced at his daughter and then extended his hand to Andy. "How are you, son?"

"Fine, sir. How is Mrs. Stewart?"

Walter nodded. "She gave us quite a scare there for awhile, but I think she's going to be just fine."

"Dad, what happened?"

Walter looked at his daughter and saw his own fear reflected in her eyes. He hugged her again, trying to erase the pain he saw. "I'm not really sure, honey. She was out in the garden checking her plants. She came in complaining of some indigestion. She took some antacid pills but it never seemed to go away. A bit later, she said her arm felt funny so I thought I'd better take her in. We brought her here and they immediately admitted her. Based on the look of things, it was a mild one, if it was a heart attack at all."

Emma leaned in and hugged her father again. "Oh, Dad. I'm so sorry this happened." She pulled back and looked at him. "Can we see her?"

"The doctor's in there now, but I think we'll be able to go in there in just a few minutes."

Emma nodded. "Okay."

She looked up at Andy, almost as though she'd forget he was with her. "Oh, God. Andy. I'm so sorry about all this-"

"Emma," he said, as he touched her hand. "I'm staying here with you for as long as you need me."

He wasn't asking to stay; he was telling her he was going to be there for her. She was so moved by that simple statement that she felt her throat tighten with emotion and all she could do was nod.

After several moments, the door to her mother's room opened and a woman wearing a white coat stepped out of the room. Her white coat was worn over green scrubs and Emma assumed she was the cardiac specialist on staff.

"Mr. Stewart?" She asked.

Walter looked up at her expectantly. "Yes?"

She extended her hand to him. "I'm Dr. Monroe. I'm the cardiologist taking care of your wife."

Walter nodded. "How is she?" He asked, swallowing hard.

"Stronger than most, I have to say," she said, chuckling. "She's going to be just fine."

Emma saw her father visibly relax at hearing those words and again felt a pang of envy knowing how close her parents were. Once again, she longed for that lifelong commitment with someone. Given the events of this evening, however, for the first time ever, her feelings of longing were mixed with just a tiny sprinkle of hope. But she brushed those thoughts from her mind. She couldn't think of anything right now other than the health of her mother. She waited for the doctor to continue.

"Mrs. Stewart suffered a very mild heart attack. She's lucky she noticed the symptoms. Most people tend to disregard the symptoms when they are so mild, thinking it's only indigestion. Luckily, the two of you did not. I'm going to review diet and nutrition with the both of you and speak to you about getting a bit more exercise. We're going to keep her here for a couple of days, just to monitor her and run a few tests. I don't believe there will be any permanent damage but I'd like to run some tests just to confirm. After that, she'll be able to go home, provided you follow the guidelines I'm going to review with you. Does that sound all right?"

"Yes. It sounds very good. Thank you. Thank you so much." Walter reached for her hand and shook it enthusiastically, causing the stethoscope around her neck to wobble. Emma placed her hand on her father's shoulder.

"Easy, dad. Let's not take her arm off."

Walter chuckled out of embarrassment. "Sorry. I'm just so grateful."

The doctor nodded and smiled as she looked at Emma. "It's okay. I get that a lot when I'm delivering good news. And you're welcome, Mr. Stewart. But I didn't really do anything. Your wife is the strong one in there."

"She certainly is." He was beaming. "Can we go in and see her now?"

"Of course. I'll check in with you tomorrow." Emma watched for a moment as Dr. Monroe walked down the hall and disappeared around the corner. She followed her father into her mother's room.

Emma wasn't sure what she was expecting but it certainly wasn't what she saw when she walked into the room. Other than being a little disheveled from being poked and prodded all night, she looked completely normal. Normal, that is, with the exception of ....well, something. Emma just wasn't quite sure what it was. She watched as her father walked over to the side of the bed and gently took his wife's hand and leaned over to kiss her cheek. Marjorie looked up at Walter with the tenderness and love that had always been there, but there was something else as well. As her father stood up, Emma saw the look in her mother's face as she looked up at her father. It was just for a moment and then it was gone but Emma saw it nonetheless.

It was vulnerability. Emma hadn't recognized it initially because she'd never seen it before on Marjorie Stewart's face. For as long as Emma could remember, her mother was the strength of the family. Now, it was a though she was faced with her own mortality which allowed her vulnerability to seep out, even if just for a little while. Emma was seeing her parents as the couple they were rather than only as her parents and it touched her deeply. It was oddly comforting to her and yet, she felt that pang of envy once again. She had always known her mother to be strong and independent but now she knew that the core of their relationship was that they depended on each other, their roles changing as their needs did.

Emma walked over to the opposite side of the bed and kissed her mother on the cheek. "You gave us quite a scare, you know."

In an instant, the strong, independent Marjorie had returned. "Pfft. Heart attack. What do they know? I'm still not entirely convinced it was a heart attack. It sure felt like indigestion to me!"

Emma sighed. "Mom. It was mild, but it was a heart attack."

"Well, if you say so." She looked past Emma and saw Andy lingering by the doorway. "Andrew! What are you doing over there? Come over here and let me see you! It's been too long." She glanced back at Emma with a knowing look in her eyes that Emma chose to ignore. She was riddled with uncertainty so there was no point in even acknowledging her mother's pointed look.

Andy took a few steps closer to the bed. "Hi Mrs. Stewart. I hope I'm not intruding. I was at Emma's place when Mr. Stewart called and thought it would be best if I drove her here."

Marjorie waved her hand as though to dismiss what he'd said. "Of course you're not intruding. It's always nice to see you. I just wish it were under better circumstances. So Andrew…you say you were at Emma's apartment this evening?" Once again, she glanced at Emma and smirked. Emma once again chose to ignore and simply looked in the other direction and rolled her eyes at Andy, trying to communicate to him to simply ignore her mother. Of course, he was far too polite to ignore her attempt at subtlety.

"Yes, ma'am. We went to a movie tonight."

"A movie, you say." Marjorie raised one eyebrow and looked at her husband. "Walter, Emma and Andrew went to a movie. Isn't that nice?"

Emma was immensely grateful for her father, who was oblivious to all the tension in the room and unable to follow Marjorie's leading question. "Splendid! Did you see anything interesting?" He asked.

Marjorie sighed and muttered under her breath. She spoke before either Emma or Andrew were able to answer Walter's question. "Walter, dear, did they say when they were going to free me?"

He chuckled. "Marji, you make it sound like it's jail. But the Doctor said they would keep you here *resting* for a day or so."

She sighed. "Well, I guess I can stay for a day. But I don't need to rest."

"Mom," Emma chimed in. "You need to follow the doctor's orders and she said you needed to rest. Got it?"

"Now don't you take that tone with me," Marjorie joked. "But fine. I'll do what the doctor said only so that I can set a good example for you."

Emma laughed and looked up at Andy standing by the end of the bed. Andy was looking down at her mother and laughing along with her. He took her breath away. She quickly looked away, unwilling to reveal her emotions despite what had happened – or nearly happened- at her apartment earlier.

What was that, anyway? For a moment, she felt certain Andy was going to kiss her. But surely, that wasn't the case. How much wine had she had anyway? She tried to recall but her mind was full of worry for her mother and wasn't able to think clearly.

Besides, she didn't even want to think about the possibility that Andy was going to kiss her. She couldn't allow herself to go in to the arena of possibility.

She turned her attention back to her mother and pulled a chair over to sit beside the bed. "I'm so glad you're going to be all right, mom. I don't know what I'd do-" She was unable to finish.

"Shhhhhhh," Marjorie said, as she took her daughter's hand in her own. "Now don't you worry, dear. I'm not going anywhere. Not for some time yet. There are some things I need to see to completion before I'm ready to leave this earth." Emma looked up at her mother and watched as she surreptitiously glanced toward Andy and then back to her daughter.

Emma grinned slightly and realized she felt better. If her mother was busy making googley-eyes at her, she was going to be just fine.

They spent a few hours at the hospital – enough time for it to sink in that her mother was going to be all right. During the drive back to her apartment, Emma and Andy were silent, save for the sound of Emma's tears which were accompanied by the occasional sniffle and hiccup. Andy, unsure of what to do, simply drove in silence, his eyes focused on the road.

Emma stared out the window, letting the tears fall. Truthfully, she wasn't even sure herself why she was crying so she was glad that Andy didn't ask.

When they reached Emma's apartment building, Andy pulled into a spot and turned off the engine.

"Emma, I'm so sorry this happened. Are you okay?" He asked, turning in his seat to look at her.

"Yes. I don't know why I'm crying, though. I mean, she's going to be fine! I'm such a blubbering idiot." She wiped her eyes with the tissue she'd been clenching in her hands.

"Come on. Let's get you inside." Andy opened his door and then walked around to her side to help her out. She walked slowly up the steps to her apartment and then let them in. Andy shut the door behind them and turns to see Emma collapse on the couch. He walked over and sat down beside her, his hand resting on the top of the couch behind her.

"Hey," he whispered. "You okay?"

Emma looks up at him. "I think so. I'm just so tired. I need to get some sleep so I can get back there in the morning."

Andy nodded, then lifted his hand from behind the couch to wipe a stray tear from her cheek. "Do you want me to pick you up in the morning? We can head over to see your mom together?"

"You don't have to do that. Besides, don't you have to work?"

"I think I can take a sick day for this."

She paused before answering. While she hated to have Andy miss a day of work on her account, she realized it would be nice to be chauffeured around by him and not having to focus any attention on driving. All her energy could be focused on her parents and getting them through this. "All right. Thanks."

Andy, for just a moment, looked as though he wanted to say something, of that Emma was almost sure. She looked at him, waiting for him to speak but instead he nodded, then stood up and walked to the door.

He opened the door and paused, looking back at her. "Get some sleep, okay? And lock this behind me."

She grinned at him. "Okay, *dad.*"

He smiled at her; then walked out of the apartment, closing the door softly behind him.

Emma stared at the door for several moments after he'd gone. She was confused, to say the least. What was it exactly that had happened earlier? She felt certain Andy was going to kiss her. *What the hell was going on?* She wondered what would have happened if her phone hadn't rung. *But it did,* she told herself. And now her mother was in the hospital. Emma knew that in all likelihood, her mother would make a full and complete recovery, but until then, whatever had happened (*or was going to happen,* she told herself) would have to wait.

She couldn't believe she had just thought that, but it was the truth. Until she knew for certain her mother was going to be okay, this *thing, whatever it was,* would have to be put on the back burner.

Emma heaved herself off the couch, deadbolted the door to her apartment, and went to bed. Bed, yes. Sleep, no. Much to her dismay, she found her mind to be swimming with thoughts of Andy. She also found that if she dug deep inside of her, she was suddenly full of hope, something she never thought possible. For the first time in a very long time, she fell asleep with a smile on her face.

Chapter 18

The next morning, Emma showered and got herself ready. Andy was there right before nine o'clock so that they could get to the hospital in time for visiting hours. When they got there, they found Marjorie sitting up in bed holding Walter's hand. As Emma walked into the room, she noticed that her mother, aside from the bleakness of the hospital room, looked as comfortable as if she were in her own bed. Emma immediately felt relief wash over her.

She sat down on the edge of the bed and took her mother's free hand.

"How are you, mom?"

"I'd be much better if I wasn't attached to all this machinery."

Emma rolled her eyes. "Mom, you had a heart attack. The doctor's need to monitor your vitals."

Marjorie looked behind Emma and saw Andy standing in the doorway. She leaned over a bit to say hello.

"Hello, Andrew."

"Hello, Mrs. Stewart. You're looking well."

"Thank you dear. And thank you for bringing Emma to me. I already feel much better."

"I'm glad to do it." Marjorie noticed that he looked over at Emma as he spoke at smiled gently at her. She noticed something different in his eyes that only confirmed what she had guessed at last night. That boy had feelings for her daughter! It was about time, she thought, smiling. She turned her gaze toward Emma, hoping to find some answers but found none. She was simply sitting beside her, looking at her with concern. Marjorie for only an instant wondered if Emma's feelings for Andy had changed but she swiftly put those thoughts out of her mind. She knew that her daughter had been in love with Andrew for too long to simply have those feelings vanish. Marjorie figured Emma was probably too worried about her condition to focus on what may or may not be happening with Andrew. She knew she needed to rectify that situation quickly.

Turning to Emma, she said. "You know I'm going to be fine, don't   you?
There's no reason for you to look so worried."

Emma shrugged. "Oh, I'm not worried. I know you'll be all right."

Marjorie chuckled. "Now don't start lying to your mother. You know I can read you better than anyone else." She patted her hand. "You father is here with me now and I need to speak with him. Why don't you and Andy go and get something to eat?"

Emma didn't look or feel like going to get something to eat but to placate her mother, she shrugged. "I guess I could grab a coffee or something. Does that sound okay with you?" She asked, looking back towards Andy.

"Sure." He replied.

"Okay, mom. We're going to head to the cafeteria but if you need anything. Just call my cell."

"I'll be fine, dear. You run along."

Walter sat beside the bed and took his wife's hand. "Now what was that all about? She just got here and you're shoo-ing her out?"

Marjorie looked over at him and raised one eyebrow.

Seeing her look, Walter broke into a huge grin. "Now, Marji, what do you have up your sleeve?"

"There's something going on between those two and I'm going to do everything I can to make sure it continues. Nothing like a good cup of coffee when you're getting to know someone."

Walter looked at his wife, bewildered, and then looked toward the now closed door. "Emma and Andrew? Surely not."

Marjorie patted his hand affectionately. "Oh, Walter. You can be so obtuse sometimes. That's just one of the many reasons I love you so much. But I can tell you with absolute certainty....there is something brewing between those two and I couldn't be happier about it."

* * *

Emma sat at a table in the corner of the hospital cafeteria, staring at the far wall. Andy was pouring them their coffee and glanced back at Emma and frowned as he noticed the look in her eyes. They'd been friends for so long that he knew her emotions practically better than his own. As much as she tried to hide it, Emma was worried and that concerned Andy and at the same time confused him. While he had always had a concern for her well-being, this was something altogether different. He felt...*protective* of her. It was as though he wanted to shield her from anything that might harm her.

Andy frowned. They'd been friends for so long that it seemed natural to help her as he'd done over the past several weeks. But during that time, his feelings had changed into something different. He couldn't quite figure out what he was feeling, only that he felt a need to make sure she was okay. Of course, he knew she would be. Emma had always been fine on her own, but he worried that without Layne by her side, she'd need someone to talk to and he was glad to be that person.

But there was something else, he thought, that was more than protectiveness. He looked at her across the cafeteria and felt his pulse quicken. It startled him and made him quickly glance away, afraid that his emotions were displayed on his face. Surely he didn't have *those* feelings for her. That just couldn't be right. He and Emma were friends. They were spending time together because it was comfortable and they had a lot in common. They enjoyed spending time with each other; that was all. Or was it?

He knew he wanted to kiss her last night but felt certain that today, things would return to normal and the feelings he had would have passed. He glanced back at her discreetly, careful to make it appear as though he were engrossed in mixing the coffee. As he looked at her, a thought occurred to him – Emma was a very attractive woman. But then again, he'd always thought she was, in that friend-of-my-wife sort of way. He looked at her again, not caring about being caught and felt his pulse quicken once again. She was most definitely attractive with her long blond hair and sky-blue eyes. She was thin but not the anorexia thin that some other women he knew favored. Emma had curves, although she she them behind her t-shirts, but he had noticed them. He frowned. It seemed he was noticing lots about Emma lately.

She was attractive, certainly. But Andy realized whatever these feelings were he had for her stemmed from more than her being pretty. What really made her more attractive to him was getting to know her; learning about how she felt about her family and the children she taught. These past few weeks he'd gotten to know her much more than ever before and what he was feeling with this new knowledge was only making him want to get to know her better. He felt drawn to her in a way that he'd never been before.

He'd definitely been drawn to her the night before. What was that, anyway? He felt certain that if the phone hadn't rung when it did, he would have kissed her. He saw each and every one of those freckles and had wanted to kiss each one individually and give them the attention they were entitled to. Come to think of it, he'd wanted to do more than just kiss her. He frowned. What would that have done to their friendship? He certainly didn't want to ruin this. He enjoyed spending time with Emma and didn't want that to change.

He picked up the coffees and turned to look at Emma. As he did, he felt a tightening of his heart and frowned. He knew he was feeling something much more than friendship for her and wasn't sure what to do about it. What if she didn't feel the same? He tried to recall the look in her eyes the night before and felt certain that she knew he was going to kiss her. He also thought she would have kissed him back. But what if she had only been caught up in the moment?

He couldn't think about this now. What Emma needed right now was a friend to help her through the situation with Marjorie. She certainly didn't need a complication like this. He nodded. He knew that his feelings for Emma, whatever they were, would have to be put aside.

Andy walked over to Emma's table and sat down across from her. "Are you all right?"

She nodded. "I think so. I mean, I am. I'm just a bit worried. My mom seems to be back to her old self but she did have a heart attack, however mild it might have been. I'm worried I'm going to lose her."

Her voice caught as she spoke and Emma found herself holding back tears. Andy reached over and took her hand in his. She felt the warmth there and for just a moment, her mind wandered back to the previous night. Would he have kissed her if her phone hadn't rung? She pushed the thought away. She couldn't think about this now. She needed to focus on her mother and make sure that everything was going to be okay with her. She realized Andy was still holding her hand. She looked up at him and watched her hand disappear into both of his. He held her hand tight within his own.

"Whatever you need, Emma. You just tell me, okay?"

"Okay," she whispered. She left her hand in Andy's, enjoying the warm and safe feeling it provided and sipped her coffee with her free hand.

They finished their coffee in silence and then headed back to her mother's room only to find her directing her husband around the room as though they were on vacation rather than in a hospital room. Emma couldn't help but chuckle as she watched her father change the channel and adjust the volume on the TV to her mother's liking. Actually, on closer inspection, her father seemed to actually *enjoy* being told what to do. As she watched, she Emma realized that her mother's bossiness was so typically Marjorie that it gave her father comfort to have some semblance of normalcy. To him, it indicated that she was, in fact, going to get better and return to their life at home.

Seeing her mother acting more and more like her old self pleased Emma beyond words and after a couple of hours, Emma felt comfortable enough to head home free from worry. The doctor had visited once again and told all of them that Marjorie would be released the following day.

Emma gave her father a kiss on the cheek and leaned over the hospital bed to give her mother a hug, telling her that she would see her the next day. Andy shook hands with her father and then leaned over to give Marjorie a kiss on the check. As her mother turned her head to receive his peck on the cheek, she winked at Emma causing her to roll her eyes. There was a look in her mother's eye that told her they'd be having a discussion once things were back to normal. Emma knew there would be no way to avoid it; she only hoped she could postpone the inevitable until she knew what was going on. Right now? She had no idea.

Emma walked out of the room with Andy trailing behind, not willing to give her mother the opportunity to have her alone for even the briefest of moments. She breathed a sigh of relief knowing she'd escaped, but only for the time being.

As they settled into Andy's car, he turned to her.

"You hungry?" He asked.

Emma nodded as she buckled her seat belt. "Absolutely. That coffee just didn't cut it for me."

"Okay, then," Andy replied as he started the engine. He put the car into reverse and placed his arm behind Emma's seat as he eased the car out of the spot. "Pizza?"

Emma smiled at him. "That would be great."

Emma called in their order to a place that was on the way home. When they got there, Andy got out of the car and ran in to get the pizza, telling her to stay put. He came back out and placed the pizza in the back seat. For the three or so minutes it took them to get to Emma's apartment, the scent of pepperoni and cheese tormented them.

"I didn't realize I was so hungry until I smelled that," Emma said.

Andy grinned at her. "I know." They arrived at Emma's and he parked the car. "I'll get the pizza. You get your keys."

She laughed, realizing they were both starving.

* * *

Not very much later, the cardboard pizza box sat empty on the coffee table, save for a few crumbs. Andy and Emma had devoured the entire pizza with Emma holding her own at three pieces to Andy's five. She leaned back against the couch and rubbed her stomach.

"That was delicious. I need to put their number in my cell so I can call them at a moment's notice."

"I wouldn't do that if I were you. You'll be calling them every day! And that can get expensive for those of you that can't...I mean won't cook."

She looked up at him and smiled when she saw the crooked grin on his face. She picked up the pillow from behind her and swatted him on the shoulder. "You know, we all have our talents. Mine just isn't cooking."

"I know. Believe me, I know..." He ducked just in time to miss getting another swat with the pillow.

Emma placed the pillow back down on the couch. She sat silent for a moment, thinking about her mother and all that had transpired. The smile that was on her face only moments ago was now gone. When she looked at Andy again, her expression was quite serious. Andy sensed the change in her mood and looked back at her, somewhat fearful of what he might see.

His eyebrows came together in a frown. "Emma? What's wrong?"

She shrugged. "Nothing," she replied. "It's just…well…"

Andy was getting worried as he watched Emma stumble over her words. "What is it?" He urged.

"Thanks for….well, everything."

Andy shook his head. "Don't thank me. I didn't do anything."

"Yes. You did. You drove me to the hospital when my father called me. There's no way I could have driven. You picked me up today, drove me there…drove me home. I really appreciate it."

He leaned forward slightly, a tiny grin on his face. "You're welcome. But you don't need to thank me. That's what friends are for."

Once he said the word 'friend,' he frowned slightly. Is that what he wanted? What about the other night? Once again the image of Emma closing her eyes and waiting for him to kiss her played over in his mind. He felt his pulse quicken and wondered again what it would be like to kiss her.

The playful banter that had been between them only moments before had vanished. Now, there was something between them…a question that each wanted to ask but was afraid to do so. Emma sensed it. She could feel the change in the room as well as she could feel the couch beneath her. She looked up into Andy's eyes and saw that something had changed. He was looking at her now differently than he'd ever done so before. Emma's heart began to pound loudly in her ears and she felt her pulse begin to race. She was locked into his eyes and found herself leaning toward Andy as he leaned towards her. Ever so gently, their lips met. Hesitantly at first, as though each of them were unsure of the other's response.

She felt his hand reach around to the back of her neck; his fingers weaved their way into her hair. The feeling was so sensual that Emma felt chills run down her spine. Andy pulled her closer to him in order to deepen the kiss. There was still some part of her that felt as though this was some sort of dream she was in but when she felt him pull her closer to him, she realized it was true. Almost instinctively, her hands reached up and wrapped themselves around his neck. Wanting desperately to touch more of him, she moved her hands down across the expanse of his chest and then around his waist. His shirt was untucked in the back so she gently slipped a finger underneath the soft cotton and caressed the skin just above his waistband.

He groaned and pulled her even closer. Her hands moved inside of his shirt and up his back, feeling the strength there. Pulling him closer to her she opened her mouth and allowed his tongue to have free reign. As she felt his tongue wrestle with hers, she was lost. Her breathing became ragged and he tugged at her mouth until she felt swollen.

Almost as soon as it began, it was over. He pulled away, gasping for air, and looked at her. "What the hell was that and why haven't we ever done that before?"

She realized that her hands were still wrapped around him. Seeing his reaction to their kiss, for the first time in her life, Emma felt bold. "I don't know but we need to do it many, many more times."

Andy could only nod as he leaned in to kiss her again...and again...

Chapter 19

Andy picked Emma up at her apartment early the next morning. Although Walter was going to drive Marjorie home, Emma wanted to be sure that she understood all the instructions that Marjorie would need to follow. She only hoped that her mother's attention would be focused on getting out of the hospital and heading home rather than on Emma and Andy. She knew it was a long shot, though, since she hadn't been able to stop smiling since the events of the night before.

Emma thought back to the previous night and the hour or so her and Andy spent kissing on her couch before moving to the bedroom. Once there, they'd spent hours exploring each other's bodies until finally they fell asleep in each other's arms. Andy had gone home very early in the morning only because he didn't want to show up at the hospital with the same clothes on as the previous day. Emma smiled as she thought of Andy trying to get dressed in the darkness of her bedroom.

Emma was ecstatic. She had loved Andy for so long but she'd never allowed herself to hope that this might happen. They were a couple. The transition from friends to couple had been seamless without any of the awkward 'are you seeing anyone else' conversations. They were both of the same mindset and they knew this because they'd been friends for so long. Much too long, in Emma's mind. But she had to be thankful. Had they not been friends for so long, perhaps things wouldn't have worked out as they now appeared to be. Yes, she was absolutely thrilled and there was no way of hiding it.

Which of course, posed another entirely different problem…her mother. She knew the minute her mother laid eyes on her, she would know that things had changed between her and Andy. It wasn't that she didn't' want everyone to know – she wanted to shout it from every rooftop around – she just wasn't' ready to discuss it with her mother. She just needed a little time to become accustomed to this new relationship with Andy.

After greeting Andy with a kiss at the door, they left for the hospital. Emma couldn't help but be amazed at how easy their relationship was. She leaned in to kiss him as though she'd done it for years.

They arrived at the Marjorie's room just as she was sitting down into the wheelchair. Walter was standing beside his wife with a worried look on his face. Emma, seeing his expression, hurried to his side.

"Dad?" She asked. "Is everything okay?"

He looked at her, confusion all over his face. "What? Oh yes, honey. I'm just making sure your mother is comfortable."

"Walter, I'm fine!" Marjorie looked over at Emma. "Would you tell your father that I'm fine? I just need to be in my own house. Well, hello Andrew. How nice to see you ."

Emma couldn't help but notice the tone in her mother's voice. She knew. Of course she knew. Marjorie Stewart didn't miss a thing.

"Emma, you didn't tell me Andrew was coming today."

Andy jumped in. "I hope it's all right Mrs. Stewart. I thought I'd bring Emma in so she wouldn't have to drive."

Marjorie waved her hand as though shoo-ing his words away. "Andrew, dear. Of course it's okay that you're here. I'm just surprised that Emma didn't mention it to me." She looked pointedly at her daughter.

She couldn't hide her happiness and grinned stupidly at her mother, which told her all she needed to know.

Marjorie nodded. "Well, then. Let's get this show on the road."

Once Marjorie was safely loaded into her father's Buick, Emma and Andy walked to his car so they could follow her parents to their house.

Andy reached for Emma's hand. "So, what was that all about?"

"What was what all about?" Emma replied, feigning ignorance.

He poked her in the shoulder. "Don't pretend you don't know what I'm talking about! That look between you and your mother! And that sing-songy tone she used with me!"

Emma felt the color come to her cheeks. "Oh, god. You noticed that? What can I say?" She shrugged. "Nothing gets past Marjorie."

The knowledge of what Emma was referring to his Andy

suddenly. "Oh! So you mean…"

Emma nodded. "Yup. She knows about this." She motioned to their intertwined hands.

"Well, does she know about this?" Andy asked, as he pulled Emma into a hug and kissed her full on the lips.

"I'm sure she's staring at us right now."

Andy leaned her back and kissed her deeply. "Then we need to make sure she gets an eyeful."

Emma giggled as she kissed him back, wrapping her arms around his shoulders. She knew she'd never been happier and truthfully, didn't really care who knew. This was heaven.

They arrived at Emma's parent's house shortly after her parents and helped Marjorie into the house, despite her protests that she could manage on her own. Once she was settled onto the couch, she patted the cushion beside her and motioned for Emma to sit down beside her. Emma rolled her eyes as she looked at Andy and then sat down beside her mother.

"Walter, why don't you and Andy take a walk outside and see how my garden is doing? I haven't been able to tend to it in, what, three days?"

Walter, who remained completely oblivious to Marjorie's intentions, turned to Andy. "What do you say, son? Care to help me inspect the garden?"

"Sure," he replied. Turning to Emma, he said. "I'll be back in a bit."

Emma replied with an eye roll.

Once Walter and Andy had closed the door behind them, Marjorie turned to Emma. "So….," she said.

Emma, who was enjoying the fact that her mother didn't know the entire situation, feigned innocence. "So…what?" She replied.

"Don't pretend you don't know what I'm asking," Marjorie said, waggling a finger at her daughter. "It's obvious to anyone who is within fifty yards of the two of you that something is going on. Now," she said, patting Emma's thigh. "Talk to your mother."

Emma grinned and released a mock sigh, placing the back of her hand to her forehead. "Oh, all right. I'm caving with all this cross-examination." She paused for effect. "I will just say that you're assumption is correct. Andy and I are together."

Marjorie grinned and Emma thought she might have heard a

squeal. "I knew it!" She said, clasping her hands together in front of her. "I knew he would realize sooner or later that you were the girl for him! Didn't I tell you?"

Emma rolled her eyes. "Yes, mom. You did mention that a time or two."

"Well, I'm just glad it didn't take too long," she said, reaching over to pat Emma's thigh once more.

Emma frowned slightly. "You don't think it's too quick, do you? I mean, Andy and Layne split up less than a year ago."

"Sweetheart, when it's meant to be, it's meant to be. You and Andy are meant for each other. Don't doubt your feelings or his, for that matter, simply because of something as silly as time. I think you and I both know that his marriage was never going to work."

Emma shrugged. "I guess you're right."

"Of course, I am!" Marjorie said. "Have you ever known me to be wrong when it comes to matters of the heart?"

"Absolutely not," Emma replied, leaning over to give her mother a hug. "I'm just so glad you're home."

Marjorie felt the tightness of her daughter's arms around her and knew how afraid she had been. "Now don't you worry about me. I'm not going anywhere."

"Promise?" Emma said, pulling back to look at her mother.

"Promise." Marjorie replied, placing a hand on her daughter's cheek. "I still have lots to see and do. One of them being seeing you walk down the aisle in a beautiful white dress!"

Emma felt the color rush to her cheeks. "Oh my god. Mom! Don't rush it or anything. Sheesh!"

Over her shoulder, Emma heard the sound of the back door open and close. Her father and Andy walked into the living room. Andy looked at her and raised his eyebrows. Emma smiled, indicating everything was fine.

As they left Emma's parents house, Andy couldn't help but ask. "So what was all that about...with your mom, I mean."

Emma looked at him and grinned. "Oh, you know my mother. She was just being nosy."

"Really? About what?" Andy was grinning and sneaking glances at Emma while driving.

Emma looked at him sideways and noticed his grin. "Ha ha ha.. What do you think?" She said, sarcastically.

For a moment, Andy looked concerned. "Well, is she okay with this?"

"Oh my god. Are you kidding?" Emma placed her head in her hands. "She's thrilled!"

Andy reached over and placed his hand on Emma's knee, squeezing it gently. "Well, I am too," he said as he looked at her briefly.

Emma placed her hand on top of his. "Me too," she said. "Me too." She rested her head against the back of the seat and turned slightly to look at Andy's profile. *How did this happen?* She thought, smiling.

* * *

As Emma and Andy spent more time together over the next few weeks, they became closer and closer. Slowly, Emma got over her concern that things had happened too quickly and that they might be rushing things. Her ease with Andy and his with hers quickly erased any fears she might have had. They seemed to slide so easily into their relationship that Emma had trouble remembering a time when they were just friends.

They settled into a routine where they would meet at her place each night after work, since she got off work before he did. She would do her part for dinner and slice of vegetables for a salad and Andy would cook the main entrée later on in the evening. They both knew Emma was dangerous in the kitchen, so unless they were ordering a pizza, Andy took care of their dinner. This routine suited Emma just fine. It was comfortable and she couldn't be happier.

On the weekends, they did mainly what they'd done in the past. They'd have coffee at Starbuck's on Sunday mornings and maybe catch a movie on Saturday and either eat out or grab something to take home. Occasionally, they'd make a trip to Lowe's or Home depot to purchase something one of them needed for their apartment and conversations had begun regarding moving in together. Things were moving along at at a pace that suited their history of a three year friendship. It seemed that once they'd made the leap from friends to lovers, there was no slowing them down. At times, they both felt as though they were making up for lost time.

Marjorie had been home now for well over a month and was

recovering beautifully. Of course, she still disagreed that she needed to recover from anything. Emma and Andy tried to visit at least once a week just to see how she was doing. Andy knew that Emma still had some leftover worry from her mother's time spent in the hospital and wanted to make sure her fears were alleviated as much as possible.

One Saturday, nearly two months after Marjorie's release from the hospital, Andy and Emma visited for the afternoon. As they drove back to Emma's apartment, they decided to stop at Murphy's to grab something to eat. They decided to get their dinner to go rather than stay and eat in the normally crowded restaurant. They were both perfectly content to pick up take out on their way home and eat it while sharing a bottle of wine in front of Emma's TV. It had become sort of a routine over the last month and Emma relished every minute of it. There was not a single day that went by where she didn't think about how happy she was. She was completely and utterly in love with a man who loved her back and the feeling was wonderful.

They pulled into Murphy's and Andy found a spot near the front, which was surprising since there were people milling about outside the front of the restaurant, seemingly waiting for their table. As she moved to get out of the car, Emma glanced over at the grocery store and realized she needed a few things.

"I'm going to run over to the store and pick up a few things. I'll meet you inside in just a few minutes." She lifted up onto her tip toes and met Andy's lips for a quick kiss, once again relishing in the fact that this was now both a normal and frequent occurrence in her life.

"Okay. See you in a few." Andy walked toward the entrance of Murphy's and Emma headed toward the grocery store. She went in and picked up the few items she needed. As she was walking toward the front of the store, she noticed a display of wine. Within it was one of Andy's favorites. Smiling, she picked up a bottle and then continued on her way to the checkout area. She paid for her items and walked across the parking lot to Murphy's, carrying her plastic grocery bag. Weaving her way in between the throngs of people, she finally located Andy inside sitting on the bench waiting for their order. As she approached, she looked at him and rolled her eyes. "Gosh, I'm so glad we got this to go. I can't stand it when it's crowded like this."

As he rose to greet her, she slipped an arm around her waist and gave a gently squeeze. "Me too. Besides, it's so much nicer at 'La Stewart's.'," he said, winking at her.

The woman behind the counter called their number and Andy pulled out his wallet and handed over his debit card. "Is there any of that merlot left at your place or did we finish it all?"

"We finished it," Emma said. "But I just picked up another bottle." She lifted her plastic bag in order to indicate its contents.

He smiled at her. "Excellent."

Andy grabbed the bag of to-go food and turned to leave. "You ready?"

Emma nodded. "Uh-huh. Let's go."

Andy reached behind him to place his wallet back into his jeans pocket then reached for Emma's hand to lead her through the crowd. Suddenly, he stopped, causing Emma to look up at him, confused.

Andy was staring straight ahead with a frown on his face. Emma followed his gaze and when she realized what he was looking at, she gasped.

Layne and Brad were coming through the door, arm in arm and giggling like teenagers. Emma could tell by her glassy eyes, wide grin and slow movements that Layne had been drinking.

Emma hoped that they'd be able to walk past the couple without being seen but that was not going to be the case. Layne laughed obscenely loud at something Brad had whispered in her ear and threw her head back, tossing her long auburn locks over her shoulder in a way that was both seductive and clearly rehearsed, although it was only Emma who knew she'd spent hours perfecting the move. She looked around the room, trying to determine if there was a way for her and Andy to leave the restaurant without being seen by the couple. Since Layne and Brad were directly in front of the door, she realized it would be nearly impossible to avoid a confrontation. Emma felt a rush of panic inside of her. Not only would this be the first time she'd seen Layne since the day she'd stormed out of her apartment, but this would be the first time Layne would realize that Emma was seeing Andy. Emma tried to swallow but found she was unable to as her throat had suddenly become very dry.

Emma watched as Layne lost her balance slightly and stumbled. As she righted herself, her gaze scanned the room almost as if she were looking to see who had seen her stumble. As she glanced around, her eyes locked on Andy. Slowly her eyes narrowed as her mind registered that she was in the same room as her ex-husband. Keeping her eyes locked on Andy's, she slowly began to walk toward him through the crowd. Brad looked at her with a confused look on his face and Emma saw him say something to Layne. Layne simply motioned for him to stay where he was while keeping her gaze locked on Andy. Emma knew by the determined look on Layne's face that this chance meeting was going to get ugly, and quick.

Emma watched as Layne stopped walking forward and for just a moment, she thought Layne might have changed her mind and thought better of a confrontation. A feeling of relief coursed through Emma but then dissipated at quickly as it came. She watched as Layne's gaze traveled from Andy's face down to his hand- which was still holding on to Emma's – and then up to look Emma in the eye. She watched as Layne's face registered the fact that it was Emma who was, in fact, holding on to Andy's hand. Although 'holding it' was putting it mildly since she was clenching it as though it were a life-line. This is exactly what Emma had feared the most. She'd known Layne long enough to know just how mean she could be when she wanted to be. And since she'd never returned any of Emma's phone calls or texts, Emma knew that Layne was far from over what she felt was a huge mistake on Emma's part. In Layne's mind, Emma had not only let her down by cancelling on their date and refusing to cover for her, but she'd broken the most sacred of all the rules of friendship – she'd fallen in love with her best friend's husband. While Emma knew she'd never said or done anything to Andy or anyone regarding her feelings, she knew that Layne still felt betrayed and there was no convincing her otherwise. Emma steeled herself for the encounter and pressed herself a little bit closer to Andy as though trying to gain some strength from him.

Layne's eyes locked on to Emma's and didn't waiver. She stared at Emma and didn't blink for what seemed like minutes. Emma felt herself go cold as she watched Layne's casual smile spread into a sinister grin.

She made her way across the room and stood in front of Andy and Emma. She crossed her arms in front of her and rested her weight on one hip as she looked from one to the other.

"Well, well, well..." she said, glancing from one to the other. "Don't you two look cozy."

Emma felt Andy's hand squeeze her own as though telling her not to worry. She tried to take a deep breath and calm herself but found that her nerves had gotten the better of her. She also found she was unable to speak. Luckily, Andy managed to make an attempt at making an awkward moment bearable.

"Layne. I hope you're doing well." His voice was more formal that Emma would have expected but oddly, the tone of his voice gave Emma a bit of comfort in what was quickly becoming very uncomfortable.

"Hello Andrew," Layne replied. "Yes, actually, I am doing well." She nodded behind her toward Brad. "We're having a great time tonight being OUT. I'm actually shocked to see you out of your apartment. What's the occasion?"

"We're actually just getting some dinner to go. Isn't that right, Emma?" He said, turning to her.

Emma managed to find her voice. "Uh-huh."

Layne managed to tear her gaze away from Andy and rested her gaze on Emma. Emma felt herself becoming very uncomfortable. Her hand, still gripping Andy's, felt slick with perspiration. She silently berated herself for letting Layne have this affect on her.

"I see you didn't waste any time stepping into my shoes. Don't let the body get cold or whatever..." Layne waived her hand around dismissively. "I guess it's what they say, 'with friends like this, who needs enemies?'"

Emma gasped at the venom in Layne's tone. She wanted to explain everything and clear the air but a part of knew nothing she could say would change Layne's opinion of the situation. Somehow, in Layne's mind, Emma had practically stolen Andy away from her, despite the fact that it was Layne who had left the marriage long before Emma had made any sort of step in that direction.

"Layne, I-"

"You know what? I really don't care to hear anything you have to say," Layne interrupted. "God, Emma! You were my best friend! And now you're standing here holding hands with my husband? What kind of person are you?!"

Up until this point, Andy had watched the situation between the two women, gauging if he needed to step in or not. Now he knew it

187

was time. "EX – husband." He said, emphasizing the 'ex.'

Layne stopped and glared at Andy. "What did you say?"

"Ex-husband. We're divorced, remember?"

Layne's eyes narrowed. "Fine. Whatever. An insignificant detail." She pointed her finger at Emma. "It doesn't make any difference. This whole situation is just a little too…too incestuous for me."

"What the hell are you talking about?" Andy asked.

"I'm talking about the fact that my best friend couldn't wait for me to step aside so she could take my place."

"You have GOT to be kidding me. Is that really what you think happened here?" Andy was beyond angry. Color had risen to his cheeks and his voice was getting louder and louder. "Layne, not that it's any of your business, but we didn't even start to see each other until you and I were divorced. Again, not that it's any of your business."

Emma was stunned watching Andy speak to Layne. She'd never seen him this angry before. His normally friendly tone was replaced with one full of disgust. Each word was enunciated through clenched teeth. Truthfully, it made her nervous that he could get so riled up by Layne and it worried her that he still might have feelings for her. She quickly brushed aside those thoughts and focused on the fact that it was her hand he was holding on to.

"None of my business? Really? Well, I happen to know that Emma's feelings ARE my business." She looked at Emma. "Don't you agree? Actually, don't you think we all ought to share how we feel? How we've felt for a loooong time?"

Emma cringed. She wasn't at all ready for Andy to know how much or how long she'd been in love with him and now it was nearly out in the open. Their relationship was so new, so fragile, that she was terrified of anything upsetting the path they were one. She feared that this revelation of Layne's would scare Andy away. After all, if he knew she'd felt this way since…well forever, surely it would make him uncomfortable.

Emma found her voice. "Just leave it alone, Layne."

Although Emma hadn't thought through the logistics of telling how long she'd had feelings for him, she did know that she intended to tell him. Of course, she wanted to wait until she was absolutely certain of his feelings toward her. The thought of someone being in love with you since the moment they first laid eyes on you was a lot of pressure and she didn't want Andy to have any idea she had felt that way since the beginning. Sure, she'd tell him....just not now. And *she* would be the one to tell him – not Layne.

Layne laughed out loud. "Leave it alone? I think you should take your own advice, Emma."

Andy looked from Emma to Layne, confused with their exchange. Emma caught his eye and spoke. "Can we just go?"

"Sure," he replied. "Let's go."

Just then, Brad came up behind Layne and wrapped his arms around her waist. "Everything okay, hon?"

"Everything's just fine," Layne replied, looking right at Emma. "Just trying to clear the air."

He nudged her toward the hostess' stand. "Well, come on then. Let's get to our table before they give away our reservation."

"Excuse me, sir?" A young woman who was clearly one of the wait staff was standing beside Brad with an expectant look on her face. Brad turned to her.

"Yes?"

"Are you the anniversary reservation? Ummmmm...Somerfield?" She dragged her finger down the sheet of paper she held and then looked up at him, waiting for an answer.

Brad, who suddenly looked extremely uncomfortable, stole a glance at Layne, then Emma, and then finally Andy, before nodding discreetly. "Uh...yeah. We'll be right there." He was making every attempt to shoo the girl away but she was having none of it.

"Great! We've got a special dinner for the two of you! Our anniversary customers get nothing but the best!" She was smiling ear to ear and neglected to notice the silence that had befallen the group. Emma was staring at a spot on the floor and hoping it would swallow her up. Brad was fidgeting with Layne's shirt sleeve, trying to get her to follow him. Andy however, was simply standing still, rooted to the spot, staring at Layne.

"Anniversary?" He looked back and forth between them. "What anniversary?"

The hostess was apparently oblivious to the tension and chimed in, ready with an answer to Andy's question. "Yes, sir!" She nodded enthusiastically. "I have here that we've got a one year anniversary celebration!" She looked between the four of them. "Should I change the reservation to four people?"

No one spoke. Andy stood, rooted to his spot as he looked from Brad to Layne.

"Andy, listen-" Layne took a step forward. Almost involuntarily, Andy backed away from her as though he had been scalded.

"Don't." He said. "Let me see if I've got this correct. The two of you have been seeing each other for a year now?"

Layne boldly lifted her chin and looked him directly in the eyes as if to show she had nothing to be ashamed of. When she spoke, however, her voice lacked any of the confidence her body language displayed. "Yes, we have," she whispered.

"Well, then. Allow me to connect the dots here. You began seeing him a year ago…while we were still married." There was no question in Andy's tone so Layne stood silent and let him many his assumptions. She wasn't going to offer anything.

"Look, man-" Brad spoke apologetically but Andy stopped him before he could utter another word.

"This doesn't concern you." He said, between clenched teeth. Turning back to Layne, he continued. "You," he said, pointing a finger at her. "Let me think that I…I failed you in some way." Andy startled Emma by laughing out loud. "That's rich. Only you would think to shift the blame for their own affair on to someone else. Come on, Emma. Let's get out of here."

He held tightly to Emma's hand and pulled her through the crowd. She stole a glance over her shoulder to see Layne and Brad walking into the restaurant, hand in hand.

Chapter 20

Emma followed Andy silently out of Murphy's and into the car. Rather than open the door for her as he usually did, he unlocked the doors using the remote as he stormed to the driver's side of the car. Emma got in to the passenger side of the car and buckled herself in, wishing herself invisible. They drove in silence for several miles. Andy's hands gripped the steering wheel and Emma's were in her lap, clenched tightly.

Finally he spoke. "Don't worry, okay?"

"Okay."

"I'm fine. Really I am. I don't want you to think I have any feelings left for Layne. I'm just pissed that she made me think the divorce was all my fault. I'm willing to share in the blame; I'm just not willing to take all of it." He glanced at her in the passenger seat. "You okay?"

She was. Andy had verbalized exactly what she'd been worrying about – that he still had feelings for Layne. "I'm fine."

"Good." He said, resting his hand on her thigh. They drove for a few more minutes in silence. "I'm starved. How 'bout you?"

The normalcy of the question immediately alleviated the tension Emma felt as a result of running into Layne. She felt herself relax but also knew that a glass or two of wine would help even further. "Starved," she said, placing her hand over Andy's.

Andy pulled into Emma's apartment complex and parked the car. They got out of the car and got their dinner out of the back seat. Emma grabbed the wine and the few items she had gotten at the store while Andy grabbed their dinner. She unlocked the door to the building and then walked up the flight of steps to her apartment with Andy close behind her. Her stomach growled loudly.

"Sheesh! I guess you are hungry!" He said, grinning at her.

Emma looked at him over her shoulder and poked him in the chest playfully. "You betcha. As a matter of fact, I'd set that food out quickly if I were you...."

"Oh, really…that sounds interesting…" He swatted her behind as she opened the door.

Emma giggled and jumped forward at the feel of Andy's hand on her. "I'll get us some wine. You set out the food."

"You got it," he replied.

She walked into the kitchen and opened up the bottle she'd just purchased. She couldn't help but think about their run-in with Layne and Brad. She was relieved, to say the least. Things could have been much worse. Not this first encounter was a picnic by anyone's standards but she knew it could always be worse. She grabbed the two glasses and walked into the living room to find Andy setting out their dinners. He'd already turned on her TV and was channel surfing. Emma smiled, pleased that he was so comfortable at her place. She'd always heard people say that the best relationships started out as friends and she was finding out herself that it was absolutely true. She and Andy were so comfortable with each other even thought they'd only been involved for a few months. Once they'd made the leap into their relationship, it had moved smoothly and at the right speed for the both of them. And if it hadn't? Well, Emma knew that either one of them would talk to the other about it.

Emma placed the two glasses on the table in front of Andy and sat down beside him, curling one leg underneath her. She was relaxed, despite the events of the evening and was glad to see Andy was feeling the same. Even though they'd run into Layne, the night wasn't a total waste. They would still be able to enjoy their evening, eat some dinner and spend some time snuggling on the couch.

Andy reached for the glass and took a sip. "Thanks," he said. "I think I need this. I hate to say it, but running into Layne and Brad was rough."

Emma nodded. "I know. I'm so sorry we had to run into her."

He looked at her sideways and grinned. "You don't have to apologize, Emma. You have nothing to be sorry for. It's not like you did the cheating."

"No. But I still hate that we ran into her at all."

He reached over and squeezed her knee. "Look at it this way. It was going to happen sooner or later and now it's over. We can still enjoy the rest of our evening." He leaned back and continued to channel surf. Emma saw several movies that she would have been happy to watch but Andy just went right past them. He seemed to be thinking of something while flipping through the channels. Sure enough, several moments later he spoke again.

"You know," he said. "It's weird."

"What is," Emma asked.

"I never noticed anything different. I mean, I was married to her. I lived with her. How could I not have known?" He glanced at her out of the corner of his eye while continuing to flip through the channels.

She shrugged. "You probably weren't thinking anything like that could happen."

"No. I wasn't. But still, I should have noticed something, right?"

"I don't know." Emma wasn't sure how to respond to his questions but she wished that he would change the subject...desperately.

"It's odd. I never even had a clue. How did she manage to see him without me knowing? I mean, all she ever did was work and spend time with you." He chuckled softly. "She was with you practically more than she was with me."

Emma's palms were cold and clammy. She rubbed them on her jeans, trying to eliminate the moisture. She released a nervous chuckle, trying to match his. "Yeah."

"I just don't know how she found the time to see him. She's a work-a-holic for Christ-sakes! How did she manage it?"

"I don't know," Emma replied, knowing that Andy wasn't even hearing her response. He was lost in his memories, trying to determine any clues that might tell him where things had gone awry. He turned to Emma suddenly, as though a thought had just occurred to him.

"Did you ever notice anything?" He asked.

And there it was. The question she feared would someday come. How in the world was she going to answer this? She realized after all this time, she still had no idea. She'd thought of it often enough-What would she say if Andy ever asked her about it- but she never seemed to figure out what her response would be. And she still had no idea. She looked at him, sitting beside her, looking at her expectantly, wanting to know that he was not alone in the dark; that someone besides him had no idea what was going on.

She was terrified. "Notice anything?" She cringed inwardly,

knowing how stupid she sounded simply repeating what he'd asked her. Luckily, Andy didn't notice anything odd about her response.

He nodded. "You know...like she wasn't around....maybe she was acting funny...God, Emma. I don't even know what I'm asking." He paused and then looked her in the eyes. "Did you have any idea?"

Staring at him, she felt as though he could see right through her. There was no was she could lie to him. She didn't need to. As she sat there, she recalled the nights, too many to recall, in which she sat home alone while Layne was out with Brad. She thought of the worry she felt wondering if Andy would ever find out. Remembering all the frustration she felt angered her all over again. She ripped her gaze away from Andy's and looked down at her hands, which were now clasped tightly together in her lap.

"Andy, I..." She looked up at him again, unsure of what to say to him.

Andy saw the look on Emma's face and immediately became concerned. He leaned toward her and rested his hand over hers. "Emma? What is it?"

She looked down at their hands in her lap and noticed how his one hand covered both of hers completely. She could barely see the pale skin of her hand peeking out from underneath his. Her hands were warm now, despite the coldness she felt running through her. She looked up at him and opened her mouth to speak but found that she could not.

He was sitting so close to her and Emma could tell he was worried. She knew him so well now; better than she'd ever allowed herself to hope and she could read his emotions nearly as well as her own. She could see the worry all over his face. His brow had come together in a frown and he was looking all over her face for some clue as to what was wrong. Emma watched as expression on his face slowly changed from worry to confusion and then finally, to understanding. She watched as the realization dawned on him.

He hadn't moved a muscle but Emma felt the change within him. He was now tense where just moments ago, he was comfortable and relaxed. Slowly, he removed his hand from hers and brought it back to his own lap. "Emma."

The word was an accusation and a conviction all at once. In that moment, They both knew she had known about the affair all along.

Emma finally found her voice. "Andy, I'm so sorry! You have no idea...I didn't...Shit..." Her voice trailed off. She really had no idea what to say, only that she needed to keep talking to him or he'd simply shut down.

He was looking past her into the depths of his memories. Emma watched as he squinted his eyes and frowned, trying to recall something in particular. It was only a moment or so later that he turned to her, having located some memory.

"That night," he said. "The night we were supposed to double-date. You were supposed to go out with Brad. That's the same night you and Layne fought, isn't it?"

Emma nodded slowly.

"You were going to let her set you up with man she was sleeping with?"

"No...I...I mean, Yes. But –" Emma's voice trailed off when she looked at Andy. He was sitting beside her, staring at her; not with a look of anger, but with sadness and disappointment.

"How long?" He asked softly.

Emma was confused. "I...I don't-"

Andy was running out of patience and released an exasperated sigh, interrupting her. "How long did you know about the affair?"

And there it was. The question she'd dreaded since the beginning. She tried desperately to think of something to say to make it all go away but there was nothing. She looked at Andy and realized that he wasn't angry. No, he was something worse. He was disappointed. Emma knew she'd never forget the look on his face, particularly because it was she who put it there. She knew she had to answer his question but, unfortunately, the only response she could give was the absolute truth, as terrifying as it was. She looked him in the eyes and gave her answer.

"Since it began." Emma knew she'd never felt this horrible before. She could feel the breath being sucked out of her knowing she'd hurt Andy this way. Slowly, a tear made its way down her cheek. She waited for him to say something, anything, even though she knew that whatever he was going to say wasn't going to make her feel any better.

He stared at her for several seconds before speaking. "You knew that my wife was having an affair the entire time it went on? Why would you keep something like that from me?"

195

"Andy, I-"

"Not only would it have saved me a lot of bullshit but it would have helped me to realize that the divorce wasn't entirely my fault the way Layne made it out to be."

"I am so sorry, Andy," Emma whispered.

"No, I'm the one who's sorry." He got up and moved to the front door. He stopped before he reached and looked back over his shoulder. "Let me ask you something."

"Anything," Emma replied. She was desperate to keep him talking. If he was talking to her, even yelling at her, at least he would still be in her apartment. She feared if he left in this state, he'd never return.

When he spoke, his voice was eerily calm, which under the circumstances, Emma found not the slightest bit reassuring. "Wasn't I your friend too? Didn't that count for anything?"

Emma couldn't come up with any words that would make this situation better. She was staring at his profile trying to think of something, anything to say to make this all right – to somehow make what she did seem less horrible than it was. But she came up with nothing.

Andy stood at the door for several moments, waiting for a response. "Forget it. Don't answer that." He chuckled sarcastically. "It doesn't matter who gets hurt as long as you cover for each other, is that it? Well, I think it sucks."

Tears were now streaming down Emma's cheeks. She knew she was mere moments from losing the man she loved so desperately. She needed to get him to understand what had happened- what she'd tried to do.

"You've got to understand," she sobbed. "I did everything I could."

At this, he turned around and faced her. "You did everything you could? I find that hard to believe. Emma, all you had to do was talk to me. I would have listened to you. But you didn't. You didn't do anything." He ran his hand through his hair and sighed heavily. "Did you even encourage her to stop? Or were the two of you laughing at me behind my back?!"

Emma gasped. "God, NO! It wasn't like that!"

"What was it like then? Huh? Did Layne tell you where she was going? Were you the one who was supposed to cover for her? Did the two of you have some sort of 'code' you'd use if something went wrong?"

Emma's eyes grew wide and she opened her mouth in surprise as she realized how close to the truth his assumptions were. When she heard it out of the mouth of the man who had been cheated on, somehow it sounded worse, much worse, than she ever thought. She sat still on the couch, rooted to the spot. In that instant, she knew there was nothing she could say that would excuse her behavior in his eyes. She was defeated.

He nodded, as though he knew everything he'd just said was dead-on correct. "I thought so."

He turned back around and placed his hand on the door knob. "Good-bye, Emma."

He walked out of the apartment and slowly closed the door behind him. Emma felt as though a part of her had been ripped from her body. She desperately wanted to go after him and plead her case, scream to him that she had no choice, but did she? Did she have to do as Layne asked? Now that she had the love of her life, was it worth it? Losing her best friend was hard enough; she wasn't sure if she could survive losing Andy.

Chapter 21

Emma had never felt so empty which, somehow, was worse than anything she'd ever felt before. For such a short amount of time, she'd been happy. So deliriously happy. She now knew what it felt like to love someone and have them love you back. The had felt the happiness of walking down the street arm in arm with someone, falling asleep with someone beside you and waking in the middle of the night to place your hand on their shoulder – touching the reality that the man you love is laying beside you. She'd felt all the happiness that comes along with knowing you are loved. But now? Now she had lost it.

The feeling of loss Emma was experiencing was worse than she could have ever imagined. She couldn't help but feel as though if she and Andy had not crossed that line of friendship, she wouldn't be in so much pain right now. If only they'd stayed friends she wouldn't have known what it was like to be loved by him. And she wouldn't know the feeling of losing that love. She'd allowed herself to hope – the infinite ocean of possibility – and now her dreams were shattered.

Because Emma knew that this turn of events was partly due to her own actions, she spent much time thinking about 'what if,' or 'if only,' and it nearly drove her crazy. The difficult part was that she knew she was partly responsible for this turn of events. Andy was right. She would have done anything for Layne...but this time, maybe she shouldn't have. Another 'what if' that continued to plague her.

Over the next few weeks, she spent hour upon hour reviewing the past year. It was an exercise in futility, she knew, but she couldn't help but review everything over and over in her mind. In doing this, though, it began to dawn on her that Layne wasn't the friend she thought she was. She had not only put her in a position where she had to keep something from Andy, but she turned on Emma when she discovered her feelings for him. One would have thought that Layne would have at that point, realized how difficult it had been for Emma to know about the affair and keep it from Andy. Layne had just glossed over Emma's pain, instead focusing on her own.

While Emma could certainly understand Layne's anger upon finding out Emma had feelings for Andy, she always thought that given some time, Layne would come to realize that Emma hadn't done anything wrong. A tiny part of her had even hoped the four of them might one day be able to sit and have a friendly conversation and put the past behind them. Well, any hope of that ever happening was put to rest the night she and Andy ran into Layne. Emma had been shocked at the amount of venom that spewed from Layne. She was positively hostile and vengeful. Emma had never seen her like that before and truthfully, it scared her.

Emma stumbled through the next several weeks in a haze of sadness. During the day, she tried to put on a smile for the benefit of her students, but they could tell something just wasn't quite right. A couple of her students, Delainey and Lila, were now prone to giving her spontaneous hugs. Some of the more rambunctious boys in her class tended to be more subdued than normal. Of course, Emma was grateful that her students were so in-tune to her feelings but she was also disappointed in her inability to hide her emotions from a bunch of six year olds. Clearly, she was wearing her heart on her sleeve and even the kindergarteners could see it had been bruised.

Emma also found that she had no appetite, which at any other time, she'd be grateful for. But once she realized her favorite pair of jeans could be pulled on and off without unbuttoning them, she knew she had to snap out of it. She forced herself to eat, even if she wasn't hungry, else she'd hear it the next time she visited her parents.

She had avoided them for over a month now and still wasn't ready to see them, her mother in particular. Each time she thought she was strong enough to visit her parents she caved, thinking of the look on her mother's face when she explained to her that she and Andy were no longer together. She needed to reach her own level of acceptance before she was able to help her mother with it. Frankly, while she was having difficulty with it, she felt certain her mother might never get over it.

After a few weeks of going through the motions of living, Emma knew she needed to get back to some sense of normalcy and put forth some effort to move on. If she didn't force herself to at least act as though she were all right, it wouldn't be long before she wouldn't be able to shake what she felt certain was approaching a severe case of depression. She slowly forced herself to get up each day with an attempt at a positive attitude. Each evening, she mustered the energy to make one stop on the way home from work. Sometimes, she'd stop for groceries; at other times, she'd simply walk through her favorite craft store hoping to be inspired by something. She told herself over and over that she needed to do something besides work and lay in her bed.

It took some time for the feelings to mimic her actions but after several days of going through the motions, Emma began to feel a bit like her old self. Granted, she was still distraught over how her life had been messed up but she now found that a pint of Starbuck's ice cream would at least dull some of those feelings, for a little while at least. This, of course, was better than her earlier days of eating practically nothing and she found that she was gaining back a few of the pounds she'd lost.

It took nearly two months, but Emma finally found herself in a place of resignation and acceptance of where she was. And that, she felt, was a very good first step. If she could accept where her life was at the moment, she could certainly move forward from there. It was the first positive thought she'd had in some time.

* * *

Andy, being the productive person that he was, had thrown himself into his work. Since leaving Emma's apartment that night, he'd barely left the office. His clients were thrilled with the level of attention they were getting, since they were receiving phone calls and emails at all hours of the day and night. Any recommendations he made on stocks, mutual funds and other investments were based on the most thorough research he'd ever done. And he felt great about it.

What he didn't feel so great about, however, was how his life had turned out. He just couldn't seem to get past the fact that Emma had, for all intents and purposes, lied to him. Technically, it was a lie by omission, but a lie nonetheless. He thought their relationship had been based on friendship and this betrayal (because that's what he felt this was) blew his idea of friendship out of the water. In his mind, it was unforgivable. He felt as though the Emma he knew (and loved?) was gone and replaced with someone who found it easy to lie...someone like his ex-wife. And that, he thought, was not something he wanted to experience ever again.

Did he love Emma? It was something he'd thought of often since their time apart. He felt certain he did, which was why their separation was so painful to him. But he knew it was for the best. He simply couldn't tolerate being lied to.

Andy focused on the screen in front of him and tried to ignore the group of co-workers standing outside of his office making plans for the evening. He knew he would be invited, as he'd been every week for the past two months. He also knew he would decline, as he'd also done every week for the past two months. He had pushed his door nearly closed earlier knowing that the invitation would come. As much as he wanted to avoid it, he knew he was running out of excuses. And tonight, the plans were a celebration rather than just an 'it's Friday so let's go for a drink' event. Chad, one of the Investment counselors, was getting married in a couple of weeks and everyone was taking him out for drinks. Andy knew that, barring cast on both of his legs, there would be no way to avoid going out tonight. Then again, he knew that even if his legs were in casts, his co-workers would drive him to the bar. He sighed, and resigned himself to one night of going out instead of heading home to his empty apartment.

Andy's co-workers had opted to take Chad to Spotlight, the newest club in town. The developers had taken an abandoned apartment building and converted it into a unique nightclub. It had been split into two distinct settings; one side was your stereotypical nightclub, complete with strobe lights and cages for girls to dance in. The other side was more simple; a long wooden bar with stools around it and booths circling the outside of the room for people to sit and talk. The club side boasted a killer sound system while the bar side boasted a bartender that could make anything and a setting where you could hold a conversation without screaming. This location was, given that he really had no choice, provided the perfect solution for Andy, since he could leave his co-workers at the dance club side and head over to the bar to sit and have a drink.

And he did just that. He was nursing his second Sam Adams

when he saw her walk in. She was all glittery and colorful and Andy knew that whatever she was wearing had cost a fortune. Luckily for him, that was no longer his concern. Typical Layne, he thought.

He was immediately filled with dread, remembering their last encounter. This time, however, she was alone and appeared not to have been drinking. He watched from the corner of the bar as she looked all around for whoever she was meeting or to find a place to sit, he wasn't sure which. As she scanned the room, her eyes met his and she smiled hesitantly, unsure of his response. He gave in out of habit and smiled back at her. She raised her eyebrows and pointed at the empty seat next to him. He surprised himself by nodding.

She began to make her way over to him, weaving through the crowd effortlessly. It was obvious she was accustomed to places like this, unlike Andy, who found a place to sit, and stayed there. As he watched her weave gracefully across the room, he noticed her skin-tight jeans and high heels. He'd never understood how Layne, or any other woman for that matter, was able to walk in those things. Layne somehow managed to look completely at ease, and beautiful, he had to admit, weaving around the groups of people in the bar. There was no doubt about it, she was a beautiful woman. If looks were all that mattered to him, they might have stayed together. The corners of his mouth turned upward slowly as he realized they never had a chance. They just weren't meant to be; there were too many differences between them, too many things that couldn't see eye to eye on. He felt a pang in his stomach as he remembered that not too long ago he felt certain Emma was the person he was meant to be with. Again, though, it turned out it he was wrong.

Layne weaved around a waiter and made her way to Andy's side. She placed her purse on the bar as she climbed into the high bar stool, taking note of the people surrounding her. He nodded at her as he took a sip of his beer.

"Hey," he said, somewhat hesitantly. He still wasn't entirely sure what had prompted him to signal her over to sit beside him. For all he knew, she was going to give a repeat performance of their last encounter.

"Hey, yourself," Layne replied. She situated herself on the stool, crossing her legs and adjusting the strap of her shirt. She seemed a bit nervous and Andy wondered if she were thinking of the last time they met as well. The bartender rushed over to her and stood in front of her, waiting expectantly for her to need something. He was looking her with a stupid grin on his face and was practically salivating over her. It was clear, at least to him, that the bartender was hoping she was single. Andy could feel a mix of anger and jealousy directed at him and couldn't help but smile, realizing that this bartender had assumed Layne was *with* him. Layne had always drawn a good amount of attention from the opposite sex and dressed the way she was, it was certainly no surprise that the bartender wanted to try his luck. She oozed sexuality. Luckily for him, the divorce had ensured he was immune to her shiny outer shell.

"Chardonnay, please," she said to the bartender, who nodded, then happily bounded off to get it for her. Within a minute, a cold glass was placed in front of her. "Thanks," she said.

The bartender grinned and lingered for a moment before finally giving up and moving to help another patron. Andy couldn't help but chuckle. Layne turned to look at him.

"What are you laughing at?" She asked, as she was obliviously to any attention that was unwanted.

He nodded to the bartender who was a mere three feet away, glancing surreptitiously at her every few seconds. The bartender appeared to be in a holding pattern, waiting to be called upon by Layne. "That guy. He's been grinning stupidly since you sat down."

She looked over at him and sure enough, caught his eye and he smiled at her. She looked back at Andy. "Now that's just ridiculous. He's just being nice. He works on tips, right?"

"He sure does," Andy said, rolling his eyes. "What are you doing here, anyway?"

"I'm meeting Vicki for a drink." Layne replied, taking a sip of her chardonnay.

"Vicki? The woman from your office?"

"Yesssss. And she was one of our bridesmaids," she chastised. "We're going to have a drink here and then head next door. I want to check out the new club. What are *you* doing here? Shouldn't you be holed up in your apartment?" Almost immediately, Layne's smile vanished and she actually looked remorseful. "I'm sorry. That was uncalled for."

Andy felt a flash of anger inside of him when he heard her comment. He felt certain things were going to head downhill quickly. Upon hearing her apology almost immediately, he looked up at her surprised to hear remorse from her. He felt the anger dissipate when he saw she did, in fact, appear to be sorry for the comment. "It's the truth, though, right?" He joked. "I never liked going to these places and you can't wait to get in there."

She thought about it. "It may be the truth, but I don't have to be such a bitch about it." She fidgeted in her chair for a moment before speaking again. "I'm sorry, Andy…for everything."

He stared at her for a moment, both surprised at her apology and afraid to believe she was sincere. Layne had never been one to admit she was wrong and this change in her was completely unexpected. Truthfully, a part of him expected her to behave the way she'd done the last time he'd seen her. He found the image of her from that night was still stuck in his mind. Was it possible that Layne was truly feeling sorry for all that had happened? He stared at her for several minutes, trying to determine what she was up to. He had to admit, he'd never seen her look this sincere and finally came to realize that she was being honest with him and truly felt sorry for how their marriage had turned out. He wasn't sure what had prompted the change and he couldn't explain it, but he knew she meant it. He waited for her to continue, sensing there was more to come.

Layne's shoulders were hunched slightly and she looked, well, insecure. She was looking down at her wine glass and nervously tapping her finger along the bottom of the stem.

"I've been wanting to see you…you know since the last time…." Her voice trailed off since she didn't want to speak about their last encounter. Andy nodded his understanding. "I really am sorry about that night. I have nothing to say, no excuses for my behavior other than to say that I'm sorry. I hope you can forgive me."

He looked at her for a moment, trying to determine if she were sincere. Satisfied she was, he nodded. "I think I might be able to manage that."

She smiled and Andy noticed her relax a bit. She sat upright and looked more like her confident self; it seemed she was glad to have the weight of her apology off her shoulders. "So, what are you doing here?" She asked.

"One of the guys from the office is getting married in a couple of weeks so everyone's taking him out for drinks. Sort of a 'before the bachelor party,' bachelor party,"

Layne grinned. "Sounds like fun."

"I guess," he replied, shrugging his shoulders.

Layne rubbed her finger around the rim of her glass, making a tinny sound. She looked as though she wanted to ask something but wasn't sure how to bring it up. "I've been wondering...."

He looked at her and raised his eyebrows at the uncertainty in her voice and wondered what she was so hesitant to ask. "Wondering what?"

"Are you okay? I know it's not my place to ask anymore..." She let her voice trail off, unsure of how to finish that particular sentence. Although she was seated beside Andy, she wasn't so foolish as to think that all had been forgiven. She was grateful for this newfound civility and wanted to tread lightly. Still, she worried about him and wanted to make sure he was doing well.

"No. It's okay. I'm fine. Thanks for asking."

Layne nodded. "I know this is probably too little, too late, but I am sorry about us – about how things turned out."

Andy looked at her, unsure how to respond. "Yeah, me too. But I think it's for the best, don't you? I mean, look at us sitting here. I can't wait to head home and you can't wait to get over there." He nodded in the direction of the club. "We never seemed to be headed in the same direction. I can see that now. Don't get me wrong. I was angry with you for a very long time and then...well, that night..." His voice trailed off.

Layne cringed, thinking of the same night. "Yeah...that night....You know, I have to say that I'm a bit surprised you let me sit down...after our last meeting and all."

Andy shrugged. "Well, it's not like you can do any more damage than you already have."

"Ouch. I guess I deserved that."

He looked at her for a moment; then grinned. "Well, I'm not going to disagree with you there."

"I really am sorry, Andy. I don't know what came over me that night. I was such a bitch."

"Again, no argument here." He looked away and took a swig of his beer.

"It was just such a shock to see you and Emma together. Not that I'm excusing my behavior or anything. Just seeing you...and her...together? Well, I guess it just gave me a jolt."

Donna Small

At this, Andy turned back to face her. "Now why would that shock you? You had moved on. Why shouldn't I?"

"I don't know. I guess...just you and Emma. That night it all seemed so unreal. But now it makes perfect sense. Actually, I can't believe I didn't see it before. You and Emma are perfect for each other."

"Apparently not," he mumbled.

"What do you mean? You're still together, aren't you?" She took another sip of her wine.

He looked at her angrily, though not because she was asking but because of the whole situation. "No, we're not."

"But I don't understand. Even with all that I had to drink that night, I could tell that the two of you were happy! What happened?"

"Layne, I really don't want to get into this with you."

"But Andy, maybe there's something I can do to help."

"You know, I think you've done enough." His voice had changed and Layne noticed that anger there.

"Now what's *that* suppose to mean?"

"Look, do we have to get into all of this again?"

"All of what? Andy, would you please tell me what you're talking about?"

"Oh, for christsakes, Layne. I really don't want to re-hash your whole affair again, all right? It's taken a long time but you and I are sitting here like two grown ups having a drink. I think we've come pretty far."

She nodded her agreement. "We have. But what does my affair have to do with you and Emma?"

"Oh for-" He muttered something unintelligible and then sighed heavily. "She knew."

"What do you mean, 'she knew'?" Layne was completely lost at the moment.

"She knew about the affair. She knew the whole time." Andy looked at Layne and waited for understanding to dawn on her. She stared back at him for several moments, trying to determine why he was so upset, then it hit her. He watched as a smile crept across her face, which only irritated him further. "What?! What?!!?"

"Okay, I know this is going to sound callous...but, so what? She knew. What did you expect? She was my best friend! Of course, I was going to confide in her."

206

"You know, I get that. But she should have told me." Andy hunched over the bar and pulled his beer closer to his chest. Layne thought that he reminded her of child pouting- minus the beer, of course.

She tried to hold her laughter in but the sight of him sitting at the bar pouting was too much for her to take. She laughed out loud, causing the people sitting beside her to jump. "Are you serious? You think she should have told you? You?!??! God, you're such a man."

"What the hell is that supposed to mean?" Andy's entire face was red and blotchy and Layne knew she needed to calm him down before he completely lost it. She wiped the image of the pouting child from her mind in order to prevent herself from laughing again.

"Andy, sweetheart," she placed her hand on his shoulder. "No woman is *ever* going to betray their best friend. *Never, ever!!!* Especially Emma. She was my *best friend.* That's something you men will never understand. We would do *anything* for each other."

"Not that best friend crap again. What about me? Wasn't I her friend? Don't I deserve some of that loyalty?"

Layne nodded. "Yes, in theory you do. But it just doesn't work that way. "

"Well, why not?" He huffed.

She pondered this for a moment. "I don't know how to explain it. It's like...your best friend is everything you'd want in a sister if you could *choose* her. And because you did choose her, you'd never do anything to harm that relationship. You'd sooner cut off your own arm."

"Well, I think it sucks."

Layne smiled softly. "I'm sure it does, from your perspective. But from where I'm sitting? Emma was the best friend anyone could ever have. She was the only one who supported me when I was doing what she and I both knew was wrong. She hated...*hated,*" Layne emphasized the word. "what I was doing but she still stood by me and let me figure things out. She knew it would devastate you but she still supported me. You can't ask for anything more than that."

Andy noticed the change in Layne's tone and looked at her. "So what happened? If she was the best friend you ever had, why don't you two even speak anymore?"

Layne sighed. "It's so…stupid when I think about it now. I mean, I see how perfect the two of you are together. I can't believe I was so upset about it."

"Upset about what?"

Layne looked at him strangely. "Uhh…Emma? How she felt about you?"

Andy was looking at her and shaking his head. "I'm lost. When did she tell you how she felt about me? I thought you two weren't speaking."

"We weren't after we fought, but…" She stopped and looked at him, finally noticing the expression on his face, which was one of complete and total confusion. "Oh, god. Wait a minute. You have no idea do you?"

"No idea about what?"

"Andy, the night we were supposed to double date? The night we fought?"

Andy nodded.

"I went to Emma's to try to convince her to go out and, well we got into it. She laid into me." Layne smiled out of sheer embarrassment. "She told me how awful it was of me to put her through this date with Brad, how awful I was for cheating on you, how I had this wonderful man at home. Blah, blah blah. Well, I knew right then something was up. So I asked her about it. And she didn't deny it."

Andy had gone pale and was sitting absolutely still, staring at Layne. "Deny it…" he said, repeating her.

Layne swallowed hard, realizing what she was about to say was going to shock the hell out of him. "She didn't deny that she was in love with you."

"She told you she was in love with me?" He squeaked.

"Yes, she did."

"I didn't know…" He sat still, staring over Layne's shoulder. Finally, he managed to pull himself together and he looked at her. "Let me get this straight," he said. "Emma told you that night she was in love with me?"

She nodded. "But Andy," she said softly. "There's more."

"What now?" He cried.

"She's been in love with you ever since she first met you. The only reason….the *only* reason she never did anything to show you how she felt was because of me. She simply stepped aside and let me take you for myself."

"Oh, God." Andy practically crumpled in front of her eyes. She'd been in love with him since she first met him? How could he not have known? He looked up at Layne and she could see the misery in his face. Her expression mirrored his.

"I know," she said, nodding sympathetically. "But do you see now? Do you see how hard this was for her? This is what Emma did for me. She loved you all that time and kept her feelings to herself. She never told anyone. She supported me knowing it would at some point hurt you terribly. Never mind how much it was killing her to know that I was cheating on you, the man she was in love with. God, I can't even imagine what she was going through all that time."

"Neither can I." Andy slammed his beer down on the bar, causing droplets to bounce out of the bottle onto the shiny, wooden surface. Layne recoiled, not wanting to get anything on her. "I've got to go and see her," he said, rising up out of his seat.

In an instant, he was up and moving toward the door. Layne watched him leave, hoping for the best; hoping that she had managed to fix one small piece of the damage she'd done.

209

Chapter 22

Emma sat in her living room with a half-empty pint of Starbuck's Java Chip ice cream in her lap in front of her. It was late – nearly midnight - and she knew she should head to bed. She had good intentions but those were quickly sidetracked once she discovered The Holiday was television. Despite the fact she'd seen it nearly a dozen times, she found she was unable to turn off the television and head to bed. She looked down and noticed the ice cream was melting and would soon be nothing but a creamy mess of coffee flavored soup. She got up during the commercial and returned it to the freezer, then decided to re-fill her glass of wine. *Nothing like being a little drunk when you have to witness Cameron Diaz trying to force herself to cry*, she thought. Other than that one scene, the movie was a gem.

She filled her glass and sat down just as the movie had returned from commercial. Jude Law and Cameron Diaz were saying goodbye in some snow covered, tiny British town after falling madly in love over the course of a two week vacation. Emma felt her heart begin to melt. God, she loved this part! She felt her eyes well up as she watched Cameron Diaz get into a black car and drive away. *Stupid girl,* she thought. *You love him and he loves you...make it work!!*

But that wasn't reality, now was it. She had been in love yet where had it gotten her? Here she was, sitting in her apartment alone on a Friday night. She'd inhaled nearly a pint of ice cream and was now working her way through a bottle of merlot. This, unfortunately, had become her Friday night ritual. By the end of the week, she was so tired that all she wanted to do was come home, put on her jammies, and sit on the couch. The ice cream and wine were just a bonus.

She took a long sip of the merlot, enjoying the momentary warmth of it as it ran down her throat. This particular brand was something new she was trying and to be honest, she found that she liked it. Of course, there wasn't much she didn't like after two glasses of wine.

Emma placed the glass down on the end table and leaned back, curling her legs underneath her. This was her favorite part of the movie – the happy ending. Boy was she ready. She would have a good cry and then call it a night. She was planning on heading to her mother's house in the morning since she'd finally realized that she'd avoided her for long enough. It was high time that she and her mother sat down and had a talk about what had happened between her and Andy. And she was dreading it. She had a feeling that her mother had already been picking up bridal magazines and inspecting wedding sites in anticipation of an engagement. She sighed thinking about how difficult tomorrow was going to be.

She leaned her head on the pillow and watched the final scene of the movie. She began to feel the pull of sleep and knew she would succumb to it. She closed her eyes and began to drift off, a smile on her face as a result of seeing her happy ending. Jude Law and Cameron Diaz were going to make it work....somehow.

Emma wasn't sure how long she'd been asleep before the persistent buzzing woke her up. At first, she wasn't sure what it was or where it was coming from. She raised her hand to her head in confusion; then realized it was the buzzer to her apartment. She was once again confused since no one came to see her and it was...one in the morning? She shook her head as she realized once again, she'd fallen asleep on the couch, too tired to even walk the few steps down the hall to her bedroom.

The lights in the living room as well as the television were still on so if this was someone who knew which apartment she was in, there would be no way to pretend not to be home.

She got up off the couch and walked over to the door, pushing the talk button.

"Hello? Who's there?"

"Emma, it's Andy."

Emma jumped back as though bitten. She stared at the voice box as though it would give her some indication as to why Andy was outside her apartment building. She was rooted to the spot. After several moments, the buzzer sounded again, jolting her back to reality.

She tentatively reached for the speak button and pushed it.

"Andy? What are you doing here?"

"I need to talk to you. Can I come up?"

Emma looked down at her old sweatpants and ratty t-shirt. *Of course,* she thought. *Come see me when I look like this.* She reached for the button to unlock the door; then stepped to look at herself in the mirror. She smoothed her hair down a bit, not that it did any good, but she felt better for trying. She heard Andy's footsteps on the stairs and opened the door about six inches.

"Er...Hi?" She said, unable to keep the question from her voice.

He noticed that she didn't open the door to allow him entry into her apartment. Knowing what he now knew, he couldn't say he blamed her. He felt his chest tighten when he saw her looking so vulnerable and afraid to open not only her door, but her heart as well. He stood there for a moment and realized he felt uncomfortable. Nervously, he ran his fingers through his hair. "I know it's late but I was really hoping I could talk to you. Can I come in?"

Emma stared at him for several moments before opening the door. Andy felt certain she was thinking about closing the door when in fact, she was taking the time to stare at him in his work clothes. Despite not having seen him in over two months, he still affected her like he always had. Slowly, she opened the door and stepped aside.

"Thanks," he said, as he walked slowly past her into the living room. He motioned to the couch. "Can we ....uhh...sit for a minute?"

She nodded and watched him sit on the couch. Rather than sit beside him, she opted to sit in the chair so she wouldn't be tempted to reach out and touch him. Emma curled her legs underneath her in an attempt to hide what she could of her sweats. "So..." She said.

"Ummm...." He took his finger and stuck it between his shirt collar and neck, trying to loosen it. Emma knew it was a nervous habit of his. What she didn't know was what he could possibly be nervous about. She waited.

He cleared his throat a few times.

"Do you want something to drink?" She asked.

"No, thanks." Andy cleared his throat again. "I was just with Layne-"

Emma wasn't entirely sure why he was telling her he'd just spent time with his ex-wife so she kept a neutral expression. "I see." She said. She tried to sound as though she wasn't at all concerned about Andy spending time with Layne but the thought that the two of them might someday get back together was at the forefront of her mind. She found, despite her best attempt, she was unable to keep the sadness from her tone, though she wasn't sure why she should feel anything about it – her and Andy were no longer together. He could spend time with whomever he wanted.

Andy was looking down at the floor and didn't notice the sadness in Emma's voice. He continued. "Ummm....we had a really good talk, shockingly..." He chuckled half-heartedly. "Anyway, after talking to her, I had to come here to see you."

Emma wondered where this was going. She knew they were no longer a couple. Was he seriously coming here to tell her that he was getting back together with his ex-wife? What was he thinking? "You spent the evening with your ex-wife and then felt the need to come here?" She couldn't help it but the sarcasm had crept into her voice. Andy noticed, and looked up, eyebrows raised.

"What? No! It's not like that. We just ran into each other at Spotlight. I was there with some of the guys from work and she was meeting Vicki. We talked at the bar." He raised his eyebrows. "You didn't think we were getting back together, did you?"

Emma shrugged. "It's really none of my business." She said, feigning nonchalance.

"God, no! That would NEVER happen." He chuckled, trying to lighten the mood. "You didn't really think that, did you?"

"I don't really know. But I am wondering why a visit with Layne would prompt a visit to my apartment."

Andy nodded. "Right. Well, like I said, we talked for a bit. She's different now...like she understands how she hurt me...and you." He looked up at her. "Emma, she told me about your fight."

Emma felt her pulse quicken slightly. "Our fight?"

He moved forward on the couch an inch or so. "Everything. She told me everything." He laughed. "She pretty much told me I was an idiot for holding you accountable for not telling me about her affair. Emma, she told me what you did for her despite..."

"Despite what," she whispered.

Again, Andy shifted forward an inch or so. "Despite how you felt for me."

Emma felt her eyes well up with tears and brushed them away

angrily. "She had no right-"

Andy continued. "Layne told me everything and I wish you could have heard her tell me how stupid I was. She told me how there was no way you'd ever betray her trust. She explained to me how she had no one to confide in but you and even though you hated what she was doing, you stood by her. And I crucified you for it. Emma, I'm so sorry."

Tears were now streaming down her face. Andy took this as a positive sign and continued.

"I think…I hope you know how I feel about you. And thanks to Layne, I know how you felt about me. The only question is: do you still feel the same? Because my feelings for you haven't changed. I love you, Emma. I'm so sorry I spent these past two months without you. I was such an idiot. Can you ever forgive me?"

Emma had not noticed but Andy had moved so close to her that his knees were touching hers. She looked down and noticed that his hands were holding both of hers tightly as though he didn't intend to ever let go. And Emma realized that was okay by her.

She looked up at him to find him staring at her earnestly, waiting for her to respond. She never thought she would be sitting here with him again. Her heart swelled. She loved him. Always had, always would.

Emma smiled at him. "Of course I can forgive you. I love you."

He grinned and pulled her into his arms, sweeping her out of the chair and into his lap. He kissed her with all the emotion he'd built up over the past two months. When finally he released her, she was breathless.

As he looked down at her in his arms, he realized he'd never been happier. He felt relief wash over him. He hadn't realized until this moment how terrified he'd been that her feelings for him had changed. What if he'd lost her forever? He shuddered, thinking of how close he'd come to exactly that. Andy swiftly brushed the thought from his mind and looked down at the woman in his arms. Emma was right where she was meant to be.

And he was never going to let her go.

Visit Second Wind Publishing

http://indigoseapress.com

www.ingramcontent.com/pod-product-compliance
Lightning Source LLC
Chambersburg PA
CBHW061322200626
46813CB00017B/2813